T0365541

Circle of Shadows

Keith M. Heim

iUniverse, Inc.
Bloomington

Circle of Shadows

iUniverse books may be ordered through booksellers or by contacting:

iUniverse
1663 Liberty Drive
Bloomington, IN 47403
www.iuniverse.com
1-800-Authors (1-800-288-4677)

ISBN: 978-1-4697-4473-5 (sc)
ISBN: 978-1-4697-4472-8 (hc)
ISBN: 978-1-4697-4471-1 (e)

Library of Congress Control Number: 2012900763

Printed in the United States of America

iUniverse rev. date: 2/23/2012

CHAPTER 1

It came out of nowhere, weaving wildly in and out of the leafy barriers that invaded the road, spraying gravel and dust at each turn. The boy had been deep within his thoughts, thoughts of his hunger, thoughts of his mother, when the car came upon him suddenly. He jumped out of the way and glanced over to see a new white 1946 Chevy with the words "Coosa County Sheriff, Morefield, Alabama" circling a gold star on the door. He quickly turned his face away from the vehicle and brought his hand up over his face as if to shield it from the rolling dust that burst up from behind the car. He was relieved when it sped on its way, its uniformed occupant seeming to pay no attention to him at all. In a moment or two, it disappeared from sight.

His heart beat wildly. Suppose the sheriff had recognized him! He was a thousand miles away now, but he'd need to be more careful. For all he knew, a lookout had been posted for him. As he trudged on his way, he glanced up from time to time to make sure the sheriff was not coming back.

The road was a virtual obstacle course. Last night's windstorm had rained leaves, twigs, and branches down, and here and there, a large limb from a tree in a nearby field had crushed a fence down and protruded into the road. The light sprinkles of the early morning had done little to forestall the heat that already pressed down upon the land by mid-morning or to settle the dust that lay heavy on the unpaved road.

The sun hung motionless above him, seeming to pulsate as its yellow heat beat down relentlessly upon his back and shoulders, making his shirt hot to the touch. He was grateful for the intermittent shade of the towering oaks along the sides of the road, if not for their debris. His heels churned up angry-looking red puffs of dust behind him that seemed to propel him grudgingly forward. Already, he had walked the six miles from the gas station on the main highway where the trucker had let him off.

Although the slump of his shoulders betrayed a weariness, there was something of resolution about him as he picked his way toward yet another strange town. He had had nothing to eat or drink all morning. Maybe, he thought, the leaves and branches would give him some work, work that would buy him at least an evening meal.

Soon, the neighboring cotton fields gave way gradually to the scattered houses that marked the outskirts of the town. The late morning heat, however, fell impartially on field and town, and after a while, he paused to rest for a few minutes in the spreading shade of a giant oak and wipe the sweat from his face. Across the street, a small, tired-looking, clapboard house with peeling yellow paint and a sagging front porch caught his attention. Rank weeds and renegade hollyhocks threatened to overpower the flowerbeds along the walk and fence, complementing the general aspect of long-term neglect the place presented.

Like the rest on the street, the yard was littered with the debris from the storm, and in one corner, a solitary apple tree had surrendered most of its promised harvest to the expectant earth below. Yellow-green apples dotted the leafy carpet, and a few of them had rolled under the fence and out into the dust of the street.

Manna from Heaven, the boy thought with a smile, and he bent down and picked one up, rubbing the dust from it on the thigh of his blue jeans. He looked up to see a heavyset, elderly woman in a faded yellow housedress sitting in a swing on the front porch of the house watching him closely. She rocked slowly back and forth as if she were carefully measuring out the moments of the morning. She looked as though she belonged there, had always been there, he thought. It was almost as if she and the house were one.

"Hey, young man, that's my apple you got there!" she called out suddenly.

The voice didn't sound angry, he thought. There was something of humor, perhaps teasing, in it. He grinned. "Sorry, ma'am. Since it was lying in the street, I didn't think anybody'd mind. I didn't mean to steal it from you, and I'd give it back to you, but I've put some labor into cleaning it up. I'd be willing to go halves with you."

The woman smiled broadly, long-established wrinkles radiating out from her eyes. "You look tired. Why don't you come sit here in the shade on the porch, and we can negotiate."

The boy readily accepted her invitation, stepping through a gate that hung wearily on one hinge and advancing up the root-plagued path to the porch steps.

The woman stopped her swinging and regarded him closely through her glasses as he sat down on the edge of the porch. He was a nice looking boy, even handsome, she thought, clean-cut, though his shirt and pants looked a bit rumpled and his shoes were badly scuffed and covered with dust. His light brown hair had the look of wheat straw burnished by the summer sun, and his tanned face and arms gave him a look of health and vitality. She smoothed a lock of silvery white hair back from her brow as if to see him better.

He smiled up at her, and she was immediately struck by his eyes, a dark blue that seemed to convey something of substance deep within. The eyes, a broad brow, and a firm chin combined to present a look of quick intelligence, of transparent honesty and wholesomeness.

The apples had been badly bruised from their fall, and he held up his prize for her to see. "I count three dents in this one, and I think the worm was killed in the fall. That ought to mean a healthy discount, ma'am." His hunger had overcome his innate shyness, but he was careful to address her as "ma'am." Midwesterners didn't generally use "sir" and "ma'am," even in addressing older people, but he remembered from a Civil War novel he had read that well-brought-up boys in the South used them when speaking to adults. It would be important to blend in as much as possible.

She laughed loudly. "You take all you want—on the house! They're about ruined. The storm last night was a real ripsnorter, and I don't guess there's any savin' 'em. Give you a good old-fashioned bellyache," she warned, rubbing her ample stomach in wide circles.

He grinned up at her, and her attention immediately returned to his eyes, eyes that flashed a quick recognition of her intended humor.

"Had a few of them myself when I was a little girl, before I learned my lesson. Eat all you want, but don't say I didn't warn you."

She spoke loudly, and he guessed she was hard of hearing. "I'll risk one. Just enough for a *small* bellyache," he said, taking a big bite and grimacing at the sour, tart taste of the nearly green apple.

The woman smiled and resumed her leisurely swinging, the rusty iron chains supporting the swing accompanying her voice with a regular squeee–squaaa, squeee–squaaa, squeee–squaaa. The late morning sun filtering through the trees and splintering off her glasses gave an impression of geniality, and he felt drawn to her.

"It's gonna be another scorcher today! Would you like a drink of water?"

"Yes, ma'am, I sure would! I'm really thirsty."

He watched as the woman pushed down heavily on the seat of the swing with one hand, straightening up stiffly to her full height and clapping her free hand to the small of her back with a grimace of pain. She walked unsteadily across the porch, pushing her feet forward as if she were wearing four-buckle overshoes, he thought. Her shoes, the low heels run over to the outside, were badly scuffed, and here and there, a rounded light spot betrayed the presence of a corn beneath. The rusty spring on the screen door whined lazily as she opened it, and a squadron of flies flew up from the screen. She waved her hands and shouted, "Shoooo!" as she ducked through the door, but a number of them escorted her inside.

The boy dangled his legs over the edge of the porch, glad to rest his own aching feet for a moment. The blooming honeysuckle on the trellis at the edge of the porch perfumed the air and brought a fresh sweetness to the hot, stuffy morning. A butterfly, its wings iridescent in the sunlight, hovered and dipped among the blossoms there.

In a few moments, the woman reappeared with a large tumbler of pale pink punch and handed it to him, holding firmly onto the glass until she was sure he had hold of it. Her every move, perhaps occasioned by arthritis, was slow and studied.

"Sorry, I don't have any ice. The man didn't show up again this week." Her tone was more matter-of-fact than apologetic.

He took a couple of gulps of the lukewarm drink, narrowly avoiding gagging. It tasted as if the recipe called for a gallon of water, six cups of sugar, and one cranberry, he thought.

"What is your name, young man?" she asked.

He hesitated for a moment. "Steve. Steven Bowman."

"Holman?"

"No, ma'am, *Bow*-man." Since he had only just now selected a last name, he smiled to himself at his need to correct the woman. Holman would have done just as well.

"Well, Mr. Bowman, I'm proud to know you. You'll have to excuse me—I don't hear so good anymore, and I get things all balled up sometimes. I'm Mrs. Pike, Awillah Pike."

"Awillah? That's a pretty name. I've never heard of it before."

She laughed. "My folks named my older sister, two years older than me, Zillah, so I guess I got mine so's to rhyme with it. Funny how people get names. Zillah comes from the Bible someplace—my Sunday school teacher told me Zillah's husband was a bigamist!" She laughed again, then continued in a more serious vein. "Actually, Awillah is a family name. My father's aunt over in Macon was named Awillah; I think they came down south from Massachusetts … somewhere up there, maybe New Jersey. They were *old family* there—grew cranberries. The punch is an old recipe handed down. The family didn't come down south to Alabama until a few years after the War Between the States. Some might claim we were carpetbaggers, I guess. The name was Baldwin, but of course I became a Pike when I married."

Steve reflected that it was good to know that the cranberry punch hadn't actually started the Civil War. She seemed to want to talk. Probably didn't have many visitors, he thought.

"A long time ago," she continued. "I'm seventy-seven years old now," she added, a note of accomplishment in her voice. "I married to this house. Fifty-four years ago come July." She smoothed her dress down around her hips.

Steve guessed from the rundown condition of the house and the overgrown yard that a Mr. Pike hadn't been around for many of those years.

"How old are you, Steve?"

"I'll be sixteen in October, ma'am."

"You're not from here, are you? Up north somewhere maybe?"

"Ohio."

"Well, I declare! Ohio … Ohio," she repeated thoughtfully, accenting the first syllable. "My husband grew up there and used to talk about it quite a bit. Never been there. Never been farther from Morefield than Mobile, and that was to attend my nephew's wedding before the war. He was killed in Europe two years ago last December. The Battle of the Bulge, you know. Right at Christmastime. He left a young wife and a baby he never got to see with no one to look after 'em."

She fell silent for a moment, then resumed almost as if she were speaking to someone else. "When I was a girl, I always thought I'd go to Europe someday—England or maybe France. Both sides came from England in the 1700's, you know. I read a lot about it when I was a young girl … royalty, castles, beautiful gardens … but I never got to go there. Wanted to …"

Her voice trailed off. She pushed the swing to and fro with her right foot so regularly that it seemed to have a momentum of its own. Her voice was soft and wistful. "Young folks have lots of foolish dreams. You hold on to them as long as you can, and then one day you realize you're getting old."

She looked off toward the wall of trees that isolated the house from the street. "Maybe it's letting go of them that *makes* you old."

Everything she said seemed to have some kind of history behind it. Her mood was not bitter. Rather, it was somehow accepting, as if the long years had made things come out right. The front porch with its peeling, yellow paint on a quiet, dusty street had become her destiny, inexorably worked out. She had become one with it, and she was content.

"Do you have relatives here in Morefield?" he asked.

She stopped swinging. "Oh, no," she said sadly, "all gone now. I lost my husband eighteen years ago come October. The fifteenth. My son Wendell lives in Memphis. A grandson not much older than you, but they don't come down to visit much. He married a girl from there. They've got their own lives, I guess."

"Well, it's a long—" He stopped suddenly as he glimpsed the sheriff's white squad car out of the corner of his eye approaching up the street, back the way it had come earlier, slowing as it passed the house. He jerked his head abruptly away from the street, avoiding discovery, wondering if the sheriff had doubled back to check him out.

The old woman had frowned slightly at his sudden movement, but in a moment, there was a twinkle in her eye as she said, "Don't worry, young fellow, I haven't reported your apple larceny—yet."

He laughed and replied quickly, "Might as well make it grand larceny while I'm at it. Guess I'll have another … No tummy ache yet." He jumped down into the flower bed, picked up an apple, and began to rub it vigorously against his pant leg. Although the apple was a little green, he finished it off quickly and bent down and picked up another, then another. As thirsty as he was, he did not relish another sip of the cranberry punch. The woman continued to gaze at him intently, and he wondered if it was because of poor eyesight, but he could not risk pouring the drink onto the nearby honeysuckle while she sat there. He decided that the best course of action was to get it over with, down the hatch. He gulped it down as fast as he could, trying to ignore the sickeningly sweet taste—and aftertaste.

This was not lost upon his benefactor. Apparently, she appreciated an appreciative guest. She got up from the swing in an unexpected surge of energy, took the empty glass from his hand, and reappeared through the protesting screen door and ever-vigilant flies in a few moments with another glass filled to the brim.

"Guess the hot weather makes boys thirsty. Wendell had a hankerin' for it too. He used to drink this by the gallon."

Steve reflected wryly that the punch might have something to do with the fact that he lived in Tennessee and didn't come home very often.

She sat down heavily on the swing again, but she did not resume her swinging. Her eyes focused again sharply on Steve. "What are you doing way down here in the South?" she asked. "Do you live here now or just visiting? Do you have folks here?"

"I live over toward the park with my aunt," he said, pointing over his shoulder in the general direction he had come from. He had never been in Morefield before, nor even in northern Alabama for that matter. He hoped that there was a park somewhere in that direction.

"Oh, that would be Thomason Park."

He nodded and breathed easier.

"I guess your parents still live in Ohio?"

"No, ma'am. My mom does, but my father was killed in a car wreck six years ago. I came down to live with my aunt and go to school. Just got here yesterday." He swallowed the last of the fourth apple, washing it down with a couple of gulps of punch. He wondered if it would be impolite to ask for a glass of water to wash that down. His stomach growled reproachfully.

"I'm sorry," the woman said. "It must have been hard for you, losing your father like that. What's your aunt's name?"

This was dangerous ground, he thought. He had only just now invented the relative. Perhaps Mrs. Pike was acquainted with the people in the park neighborhood. He got up suddenly, pretending to wipe a tear from his eye, and asked, "Do you need someone to help clean up your yard, ma'am?" The ruse had another purpose—he desperately needed some way to earn some money.

"Yes, I could use somebody. It's a real mess! I'd be glad to pay you whatever you think is right."

He hesitated. "Would a dollar be okay?" He was afraid to ask for too much.

"Fine with me. There's a rake in the shed out back, and you'll find a saw hangin' on the wall, I think. With my foot trouble—diabetes, you know—I haven't been back there in a two, three years now, but I think that's where they are. Should be there somewhere anyway. There's a couple of trash cans back there too. Maybe later, I'll have you carry some boxes from the spare bedroom up to the attic for me. I haven't quite made up my mind about that yet."

He got up, thanked her for the cranberry punch, trying to sound grateful but not too enthusiastic, and hurried quickly around the house toward the shed. Out of sight of the old woman, he knelt down suddenly by the path and vomited up his lunch of apples and punch. He hadn't eaten since the hamburger at the truck stop east of Indianapolis—the one Marvin had bought him. That was three days ago. He was still shaken. The memory of the incident came back vividly, and he quickly blocked it out.

He stared down at the apples, which now lay in a pinkish mess among the weeds by the path. "I don't care how hungry I get; I'll starve before I go back," he said aloud. He got to his feet and went quickly to the shed to find the tools Mrs. Pike had mentioned.

The shed was a large, frame building in an even more desperate state of disrepair than the house, its peeling, yellow paint matching its neighbor. It was almost completely surrounded by tall cedars, grouped thickly as if trying to shield its shame from the neighborhood. *A pariah*, he thought. Like the front gate, the door hung rakishly half open on one hinge, and piles of junk half lost in the high weeds—an old axle and rusting wheels from some kind of vehicle, a couple of bald truck tires, stray pieces of weathered lumber, a storm window without glass, a big spool of wire—leaned against the sides of the shed, seeming to shore up the old building from imminent collapse.

He pushed the door open and went inside. The windows, one on each side of the door, were covered with dirt and cobwebs, letting only a dim light into the interior. The large room was filled with what could only be termed eclectic junk—things that had been discarded or stored away years ago with the thought that they might come in handy one day. But that day had never come, and now they littered the room, protruding from each other at difficult angles, gathering rust and dust as the years went by. An old sofa along the front wall was piled high with "things"—a car battery that had long since leaked its acid through one of the cushions, a washtub full of various rolls of flowered wallpaper, a cardboard box full of old rags that might have been dresses and men's overalls, a waffle iron with a frayed cord, a picture frame squashed into a parallelogram, a cellar window with one of its two panes broken out, and a box labeled "SAVE—TAX RECORDS 1931–1936." In a corner, a battered Victrola minus its doors stood silent, a roll of badly worn carpet balanced on top of the lid and a pile of automobile springs leaning against it. Next to it, half a dozen curtain rods, sans curtains, poked up jauntily from an oil drum like rank seedlings seeking whatever light the grimy windows afforded them. A tool bench in another corner was littered with nails and bolts, pieces of rusty wire, and a variety of tools long since laid down by hands now still. Articles of all descriptions filled almost every possible space in the room.

A set of wooden steps led upward from the jumble, and he could see that there was some kind of a room at the top tucked under the high-pitched roof. He climbed the steps, testing them one by one as he went, making sure they would bear his weight. At a small landing near the top, he turned to the right and ascended the final three steps to a wooden door. He pushed it open.

He stepped into a small room not much more than a dozen feet square with a single window in the south wall. The same grime and cobwebs as downstairs admitted a dim, almost ghostly light even in broad daylight. Overhead, he noticed a skylight, its grimy panes censoring the sun almost completely. He looked slowly around the room. It must have been used by someone for a retreat or a hideaway of some sort at one time, he thought. There was a wooden shelf on one wall with a rod for hangers beneath. Tattered print curtains festooned the window, and an iron cot with rusty springs occupied another wall. A small, rickety table stood in a corner with a wooden chair, minus the last three inches of one leg, pulled up to it, incongruously ready for use by someone who had gone away years ago.

As he moved about, he stirred the carpet of dust and it billowed up, settling down on his shoes and pant legs and causing him to cough.

He walked gingerly down the stairs and quickly found a crosscut saw hanging on two nails on a wall and a rake leaning nearby. He dumped the contents of the trash cans on the seat of an old one-armed rocking chair. Then he took the cans and the tools to the front yard and went to work. Mrs. Pike had apparently gone inside, and he worked without interruption, sawing off the larger limbs and gathering the brush into a big pile out by the curb in front. It was more work than he had bargained for. When it began to get dark, he went to the screen door and called to the old woman, "I'm going home now, ma'am. I'll be back in the morning to finish up."

"All right, Steve," she called out from somewhere within. "See you in the morning."

He wished she could have paid him then for the work done so he could buy something to eat. He didn't need the strenuous exercise to work up an appetite. Hunger had dogged him all day, and it was difficult to concentrate on anything else. It weighed down heavily in his stomach like a rock. He would have been better off without the apples, he reflected. Although he was thirsty, he was grateful that Mrs. Pike hadn't thought to get him another glass of cranberry punch!

He returned to the shed, and as he opened the door, he noticed a hand pump for a well in a corner of the yard, half hidden in the weeds. When he pushed down on the handle several times, cool water belched out. He continued pumping until the rust cleared from the water, then he cupped his hands and drank until he had quenched his thirst. After he had put the tools back in the shed, he headed on up Decatur Street, back the way he had come, toward Thomason Park. It was just for Mrs. Pike's benefit. There was nothing there for him, and a lie wouldn't provide him a place to stay.

He desperately needed to find a place for the night. He missed his jacket, and he didn't relish another night in the open. No matter how hot it was when he went to sleep, by dawn it was chilly and uncomfortable. He thought about the room at the top of the steps in the old shed. There was the iron cot with its rusty springs. It would be better than nothing, he reasoned.

He circled back through the alley that ran behind Mrs. Pike's place and entered the lower floor of the shed. He retrieved the rug from the top of the Victrola and took it outside. He unrolled it and struck it several times against a clothesline post to get some of the dust out. Then he carried it upstairs and spread it on top of the bedsprings. It was hot and stifling in the room, and his sweat made rivulets in the dust on his arms and face. With some effort, he managed to raise the window to let some air into the room. Then he lay down wearily on the cot with his clothes on.

He kicked his shoes off, but he decided it would be too cold by morning to sleep without his clothes. He was thirsty again, but he was too tired to go back down to the well. Besides, it was nearly dark now, and stumbling around in the unfamiliar mishmash downstairs could be dangerous.

Although he was dog-tired, he couldn't fall asleep right away. His stomach growled constantly, long ropes of squeezing sound testified to the fact that for almost six days now he had had only the one hamburger to eat. He tried to put thoughts of food out of his mind. Back home, his mother would be finishing the supper dishes. She was thinking of him, no doubt, wondering where he was and if he was all right. His father would be sitting in the front room reading the newspaper or a love story in *Redbook* magazine. Perhaps he too was wondering where he was—not out of any real concern, he thought bitterly, but angry that the son he had counted on to work on the farm that summer might not be around.

His father was a hard worker and a good provider, he had to admit, and they never went without the necessities, except, of course, for understanding and love. He had learned early on to expect neither from him. He had no doubt about his mother's love for him. She was quick to praise him, supporting him when she could, trying to shield him as best she could when she witnessed her husband's frequent onslaughts of rage. He did not need his hunger pangs to remember the good meals she always had ready for them. That evening, they might have had hot, homemade biscuits with fresh churned butter, mashed potatoes and rich brown gravy, beef or ham butchered that spring, creamed peas, maybe a Jell-o salad, and some kind of pie. Often it was cherry pie, his favorite.

He shifted his thoughts to his plight. He needed to find work right away to earn money to buy food and find a place to stay. Tomorrow, he'd finish up Mrs. Pike's yard, then look around downtown for some kind of a job. Maybe a couple of part-time jobs. And he needed to find a way to get into school in the fall. If he were to make something of himself, he'd have to finish high school, and he had planned to go to college too. Maybe study engineering. He was on his own now, and he was starting from scratch.

I don't care, I can make it on my own, he said to himself. *No matter what happens, I'm never going back, and that's for sure!* He lay there in the darkness for a long time thinking of home and his mother and then finally drifted off to sleep.

CHAPTER 2

He awoke with a start before seven, the morning sun flooding in through the open window doing little to overpower the gloom but beginning already to heat up the room. The gnawing hunger in his stomach had not slept, and it got up with him. He swung his legs off the cot and stuffed his feet into his shoes. He needed to get an early start.

He looked around at the room where he had spent the night. Rain had leaked in at various times, leaving garish brown stains running like stalactites down the plaster walls, which gave the room a cave-like atmosphere. Looking at them and letting his imagination run, he could picture all sorts of strange things, and they did nothing to lighten his mood. The dreary impression was almost overwhelming, but the room would have to do until he could find another place. If he could not, he would simply have to make the best of it. Perhaps he could find things to fix it up and make it livable—but there was no electricity and it would be impossible to have any kind of stove. Here and there, he could see daylight through cracks and chinks in the walls and roof. It would need lots of work if he were to live there for very long. In the meantime, it needed to be cleaned up. He went downstairs and retrieved a lopsided broom from the clutter and returned to the loft. Despite his best efforts, he did little more than rearrange the dust, and he stopped when it induced a fit of coughing.

He thought about Mrs. Pike. She seemed like a kindly, sympathetic person. She had mentioned a spare bedroom, and he thought about asking her if he might stay there, offering to do work around the house and yard for her to pay the rent. He quickly rejected the idea. The incident with Marvin came forcefully to mind. He had seemed friendly and had even bought him a hamburger. It would be best to go slow in trusting anyone. Besides, she would know that the story about his aunt was a lie, and she just might figure things out and think it was her duty to turn him in to the police. She had said she hadn't been back to the shed in a couple of years because of her feet, so it might be safe to stay there for a while. With her poor eyesight and hearing, the thick grove of cedars ought to be enough to protect him from discovery, and he hadn't noticed any lights on the back side of the house that night.

Emerging from the shed, he went to the pump and pushed down on the handle. This time, he stuck his face under the gushing torrent, drinking long drafts of the cold water as it splashed over his face, neck, and arms. He felt refreshed as he retrieved the tools from the shed and started up the path toward the front yard. He noticed that a caravan of black ants was already crossing the path single file and working on the vomit he had left in the weeds the afternoon before.

Enjoy the cranberry punch, he laughed to himself. *Mrs. Pike will give you some more if you get thirsty.*

As the morning progressed toward noon and the sun began to bake the yard, the cramping feeling in the pit of his stomach was relentless, and the hard work and the oppressive heat made him sweat profusely. He made several trips to the well, monitoring the progress of the ants as he went. The water not only quenched his thirst, it helped to placate his hunger to some extent.

He worked steadily, and by noon, he had finished the job. He knocked lightly on the front door, and in a moment Mrs. Pike opened it.

"Good morning, Steve," she said brightly, the light reflecting gaily from her glasses once again.

"I'm all done, ma'am."

The woman surveyed the yard approvingly. "Bless your heart, young fellow; it looks real nice. You worked like a Trojan."

"Do you have anything else you want me to do? You mentioned some boxes in your spare room."

"No, nothing else. I think I'll wait with the boxes."

He had taken off his shirt while he worked, and the old woman looked at him closely. "Those are nasty bruises you've got there. How'd you get them?"

He flushed as he looked down at the purple-black bruise that ran diagonally across his right chest and bicep and another that ran across his collarbone and right shoulder. He tried to choke back the memory of the violence of that last evening at home as he felt the bruises and winced in pain.

He recovered quickly and tried to pass it off. "Oh, about a week ago someone opened a truck door suddenly and smacked me hard across the arm and chest. It's still a little tender, but it'll heal."

"Well, you sure worked hard and the yard looks real nice, nicer than it has in a good many years. Sit down on the porch there, and I'll bring you a cold drink."

Before he could think of a tactful protest, she disappeared through the screen door and reappeared in a moment with a large tumbler of the house specialty and a china plate on which she had carefully arranged two sugar cookies, each with a raisin in the middle, eight purple grapes, and half of a ham sandwich.

"I expect you're hungry too, a growing boy," she said as she handed it to him.

Steve had learned from his experience the preceding afternoon, and he sat down on the edge of the porch and sipped the drink slowly. Obviously, the ice man was still on vacation somewhere. He nibbled down the grapes and spent some time chewing the half sandwich before finishing off the cookies in several small bites. The food assuaged his hunger only slightly, and he reflected briefly on the half sandwich. Still, it was nice of her. Perhaps it was part of her own lunch.

"Anna Meyer, the lady next door, asked me if you'd want to take care of her yard too. And if you need more to do, you might check with the lady over yonder across the street."

"Yes, ma'am, I sure would. My aunt just has her Social Security, so I need all the work I can get to help out." He wondered if she considered the food as payment for his hard work.

In a moment she said, "I don't guess you'd take some more of those green apples in payment for your work, would you?"

He caught the twinkle in her eye and smiled. "I would, but I don't know how I'd account for them on my income taxes. Do you think the worms would be assets or liabilities?"

"Depends on whether you eat them," she laughed. She fished into her apron pocket and carefully pulled out five quarters, which she counted out into his hand one by one, as carefully as if they were gold pieces. "Twenty-five, fifty, seventy-five, one dollar, and a dollar and a quarter—a little something extra for your hard work. If you stop by now and then, maybe I'll have things for you to do … no man around and all."

"All right, I will," he agreed, slipping the coins into his pocket. "Thanks for the lunch, ma'am. G'bye."

With that, he returned the tools to the shed and slipped into the neighboring yard. His knock was answered by Mrs. Meyer, a tall, angular woman of about sixty with steel-gray hair parted severely down the middle and well-defined wrinkles drawing her mouth down into a perpetual frown.

Before he even had time to announce his purpose, she launched into a heated tirade as if following a well-rehearsed script. "Regular boy didn't show up as usual. Niggers! You can't depend on them! They say they'll show up and then don't. Lazy! If you don't keep your eye on them, they'll hide out in the shade and expect to be paid even though they don't finish the job. Shiftless! Anybody'll tell you that. Steal you blind. That's just the way they are—inbred into them. Well, I expect you to earn *your* pay! I've been watching you from the window, and you do work hard, but if I pay you good money, I expect you to follow my directions so you do things right."

Her broad brush of the Negro race made Steve uncomfortable. He had heard of racial prejudice and segregation, of course, but he had never actually encountered them. He was spared the necessity of making a response, however, when she continued, almost without pause, explaining in great detail exactly how she wanted the yard and flower beds raked, where to put the harvest of leaves, weeds, and grass, how long to saw the limbs, where to stack them so that they didn't block the front gate and protrude into the walkway, the need to be careful so he didn't break the rake like the regular boy did the last time, and on and on.

That finished at last, she began to ask him a number of questions—questions about where he lived, what he was doing in Morefield—enough of them, he thought, to have qualified him for a position in some big corporation. All the while, she looked at him intently, sharply, suspiciously, as if she were recording the data in an inward notebook and seeking to trip him up in his answers. He squirmed under the relentless interrogation, trying to avoid disclosing much about his past. Finally, he interrupted, saying that if he was to finish the work that afternoon he'd need to get on with it. He had the feeling that his answers had not been entirely satisfactory.

Two and a half hours' work earned him another dollar and a couple of blisters, but no food. Then he cleaned up a small yard for the woman across the street. He finished at a little before five, collected his third dollar for the day, and headed down the street toward where he presumed downtown might be. As he passed her house, he noticed Mrs. Pike at her station on the porch and waved to her.

"Steven, would you mind bringing the mail in from the box for me?" she called loudly. "It's hard for me to get up and down the walk."

He retrieved the mail, a couple of letters and a newspaper, and started up the walk. Glancing toward the house next door, he caught a glimpse of Mrs. Meyer standing at the kitchen window, half hidden by the closing curtain. As he handed the mail to Mrs. Pike, he glanced at the address on one of the letters. 1126 Decatur St. He might need to remember that, he thought. Feeling faint from the day's exertion and the ever-present hunger, he sat down for a moment on the edge of the porch.

Mrs. Pike regarded him thoughtfully, pretending to be absorbed in her letters. After a few moments, she put them down. "How did things go with Mrs. Meyer?"

He shrugged and made a face.

"You don't need to tell me. I've lived next door to her for goin' on twenty-five years now. Isn't anything that goes on in this neighborhood that isn't her business. She wanted to know if I knew your aunt. I said I hadn't asked her name—I've forgotten, what did you say her name was?"

Steve hadn't mentioned a name, but he quickly came up with one he thought would serve the purpose. "Aunt Mildred." Hoping to preempt an inquiry as to her last name, he added quickly, "She's a little forgetful, but she's doing okay. She's got lumbago and has migraines once in a while, and she's got rheumatism in her knees and fingers too. You'd think the hot weather would cure that."

He'd need to remember Aunt Mildred's name and her array of ailments in case of future inquiries. Dealing with phantom identities could get a little confusing. He got up quickly before she could ask any more questions. "I'd better be going. She'll be wondering where I've been all day. She gets upset about things. I'll just cut through the backyard and go out through the alley. Bye now, ma'am."

He walked quickly to the backyard, looked around cautiously, glad that the cedars there shielded him from Mrs. Meyer's window, and stepped out through the back gate into the alley. A high privet hedge entwined with honeysuckle lined one side of the alley, and a six foot wooden fence interrupted now and then by a gate, the other. It should be fairly easy to come and go to Mrs. Pike's shed without being seen. He'd have to be careful, of course. Mrs. Meyer might be a problem. A plan was beginning to form in his mind. He would need some sort of guardian in order to get into the local high school, and Mrs. Pike just might be the answer for that too. But for now, finding steady work—and something to eat—was the first order of business. When he reached the end of the alley, he took a left and headed down a busy street toward the city center.

In a few minutes, he found himself in the town's business district. Hoping to see a help-wanted sign somewhere, he began a quick canvass of the store windows. He paused longingly in front of a bakery window, attracted by the smell of fresh-baked bread. A tray of sticky cinnamon rolls dotted with pecans caught his eye, reminding him of the homemade rolls his mother usually had ready for him when he got home from school. The aroma was almost overpowering, and he quickly entered the store and bought two of the rolls. Devouring them as he went, he resumed his survey of the business section. His thoughts returned to his mother. He wondered if she was thinking of him, wondering where he was, wondering if he was all right. And he thought about his older brother Dave. Dave would have to shoulder more than his share of the farm work this summer because Steve was not there to help. He felt sorry for that, but he quickly turned his thoughts back to his search for his own work. What was done was done.

Near the far end of the business district, he spotted a big red-and-yellow sign spread across the front of a building proudly proclaiming, "BANFIELD'S FINE FOODS AND NOTIONS." He had three dollars and fifteen cents in his pocket, and he would need to pick up a few things to eat. If he was going to work, he'd need to keep up his strength. And it wouldn't do to get sick—he couldn't afford a doctor or medicine.

Inside Banfield's, Steve bought a loaf of Wonder Bread, a half-pound of sliced minced ham, a quarter pound of cheddar cheese, and three oranges. The bill came to sixty-three cents. He counted the change as carefully as Mrs. Pike would have done and slipped the coins slowly into his pocket. The clerk, a plump, middle-aged woman with heavily rouged cheeks and billowing hair obviously self-dyed coal black, smiled at him as she handed him the paper bag with his groceries. She seemed friendly, and he decided it wouldn't hurt to ask.

"Ma'am, do you have any work I could do here?"

"I don't think so," she said doubtfully, "but I'll ask my husband. He does the hiring." She went into a back room, and he could hear her talking to someone. Soon, a stout man in his late fifties with gray hair receding from his temples and a roll of stubble-covered fat bulging over his collar came to the counter where he waited.

"Can you do hard work? Hard work is what I got and only for a couple of hours or so this afternoon. The regular boy didn't show up today. Kids! If you want to work, you can help me unload the truck out back. The boxes are heavy, I can tell you, and then sweep out the store just before closing. The pay is six bits. There's work if you want it. Hard work."

"Okay, I don't mind hard work … sir," said the boy quickly, and he took a step toward the back door where the truck waited. "Just show me what you want me to do."

The boxes, full of canned goods, were heavy indeed, though not nearly so heavy or unmanageable as the big alfalfa and red clover bales he was used to lifting on the farm. The man, Ed Banfield, as he introduced himself, said little as they worked, but at least he wasn't constantly bawling him out like his father did.

As he worked, Steve thought about his father. He had often wondered why they didn't get along. He had tried to be an obedient son as the Bible ordained, but his father seemed to resent him, to resent his very existence. It wasn't just his imagination. A number of times when he lost his temper, his father had exclaimed, "When you get to be twenty-one and are of age, you can clear out of here. I won't be responsible for you anymore!" Even more hurtful was, "I wish you'd never been born!" Steve had come to believe that he meant it. He'd said it often enough.

He was fifteen years younger than his half-brother David, who was the youngest of five children from his father's first marriage. Perhaps he had not been wanted in the first place, although he was sure that his mother entertained no such thoughts. He remembered fondly the countless little things she did for him—the long evenings as a child when he sat on her lap after the dishes were done and she read to him—*Tom Sawyer*, *Robinson Crusoe*, *The Three Musketeers*.

She had been an English teacher in the local high school before her marriage, and Steve's proficiency in English grammar and love of literature were no accident. Though loving, she was a quiet, submissive woman where her husband was concerned. Sometimes she tried to take up for Steve during his father's violent rages, but she could do little to leaven the anger and the physical abuse he vented upon him regularly. When his father flew off the handle, there was no reasoning with him. Nevertheless, the boy could not help feeling a little guilty. Perhaps he had not been quite the dutiful son the commandment required. Perhaps he could have tried harder.

He pondered all of this as he worked hard to please his new boss. His muscles ached from the strain, and he reached up now and then to massage the knot on his rib, still painful though it had been more than three months now since his father had struck him. The purple-black bruises on his right shoulder and upper arm, a couple of them bruised to the bone, throbbed insistently.

He sweated profusely even as the setting sun began to cool things off. When they had brought the last box inside and unpacked it, he swept out the store, finishing just as Mr. Banfield completed adding up the day's receipts. His wife, Ardella, the woman with the coal black hair, had put his groceries in a walk-in cooler, and she handed the bag to him.

"Here's your things, and here's your pay. Three and a half hours." She handed him two dollars, adding, "You're a hard worker, young man. Not many young folks are willing to work for their pay these days."

He stuffed the bills into his pocket with the rest of his earnings. "Thanks, ma'am. Do you think you might be able to take me on, on a regular basis?"

"Ed?"

"Tell you what. You come back at five tomorrow and if the regular boy don't show up, you can have his place. Three afternoons a week for three hours, fifty cents an hour. How's that sound?" His tone was businesslike but friendly enough.

"Fine. I'll be here tomorrow. 'Night, sir. 'Night, Mrs. Banfield."

There was still about an hour of daylight left when Steve headed toward home. He spotted a bunch of carrots in the trash bin behind the store, their tops just starting to rot. He retrieved it and started up the alley, hurrying on, not wanting to have to find his way through the unfamiliar streets in the approaching darkness. The cinnamon rolls he'd eaten earlier had been only a token gesture to his stomach, which continued to bid loudly for his attention. He was anxious to get some of the food he had bought at Banfield's into it. As he crossed a side street and stepped up onto the curb, he found himself face-to-face with a paunchy policeman wearing a set of khakis. His chest was conspicuously adorned by a large, shiny gold star that reminded Steve of the Jack Armstrong decoder badge he'd once gotten for a dozen Wheaties box tops.

The deputy looked at him searchingly, perhaps because of the look of alarm that had involuntarily crossed his face. "On your way home, young fella?"

"Yessir," Steve replied, hoping that his Midwestern accent wouldn't give him away. He tried to affect a local drawl. "Jest a'goin' on home."

"Haven't seen you around here b'fore."

"Nossir. Jest moved here."

"Them carrots you got there? You like carrots?"

As a matter of fact, Steve was nearly as fond of carrots as he was of sugary cranberry punch, but they were something to eat. "They're for Peter, m' pet rabbit," he said quickly. The invention came out of nowhere, but it served the purpose. The policeman did not reply, and Steve hurried on, hoping to avoid further conversation. He was relieved that the policeman hadn't asked him any questions such as where he lived or who his family was.

That encounter and Mrs. Meyer's thorough interrogation made him realize he needed to spend some time right away inventing a new identity and a plausible story that would justify his presence in Morefield. He'd need to get it down pat. The name Peter was a bit obvious for a rabbit, even an imaginary one. He'd need to do better than that—and also to get some sort of identification papers.

He found the alley without trouble and entered the darkening yard. The shadows of the protective cedars advanced boldly as the sun retreated, beginning to engulf the shed. He broke off the tops of the carrots and rinsed them off at the well, then stumbled up the steps and entered the room. It was stuffy and beastly hot. He sat down on the cot, unwrapped the lunch meat, and made a sandwich of two slices of bread. He ate it hungrily and made himself close the sack up again and save the rest of the lunch meat for the next day. The cheese, he decided, would keep for a few days along with the bread. For dessert, he managed to down two carrots.

Exhausted by the day's hard work and the strain of his new existence, he rolled over onto the cot and stretched out. An errant spring that had tormented him the night before found him again, and he decided to do something about it. To cut the heavy wire and bend it back he would need a pair of wire cutters. He remembered seeing one on the workbench downstairs the day before, but when he went to get it, it was not there. In the dimming light, he sorted through the miscellaneous items that covered the bench, and, not finding the wire cutters, he bent down to see if they had fallen to the floor.

They were not there either, but what caught his eye were a couple of footprints in the dust. They were the prints of boots with a distinctive pattern on the heels—like rays of a rising sun—and they had not been there the day before when he noticed the wire cutters lying on the bench. He was certain of that.

A parade of questions ran through his mind. Could the visitor have taken the wire cutters? Who was he and what was he doing in the shed? Did he live in the neighborhood? Would he come again? Most importantly, did he go upstairs? Steve didn't think so. He would have noticed the strange footprints in the dust on the steps. Perhaps, he thought, he should install a padlock on the door at the top of the stairs to prevent anyone from entering and discovering signs of his presence there. He quickly rejected that idea when he examined the door and doorjamb. The wood was rotten and would not hold screws, and, besides, someone who was familiar with the shed might wonder why a lock had been installed there and decide to investigate. Anyway, the thought occurred to him that possibly someone who knew Mrs. Pike had simply borrowed the wire cutters and would return them.

Nevertheless, the strange boot prints and their possible threat to his security troubled him as he set about fixing the offending wire. The lack of the wire cutters proved to be no real obstacle. He simply bent the rusty wire back and forth until it broke in two.

He lay down again, glad to be free of the wire's torment, but in a moment he realized that since he had only the clothes on his back to go to work in, he'd better not sleep in them again no matter how chilly it got toward morning. Tomorrow, he would need to see about finding a change of clothes. So many things he needed! He undressed and then lay down again. His right shoulder and arm resumed their throbbing, and his rib and muscles were still sore. He lay awake for some time mulling over the meaning of the boot prints and trying to concoct a reasonable past that would suit his new life. After a while, he fell asleep and slept through the night, dreaming fitfully of home in Nebraska.

Chapter 3

Breakfast consisted of an orange, two slices of bread, a slice of lunch meat, and a carrot. He reflected that he needed to get basic things like a knife, fork, spoon, plate, toothbrush, toothpaste, soap, a towel, flashlight, and a water glass. He took his earnings out of his pocket and counted them slowly, one, two, three, four dollars—four dollars and fifty-two cents. He was proud of the feeling of self-sufficiency the money gave him, but he realized it wouldn't buy much of what he desperately needed if he was to set up a new life and make it on his own.

Looking around the room, he decided that his present lodging, primitive as it was, would have to be his home for the foreseeable future, and he began to plan how he might fix it up to make it more livable. And what about winter? It was several months away, but it wasn't too early to begin to think about it. There was no stove, and the walls were thin. Mr. Banfield had said it sometimes got down to well below freezing, and once in a while there was snow.

He brought the broom upstairs again and made an attempt to sweep some of the dust down the stairway. He only half succeeded, stopping again when the billowing cloud made him cough loudly.

He'd have to be careful about making noise. Outside, he paused at the pump to wash his face, then walked up the alley and around the block, approaching Mrs. Pike's house from the direction of the park. She waved from her post in the swing, and he stopped a moment to say hello.

She was sipping her morning coffee. "Would you like something to drink to wake you up, Steve?"

Fearing another round of the house specialty, he quickly shook his head. "Wake me up? What have you got, hard cider you've squeezed out of those apples I raked up? Bet you've got a still somewhere!"

She laughed. "You'd be surprised what's hidden back there in that old shed."

"Maybe I will check that out," he replied, reflecting on the irony of her remark. "But don't worry, your secret is safe with me. I won't turn you into the Feds since you didn't turn me in to the sheriff. Gotta go now. I'm trying to earn an *honest* living."

Chuckling to himself, he trotted on down to the foot of Decatur Street, where he contracted with one of the residents to clean up his yard and spade a flower bed. Another dollar and a quarter.

He headed for downtown looking for work. The part-time job at the grocery store, if he got it, would not be enough. He needed another, but with school out for the summer he supposed there were plenty of boys looking for work. He asked at several stores but found nothing. At noon, he stopped at a small cafe on the courthouse square and had a bowl of steaming vegetable beef soup and a glass of milk. Twenty-five cents. He crushed six packages of crackers into the soup, stopping the process of stretching it into a full meal when he caught the disapproving eye of the waitress behind the counter. He folded the unused paper napkin and stuck it in his back pocket for a handkerchief.

He rested on a bench under the trees of a small park down the street from the cafe, feeling a little weak, before continuing his canvass of the business section. The sun beat down mercilessly on the pavement, burning his feet through the soles of his shoes. The heat reflected up from the cement in waves, distorting objects and giving them an aspect of unsteady unreality. This, combined with his hunger and fatigue, made him slightly dizzy, and he sat down weakly on the narrow ledge of a store window in the shade of a red-and-green-striped awning to regroup his senses before continuing his survey of job opportunities in the business district. Shoppers and tradesmen passed by, intent on their own concerns, and took no notice of him. He felt invisible and alone, and after a while, he got up wearily and resumed his search for work.

Mid-afternoon, he entered the office of the local newspaper. The big sign over the entrance read "MOREFIELD TIMES-ENTERPRISE—JOB PRINTING" in black gothic letters. He asked a man hunched over a linotype about work and was directed to the office of the editor-publisher, Mr. Benjamin, who sat at a roll-top desk with his back to the door, entering figures in a ledger and eating a sandwich.

Steve found the question hard to ask although he had asked it already more than a dozen times that afternoon, but he cleared his throat and began timidly, "Sir, I need a job. Would you have any work I could do?"

"No, sorry, we don't have anything," the man replied curtly without turning around.

Steve's face fell, although the rejection was hardly new to him. "Anything at all, sir?" he persisted. "I really need work, sir. I can sweep out, unload trucks—I'd like to learn the printing business if I could."

The man swiveled around in his chair. He peered at the boy over bifocals from beneath a green eyeshade—just like in the movies, Steve thought.

"Are you new around here? You sound like you might be from up north."

Steve was glad he had spent some time the night before working on his new persona. "My name is Steven Bowman, and I've been living in Dayton, Ohio. My dad was killed in a car wreck five years ago, and I lived with my mom and stepfather till last week. They've sent me down here to live with my grandmother and go to school. I just got here day before yesterday."

"How old are you? Why do you want to work here?"

"I'll be sixteen in October, sir. She's not my real grandmother. She's my stepfather's mother, and she didn't much want me here in the first place. She gives me a place to stay and that's about it. So I pretty much have to earn my own way. I really need a job, and I think the printing business would be something I'd like to learn."

"You mean you have to provide for your own food, clothes, and things?"

"Yes, sir. She's on Social Security. She gives me a place to stay, but I have to provide for everything else I need. Everything …" His voice trailed off. He wondered how convincing his story sounded. He was not used to telling lies, his recent success with Peter Rabbit notwithstanding.

Something about the boy—his apparent sincerity and the sense of urgency in his voice caught the interest of the man, and he felt an instant sympathy for him. The boy was clean-cut, respectful, and well-spoken, and he looked him straight in the eye when he spoke. His deep blue eyes seemed to flash with intelligence and integrity, perhaps character within, he thought.

Against his better judgment, the man heard himself say, "Well, I guess we could give you a little work. Not a whole lot. Just a few hours a week. The pay isn't good—how would fifty cents an hour sound, maybe fifteen hours a week? You look pretty strong—some of it will be heavy work—paper stock weighs more than you might think. And I don't know how long I can keep you on—depends on how things go with the printing jobs and how you work out."

"That would be great, sir!" the boy said with feeling. "Thanks! When can I begin?"

"How about Monday right after lunch—12:30? Work until 4:30."

"Fine, I'll be here. I'd like to learn the printing trade. Would there be a chance I could help with the printing end of it sometimes if I get my regular work done first? I could do it on my own time."

"We'll see how things go," the man replied. He was impressed by the boy's offer, and he resolved to do what he could for him if his work panned out. He looked like a good bet.

* * * * * * * *

Steve hurried on down the street. It wouldn't do to be late at the grocery store if he expected to get the job there. He hoped that the regular boy would not show up.

Mr. Banfield was not in, but Ardella gave him the good news that the regular boy had had a chance to go down to Mobile with his uncle for a few days of sailing on the bay, and his mother had called to say he wouldn't be coming back.

"Does this mean I can have the job?" he asked.

"I imagine so," she said, "but we'll have to wait until my husband gets back from Birmingham to be sure. He makes the decisions around here."

Without being asked, Steve went to work carting in heavy boxes of canned goods and cases of Dr. Pepper, Squirt, and root beer that were piled high on the loading platform and stacking them in the store room. Anxious to prove himself, he went to work with a will, straining to carry the heavy boxes and cases. He worked up a good sweat, and he was glad when that task was finished. Then he began to restock the shelves. He was sweeping out the store just before closing time when Mr. Banfield arrived. He stopped by and clapped Steve on the right shoulder, letting his hand rest there for a few moments. He smiled kindly. "You sure worked hard today, Steve. You'll get on here just fine."

Steve shuddered, not from the pain of the deep bruise to his shoulder but from a vague, discomforting feeling that came flooding back from somewhere in the past. He tried to shake it off and managed a smile.

"Does that mean I can have the job, sir?"

"You bet! My wife will pay you every two weeks."

Steve finished the sweeping and left by the back way instead of the front, passing by the garbage cans in the alley where he retrieved a package of stale cookies and an empty jelly jar and headed home. As he walked up the street, he noticed the policeman he had seen the evening before standing in front of the drugstore watching him intently. He pretended not to notice him, but as he passed by, the officer called out, "Say, how's that bunny rabbit of yours doin'?"

"Jest fine, I reckon. He didn't eat none o' them carrots last night, and I didn't see 'im this mornin'. It's like he's invisible most o' the time. I think he might be a hidin' under some o' the furniture downstairs."

The policeman did not respond, and Steve hurried on, grinning inwardly at his little joke. *Easy does it,* he said to himself. *Doesn't pay to get too flip.* He reminded himself that if he was to remain as inconspicuous as possible, especially where the police were concerned, he needed to play it straight. He wondered again if his picture was on the wall at the police station or the post office. Not likely, he decided finally. Nebraska was a long way from Alabama. He couldn't be too careful though.

He turned into the alley and slipped into Mrs. Pike's backyard, grateful that the hedge and the cedars had turned the alley into a protective tunnel of dappled gray and black. It appeared that the alley was seldom used, but he'd have to be on the alert and try to stay in the shadows.

He should have been in high spirits having landed the jobs at Banfield's and the newspaper, but the gathering gloom seemed to deepen his mood, and his spirits flagged. Perhaps it was the anticipation of the Spartan room that awaited him.

At the well near the shed, he stopped for a drink of water, washed out the jelly jar he'd brought home, filled it, and took up it to the room. He took his clothes off in the darkness before falling onto the cot. They were getting dirty—he had only the clothes on his back. He had to get some more somehow, and he had to find a way to wash them.

He continued to feel uneasy and nervous, almost depressed. He lay back on the cot and thought back over the events of the day, trying to figure out the reason for his mood. It was not long before he remembered the incident at the store when Mr. Banfield had let his hand rest on his shoulder. A friendly gesture to be sure, but it had brought back the incident with Marvin. Although he had tried to suppress the memory of that afternoon, it had continued to seep back into his consciousness and subvert his mood at odd moments. Perhaps it was time to try to sort out his feelings.

As he lay there, the incident came back in vivid detail. He had been walking along the highway just east of Charleston in Illinois when a Mayflower moving van screeched to a halt in front of him and backed up. He had been deep in thought and was not thumbing a ride, but he thought it was nice of the driver to stop and pick him up anyway.

The driver, a big, beefy, red-faced man in his early forties with a week's growth of black whiskers, rolled down the window and looked him over. "Need a ride, young fellow?"

Steve, footsore and tired, accepted the invitation without hesitation. He ran around the front of the truck, opened the door, and pulled himself up onto the cracked leather seat.

"Where you headed?" the man asked.

"Columbus." Columbus was no better than a dozen other cities he might have chosen, but it served the purpose of being somewhere east of Indianapolis.

"Well, you're in luck," the man said, patting the boy lightly on the shoulder and letting his hand rest there for a moment or two. "I go right through there on my way to Pittsburgh. I got a load of furniture to deliver there." He shifted into low, pulled onto the highway, and the boy began the next leg of his trip to somewhere.

"You live in Columbus?" the man asked.

"No, Omaha. My grandma lives in Columbus. She lives by herself and had a bad fall and broke her hip. I'm goin' there to stay with her till she can get around again." He had used the same story three times already in thumbing rides, and it seemed eminently serviceable.

"What's your name?"

"Steven, Steve."

"Steve. Well, I'm Marvin."

"Glad to know you, Marvin," he said, accepting the man's outstretched hand.

As they rode along, the man kept up a running conversation and began to ask a lot of questions, questions about his grandmother, about school, friends, things he liked to do. He had a habit of talking out of the right side of his mouth, and his conversation was peppered with sideways glances toward Steve as he talked. A couple of times he patted Steve on the shoulder, letting his hand rest there for a moment or two.

As the questions became a little more personal, Steve began to feel uncomfortable, but he decided that the man was just being friendly.

At noon, Marvin pulled his rig into a truck stop not far from the Ohio line and said, "Let's go in and get something to eat."

Steve said he wasn't hungry, but the man persisted. "A big, husky boy like you not hungry? C'mon with me and we'll get a bite."

Finally, Steve protested that he did not have any money, although he remembered that he had tucked a five-dollar bill into the top pocket of his overall jacket a couple of weeks earlier when he expected to go to the weekly free picture show in town. He planned to meet Barbara, his girlfriend, there, and they would sit together on a blanket in the darkness watching a black-and-white cowboy shoot-em-up shown on a white sheet stretched against the brick wall of the drugstore. Later, they would have an ice cream soda inside. But that evening, his father had made him stay home and help spray the apple trees, and the money was still in his pocket.

Although he was hungry and the truck stop looked inviting—a

red neon sign flashing "Good Eats," alternating with a sign that flashed "Open" in blue, he decided it would be best to save the money in case he needed it worse later along the way. He stayed in the cab while the trucker went into the cafe. When the man returned half an hour later, he handed him a hamburger. The boy thanked him and ate it down quickly, his first meal since he had left home.

Marvin watched him eat it, then eased the van back onto Route 40 headed east. Steve had been on the road for three days with little sleep, and after a while he dozed off, lulled to sleep by the rhythmic thud, thud, thud of the tar strips on the pavement. How long he had been asleep he could not say, but he awakened with a start to find the man's hand moving up on his upper thigh. He pulled away sharply.

"C'mon, boy," the man said, "nothin' to it, and there's a couple of bucks in it for you. Buy you a bunch of them hamburgers."

The man had pulled his truck into a roadside park near Dayton. Steve yanked down hard on the door handle, pushed the door open, and prepared to jump out. Marvin grabbed his jacket, but Steve straightened his arms behind him and peeled out of it, pitching headlong into the weeds at the edge of the parking lot and rolling down into a ditch. He jumped to his feet, vaulted a low fence, and darted into a thorny thicket nearby. He dived into a depression in the ground that was surrounded by high grass and caught his breath. After a while, he could hear Marvin honking the horn in the distance and shouting, "Come back! C'mon back, boy! I won't bother you! I didn't mean no harm! Come on back, boy—I'll have you in Columbus b'fore night!"

When at last he heard the truck grind into low gear and rattle into the distance, he crept out of the thicket and began to walk across the fields toward Dayton, thankful that the encounter had inflicted only a couple of minor scratches on his left arm. As he walked along, he had time to take stock of his situation. With a start, he realized that he had left his jacket in Marvin's grasp and with it the five-dollar bill he had saved for an emergency. He was in the middle of nowhere with only the clothes on his back. He hadn't a cent to his name, and he did not know where he was going.

That was six days ago, and the incident continued to upset him at odd moments in the day. He lay there in the darkness for a long time, turning it over and over in his mind, trying to assure himself that it had not been his fault in any way. He should not have been so trusting.

The room was hot and close, and he was sweating profusely. Finally, he fell into a fitful sleep, awakening several times in the night in the strange, frightening surroundings.

Chapter 4

When he awoke just after dawn, shivering in the cold, the morning light and the surreal images on the walls did little to dispel the lingering feeling of depression. It was Sunday. The stores were closed, and he wouldn't work on the Sabbath anyway. No matter what his difficulties with his father had been, he had also inherited many of his values from him, and they would guide him the rest of his life.

On the way downtown, he had noticed a Methodist church, and he set out for morning services just before eleven. He approached it cautiously and stood for a while surveying the scene from the shade of the trees across the street. A brand new black 1946 Buick, drew up to the curb in front of the church, and a woman in a broad-brimmed, flowered hat and a boy and a girl about his own age got out and headed up the walk. The boy was wearing a neatly pressed tan suit with a vest, and the girl a beautiful light blue dress with a red sash, pocketbook, and shoes. Others he saw waiting to enter the church were similarly dressed in their Sunday best.

He looked down at his own clothes, then walked to a nearby bench and sat down in the shade, watching the worshippers going into the church. He listened as the organ played the prelude and the congregation began to sing the opening hymn, "Be Still, My Soul." It was a favorite of his, one they often sang in his church at home. The words came back to him as they sang,

Be still, my soul: the Lord is on thy side;
Bear patiently the cross of grief or pain;
Leave to thy God to order and provide;
In every change he faithful will remain,
Be still, my soul: thy best, thy heavenly friend
Through thorny ways leads to a joyful end.

He followed the words through the third verse and its poignant ending, "When change and tears are past, all safe and blessed, we shall meet at last." His thoughts turned to home, tears welling up in his eyes whether from the words or the familiar tune. He got up and walked slowly back to the shed. Reluctantly, he climbed the steps to the room and lay on the cot for a long time, feeling tired and alone. He had to admit that for the first time since that evening when he left his life behind, he was homesick.

His mother and brother Dave would be worried sick about him, and he was sorry for that. Barbara would be worried too. He hadn't called her that last evening as he'd promised, and there had been no time to say good-bye. He wondered if he should send his mother a letter to let her know he was safe, but he quickly rejected the idea. It could easily be traced back to Morefield, and he couldn't risk that. Still seeking a solution to that problem, he ate the rest of the minced ham, now warm and greasy and beginning to turn gray, three slices of dry bread, and a carrot. Then he went down to the well to drink his fill of the cold water and wash the taste out of his mouth.

He sat down on the cot and thought about his situation for a long time. When the shadows of the cedars outside stole through the window and across the room as if searching for him, he decided to go to bed. With the room nearly dark now, there was nothing else to do. He removed his clothes, placed them carefully on the broken chair and rolled onto the bed. His rib hurt and his shoulder ached, and he massaged them gently until he fell asleep.

* * * * * * * *

He got up before daylight and in the anonymity of the early dawn went outside in his shorts. Looking around cautiously, he removed them and bathed himself as best he could under the cold water at the well. Now wide awake, he went upstairs, dressed, and resumed sweeping the dust from the room, stirring up clouds of it that soon coated his arms and settled on his pants and shoes. *That wasn't too smart,* he laughed to himself. *Now I need another bath!*

It occurred to him that it would be easier to keep clean if he kept a bucket of water in his room. He had noticed a shiny galvanized bucket on the end of the workbench downstairs, and he decided that Mrs. Pike wouldn't mind if he borrowed it. But when he went to get it, someone else apparently had gotten there before him. Like the wire cutters, it was gone, replaced by a new heel print in the dust bearing the telltale imprint of a rising sun. Apparently the thief had made his rounds again, something he was to do frequently in the coming months.

Although he had not yet found a mirror in the junkyard downstairs, Steve could imagine what he looked like. He desperately needed a change of clothes and a haircut. He couldn't continue to work at the grocery store or at the newspaper looking like a vagrant. He remembered seeing a sign outside the church Sunday advertising a rummage sale on Tuesday afternoon. Maybe he could find something cheap there. He needed a flashlight and a bath towel, among other things.

He swung around the block so he could pass by Mrs. Pike's front porch from the direction of the park. He needed to establish a relationship with her. He waved and called out, "Morning, Mrs. Pike," as he passed by the mailbox.

She returned the greeting from the swing. "My, you're up early this morning! You know what they say, 'The early bird gets the worm!'" She laughed.

"If you are trying to peddle some more of your prize apples off on me, sorry, no sale," he replied in kind. The sound of her laughter echoed in his ears as he continued on his way down the street.

As he passed the house next door, he caught a glimpse of Mrs. Meyer, standing on her porch, arms akimbo—looking at him darkly, he thought. Not wishing to become engaged in another interrogation, he pretended not to notice her and hurried on down the street.

He wasn't due at the newspaper until half past twelve, so he decided to reconnoiter the business section near the square.

In the center of the square stood the county courthouse. A four-columned portico dignified the entrance to a rather ordinary-looking red brick building, and the roof was topped by a cupola with a clock stuck perpetually at 11:21 in all four directions. Whether this was a.m. or p.m., he couldn't tell. Out front, the building was guarded by a tall, stone statue of a young confederate soldier standing rigidly at attention, his eyes fixed straight ahead, his stone musket at order arms. Steve smiled up at the statue and softly gave the command, "War's over. Fall out!"

Just down the street was the Carnegie Library, squat and symmetrical, set back in a grove of pecan trees. With its ornate columns and cornices, he thought it looked like a frosted one-layer wedding cake. He made a note to visit it when it opened at ten. He asked a store clerk sweeping the sidewalk where the high school was and set out on the short walk.

It was a new-looking, tan brick building, three stories with a gym attached on one end, and he could make out the bleachers of the football field out back. "Morefield High School, 1940," the sign in the cement over the main entrance read. It was much larger than the small high school he had attended back in Nebraska, probably well over a thousand students, he guessed. That was good, he thought. It would be easy to keep out of the limelight. He walked up the long sidewalk and tested the front door. It opened and he entered quietly and walked slowly down the hall, carefully observing everything as he went. He needed to find out as much as he could about the school. It might come in handy later when it was time to enroll. The halls, filled with chairs and desks moved out of the classrooms so that the janitors could oil the floors, reeked of Pine Sol and furniture polish.

A squarish, middle-aged woman in a navy pinstripe suit with wide lapels, her straight, gray hair cut short just below the ears and parted down the middle, came out of one of the offices. She reminded him of a picture of a female Communist party functionary from Romania he had recently seen in a newspaper. He smiled at the thought.

"Did you want something, young man?" she asked briskly. "I'm Myra Edwards, assistant principal."

"I just moved here to live with my grandma and will be going to school here in the fall, ma'am. I'll be a junior, and I guess I'll need to register. I just wanted to know what kind of papers I need to bring."

The woman regarded him intently, noting his somewhat disheveled appearance. "New in town? Where did you come from? You sound like you come from up north somewhere."

He guessed he'd have to get used to the question. "Yes. Yes, ma'am. I'm from Dayton, Ohio."

"We don't get many northerners down here, not since the carpetbaggers." She smiled grimly. "You'll have to fit in," she added with a slight frown. She was silent for a few moments, and he decided it was advisable to let her carry on the conversation. Apparently resigning herself to his presence in the school, she continued, "You'll need to bring an official transcript with the courses you've completed and your grades at your high school in Dayton … and a birth certificate, of course. Is your grandma your legal guardian?"

Steve nodded. "Yes, ma'am." The arrangement seemed logical to him.

"Then you'll need to bring proof of guardianship, and she'll need to come with you when you register."

"Yes, ma'am," he answered, his heart sinking. He couldn't bring any of those things, especially his "grandmother."

"Registration is August twentieth and twenty-first," the woman said, continuing to look at him intently. "Be sure to bring everything with you or you can't get registered." With that, she turned and walked back into her office.

Steve trudged back toward the town center. He felt as if a heavy, steel door had just been slammed in his face. As far as the documents were concerned, he mused, he just might be able to come up with them, but his "grandmother?" He had invented one, but he couldn't exactly bring an imaginary old woman to school with him. It would be easier to bring Peter Rabbit.

He still had some time before reporting for work at the newspaper, so he ducked into the public library. He reasoned that it might be difficult for him to keep up with his subjects in the fall because of having to work long hours to provide for himself, so he selected books on math, history, and science and brought them to the checkout desk.

Another hurdle. He hadn't thought about a library card. His hometown didn't even have a public library. It seemed to him that his whole life was now concerned with overcoming obstacles. Fortunately, the librarian, a young woman barely into her twenties, was sympathetic, and she finally agreed to give him a card without requiring identification. But he had to give a home address. He decided the imaginary Aunt Mildred's address wouldn't do. He didn't even know the names of any streets in that part of town. Reluctantly, he gave her Mrs. Pike's address—1126 Decatur Street—even though he knew that could lead to trouble.

He still had a few minutes before work, and he went to the current newspaper section. He had a special purpose. The library subscribed mostly to papers from Alabama and the Deep South, but he was pleased to see the *St. Louis Post-Dispatch* on the rack. He thumbed quickly through the section with national news until he spotted a headline:

SEARCH FOR MISSING NEBRASKA BOY FRUITLESS

He sat down at a nearby table and began to read the article eagerly. It read, "Steadman Falls, Nebraska, June 12, 1947. More than 200 neighbors and friends along with law enforcement officers searched a wide area north of Steadman Falls Friday and Saturday for Joseph Whitfield, a 15-year-old farm boy and high school honor student who disappeared from his home June 8."

The article went on to say that the county sheriff speculated that the boy had run away from home after a quarrel with his father, although the investigation had failed to turn up anyone who might have given him a ride—the federal highway ran within half a mile of the farm home. His mother was described as distraught, making a plea for his safe return or any information that might lead to finding him. A reward of $250 had been posted.

With a sense of detachment mingled with unreality, he read about his own disappearance more than a week before. He sat there for several minutes, trying to digest the strange emotions the article evoked in him, feeling a little like Tom Sawyer attending his own funeral. Who was he now? Steven Bowman or Joseph Whitfield? They were different boys. He could see that. And he was both of them. After a few moments, he decided that he would have to stick with Steven Bowman for now.

He folded the paper and put it back on the rack. At the front desk, he asked the young woman if the library kept the St. Louis paper permanently. She replied that it was discarded after a month. He asked if he might have it then, and she agreed to put it aside for him. Books under his arm, he headed for his afternoon's work at the grocery store glad that she hadn't asked any questions.

He had no doubt that his mother was upset by his disappearance as the article had reported, but he knew she understood his reasons for running away. She had witnessed his father's abuse enough times. He wished he could find a way to let her know he was safe.

As he walked along, he indulged himself in fantasizing about his father's reaction when he failed to appear at the supper table that evening and didn't show up to milk the cows the next morning. He relished the growing sense of alarm, the frustration, even anger his father must have felt at the realization that his son had defied him and run away. He felt a little guilty about such feelings, but the long-term situation between him and his father produced a delicious little feeling of defiance and triumph, of self-assertion, deep inside, which now came boldly to the surface.

With an effort, he shook off the fantasy. He needed to cut off memories of his past and concentrate on his new life and identity. With this in mind, he reflected that it was perhaps a little strange that he wanted to keep the newspaper clipping about his disappearance.

* * * * * * * *

Steve could have only half imagined the sense of frustration, growing desperation, and disappointment that the search for him had engendered among the army of family, friends, and neighbors who combed the fields, hills, and valleys near Steadman Falls for two days. When the search for Joseph had been called off at last, when the last of family and neighbors had gone home, John Whitfield and his wife, Edith, and John's son by his first marriage, David, sat at the kitchen table after supper. The reality that Joe was probably not coming back, at least not any time in the near future, had set in.

"I don't think there's any possibility that he could be anywhere in this area," David said. "The searchers combed every square foot in a radius of six miles, and flyers with his picture have been posted in every town around."

"Yeah, he's taken off, that's for sure," his father said. "Trust him to leave us in the lurch just when we need him for the wheat harvest. Now I'll have to hire somebody to fill in. Then there'll be the hay."

"Don't you feel anything for the boy, John?" asked the mother. "He's your *son*, for goodness sake! For all we know, he may be hurt somewhere, or ... and all you can think about is the work you could have gotten out of him. That's the only reason you agreed to offering a reward."

John scowled. He was a large, intimidating man whose brooding features betrayed a single track mind. "Work is what puts food on the table, Edith. Work is what pays the mortgage on this farm. Work is what pays the bills. I have to scrap from dawn till dark to keep us out of the poor farm. If I didn't keep after him, he wouldn't do a lick of work—always some excuse to get out of it. Now he's lit out just when I need him most. Just wait till I get my hands on him, I'll straighten him out."

"That's just it, John," interrupted Edith, who usually deferred to her domineering husband. "You lay your hands on him at the slightest provocation. What about last spring when he accidentally knocked over a bucket of oats and it spilled on the ground? You flew off the handle and hit him in the chest with a piece of two-by-four—you broke one of his ribs! The authorities ought to have been called on you," she said. "And when the tractor got stuck in the mud down by the pond, you laid into him with a harness tug, and he's got a scar on the back of his leg where you pushed him into the hay rake. It wasn't his fault. Anyway, he's still a boy! And the other night when we were down in the cellar—over *nothing*! *Nothing*! I don't blame him for leaving, not one bit. I can't count the times you've beaten him with anything you could find!" She began to cry.

"You go too far, Dad," David began, but his father interrupted him sharply. "You keep your nose out of this, David!" he shouted, half rising from his chair. "It ain't none of your affair!"

David, now in his early thirties, bit his lip and looked away, then got up and went over to his stepmother and put his arm around her.

"You had no cause to do those things, John," she said. "He's a good boy and now he's out there, God knows where..." The rest was swallowed up in sobs.

"That's the trouble with you, Edith, you always take up for him," John said angrily, slamming his fist down on the table. In a moment, he stood up suddenly, tipping his chair over backward to the floor, and stormed out the back door, banging the screen door loudly as he went.

* * * * * * * *

Steve was still a few minutes early for work at the newspaper, so he sat down to rest on a bench in front of an appliance store a few doors down the street from the grocery store. Only a few shoppers passed by as he sat thinking about Miss Edwards's requirements and wondering how he might manage to meet them and get into school. He was deep in thought when he looked up and saw an elderly black man approaching, carrying an unwieldy box that apparently contained a radio of some kind. Suddenly, two white, teenaged boys coming from the other direction accosted him. The taller of the two reached out and snatched the man's cap from his head and tossed it into the gutter, snarling, "You take your hat off when you meet your betters, black man! Niggers belong in the gutter, now git there!"

The other boy, shorter and heavyset, gave the old man a shove, causing him to nearly drop the box as he stumbled into the gutter.

"That's better," the first boy said. "Next time, you'll know your place." With that, the two pranced, almost skipped on down the street, apparently well-pleased with themselves.

The old man stood for a moment, looking after them, a look of sad resignation on his face. He shifted his load so that he could reach down to retrieve his cap, and went on into the appliance store.

Steve had sat there on the bench, taking the incident in, immobilized by the shock of the sudden violence that had played out right in front of him. As he sat there, reflecting on it, he felt sympathy for the elderly man, then indignation at the boys, then outrage, then guilt that he had done nothing to defend the man. After wrestling with the incident for some time, he finally decided that there was little he could have done. He needed to keep himself out of the limelight, given his own situation. It was a rationalization, he supposed, but a necessary one. After a while, he got to his feet and went on down to the newspaper for his afternoon's work.

All afternoon as he worked at the newspaper, he mulled over the incident and the feelings the newspaper article had stirred up in him.

He found no satisfactory resolution to either. In regard to his own situation, it had become clear that he needed to figure out a way to let his mother know he was all right without giving the authorities a clue as to where he was.

His job at the paper had been created largely out of Mr. Benjamin's feeling of sympathy for him rather than any immediate need for him, and his duties had been cobbled together from bits and pieces of tasks around the office and printing plant. However, he seldom worked directly with Mr. Benjamin. Howard, who was the chief typesetter, was nominally his supervisor. He was easy-going and amiable, and Steve took an instant liking to him.

Steve's duties that first afternoon were typical of what the job was to entail: cleaning type, bringing rolls of newsprint from a storeroom to the press room, picking up an ad from a jewelry store down on the square, emptying wastebaskets, and sweeping out the newsroom. His tasks took him to every corner of the business, and he soon was on a first-name basis with all of the employees. Steve enjoyed his work and the friendly atmosphere there, and as time went on and he proved himself, Howard expanded his duties and taught him how to set type and lay out ads.

* * * * * * * *

If he needed to be reminded of the continual need to protect his real identity, he got a pointed reminder the next afternoon. As he was sweeping the sidewalk in front of the grocery store, a tan, 1940 Ford sedan with a couple in the front seat and four kids crammed in the back drew up in front of the store. The woman leaned out of the window. "Can we get some cold pop inside?"

"Pop!" Steve stiffened. That's what they called soda back home. He took a quick glance at the car's license plate—it was from Nebraska, County 19. He looked away to hide his face and replied in the best Southern accent he could muster on the spur of the moment, "Yeah, y'all can git some in 'ere, ma'am. Got Orange Crush, Dr. Pepper, an' Co-Cola."

He moved quickly on down the walk a ways and resumed sweeping, keeping his face averted from the visitors. They piled out of the car and trooped quickly into the store in quest of their pop, the two younger boys shoving each other to get through the door first. In a few minutes, they all reappeared with their liquid trophies and piled into the car. Steve noticed that the kids had already half finished their bottles. The father started the engine but sat there for a moment sipping his root beer. Steve wished he would hurry up.

Suddenly, one of the boys said in a loud voice, "Hey, I seen that boy somewheres before!"

"Who?" asked his brother.

"That boy over there sweepin' the sidewalk. I seen him somewheres."

"You're crazy!" said his brother, pushing him roughly on the shoulder. "You ain't been here before."

"Mom, Jerry pushed me again!" The younger boy gave the brother a hard punch on the shoulder, apparently taking his explanation to the parent as his legal authorization for retaliation.

"Look out! You're spillin' your pop on the upholstery!" the mother warned sharply. "You two behave yourselves or this is the last you're gettin' till we get back home."

With that, the father shoved the car into gear, and it lurched sharply away from the curb, nearly colliding with a boy on a bicycle. In another moment, it had sped safely on down the street and disappeared into the street leading back to the main highway.

Steve's heart was stuck in his throat. He didn't know them. County 19 wasn't that far from Steadman Falls. Probably his photo had been in the newspapers or on flyers back there after he disappeared. His mind raced. What if they figured things out later? What if they went to the authorities when they got back to Nebraska, and they contacted the police in Morefield?

Although nothing came of the incident, it was some time before Steve could put the close call out of his mind. He'd need to be careful when he was out in public. As he passed an army-navy surplus store after work, he decided to see if he could find a pair of cheap sunglasses there. He was in luck, and, to complete his disguise, he found a baseball cap with the word "Seabees" on the front. He could pull it down over his eyes if need be, and maybe he could get his hair cut short—when he had the money. Crew cuts were popular.

While there, he also picked out a Swiss army knife, a comb, a fork and spoon, a dollar pocket watch, a small flashlight with the batteries in it, a pair of khaki pants, a dark blue T-shirt that wouldn't show the dirt or need to be ironed, two mattress covers, and an army blanket marked down to thirty-five cents because of several moth holes in it. The bill came to three dollars and ninety cents.

Emerging from the store, he donned the cap and sunglasses although the sun was just going down. As he passed a trash can at the rear of a furniture store, he spotted a large cardboard box that had held a mattress for a twin bed. He put his books and purchases inside the box and managed to lug it through the darkening alleys back to the shed without encountering the policeman or Mrs. Meyer. He leaned the box against the Victrola on the lower floor and took his purchases upstairs.

For supper, he ate two slices of bread, a slice of the minced ham he had bought at the store, and a slice of cheese he cut off with his new knife. Reluctantly, he finished off his meal with the last two carrots. "If I keep swiping your carrots, Petey," he said aloud, "I won't need this flashlight. I'll be able to see in the dark." He grimaced as he chewed them carefully and washed them down with a jar of water. A horrible thought crossed his mind. What if Mrs. Pike also knew how to make carrot punch?

He picked up the flashlight and flipped it on and off several times, testing it. Then he went down to the lower floor and managed to find a broken spade handle he had noticed earlier, some rusty baling wire, and the crosscut saw he had used in cleaning up Mrs. Pike's yard. Upstairs, he sawed off a piece of the wooden handle and spliced it to the end of the broken leg of the chair by winding the wire around the two pieces. He sat down on the chair to test it. It wobbled, and he unwound the wire, adjusted the length of the leg, then tightened the wire again. He sat down on the chair again. Serviceable, he decided, but he'd have to be careful or it would break again and dump him on his head.

He opened the history book he had checked out of the library and began to read by the light of the flashlight. After half an hour, he grew tired and his eyes began to water and burn in the dim light. He lay down on the cot, said a quick prayer, and soon fell asleep. It had been a long day.

* * * * * * * *

Just after midnight, he awoke suddenly to the sound of someone rummaging through the sack of groceries he had brought home that afternoon. His heart beat wildly as he reached noiselessly for the flashlight that he had stood on end on the floor near the head of the cot. Had the intruder returned? He aimed the flashlight at the sound and switched it on quickly. His eyes took a moment to adjust to the light. There crouched on the table, hungrily devouring a slice of lunch meat, was an orange-striped cat not much more than a kitten. Hearing the click of the flashlight, it turned and regarded him without blinking. When the boy did not move, it returned to the minced ham and continued clawing at the wrapper.

Speaking softly in a low voice to avoid alarming it, Steve slipped his feet quietly to the floor and advanced slowly toward the kitten. It kept on at its business while keeping an eye on him. Steve reached out slowly, placed his fingers on top of its head, and began to stroke it gently.

"Hi, there, little fellow! Where'd you come from?" The kitten stiffened and arched its back but kept on at the meat.

"Judging by your ears, I'd say you're not my bunny Petey who has materialized and come for his carrots." He chuckled and let his hand drift down over the animal's body. He could easily feel its shoulder blades and ribs, and its hunger had obviously overcome any fear it might have had for the boy. It apparently was used to human beings. It had obviously been someone's kitten, but it had been neglected, probably dumped in the neighborhood.

"You must really be hungry," he continued softly, hoping that the sound of his voice would soothe the kitten. "You go ahead. Looks like you haven't had a good meal in a while either. Where's your mama? Don't you have a home? Here, let me get you some more meat." He opened the wrapper and put a slice on the table. The kitten picked it up and moved to the far corner of the table where it placed both front feet on it and began to nibble hungrily at it, monitoring the boy as it devoured the offering. Steve sat down on the chair, and when the kitten had finished its meal, he picked it up and held it in his arms.

As he stroked it tenderly, it looked up at Steve, eyes wide as if to gauge his intentions. Steve apparently passed the test and, satisfied with its new circumstances, it began to purr loudly.

"Here, let me check out your equipment," he said after a while, lifting the kitten up above his head. A quick examination revealed that it was male.

"Hey," he announced, "you're a little mister!"

The kitten pressed its eyes shut into two diagonal slits for a moment, then opened them nonchalantly as if to say, "I knew that all along."

There had been plenty of cats and kittens on the farm, Steve remembered, but they had stayed out at the barn, and he usually had dogs for pets. He hadn't thought he liked cats much, but the softness and warmth of the kitten and its vulnerability and independence wrapped up in one little body intrigued him. Into the wee hours of the morning, he sat there in the dark, holding the little animal, stroking it and talking to it quietly. He decided that the kitten was to be his companion, and he promised it aloud that he would manage somehow to feed and care for him.

He wondered about an appropriate name for him. "If you were a pure black cat, mister, I'd name you Spot," he said playfully, "but we need to get you a better name. How about Tiger? No? Don't like that either? That's too obvious anyway, like Peter Rabbit."

Reflecting on his own solitary circumstances and his need to provide for all his wants from scratch, he smiled. He was a latter day Robinson Crusoe! If the kitten was to be his companion, then his name must be Friday, and in view of the recent examination, he decided the full name should be Man Friday.

He took the kitten to bed with him, and it crawled into a ball in the crook of his elbow and began to knead his newfound friend with a fixed concentration. After a while, both fell asleep, and they shared the first of the many nights they were to spend together.

Steve awoke next morning to find Friday sprawled on his chest, watching him intently as he blinked awake. "No wonder I was dreaming I was suffocating," he complained, "with you weighing down on my chest! I suppose I'm just a convenient mattress to you."

He was a bit surprised and pleased to see that the kitten had hung around until morning, and he talked to it as he dressed. It watched his every move, turning its head and cocking its ears, seeming to understand what the boy was saying. Steve fed the kitten a slice of bread and the last piece of lunch meat. Man Friday gobbled them down without pausing.

"Sorry, my Man Friday cat, that's all I've got for now. Maybe you can ambush a little mouse today, huh?"

CHAPTER 5

Tuesday morning and into the afternoon, Steve worked at cleaning up three more yards in Mrs. Pike's neighborhood. He had decided the local market could bear a slight increase in price, and he collected four dollars and fifty cents for his labor. Passing by Mrs. Pike's house on the way up the street, he decided to stop for a brief chat. He sat down on the edge of the porch, and the old woman grinned down at him from the swing.

"What's with those sunglasses? Are you pulling a Hollywood? Who are you supposed to be, Errol Flynn?"

Steve chuckled at the sally and replied, "Yeah, that's me, Errol, the neighborhood Romeo."

"Well, you better watch your step, Romeo. If your Aunt Mildred finds out, she'll bounce you out on your ear."

Steve grinned, blushing a little, and he reflected that it was much more likely that Mrs. Meyer, no doubt on duty at her sentry post, would want to know what was going on. In a few moments, he continued on his way up the street.

Toward five o'clock, he approached the First Methodist Church on North Fourth Street where he had noticed the sign advertising a rummage sale. He had purposely delayed coming to the sale until late in the afternoon, reasoning that the women running it would prefer to mark some of the items down to sell rather than have to box them up and find a place to store them for the next year's sale.

Looking over the items on the long tables along the front sidewalk, he selected a bath towel, a five-gallon bucket that had held a caulking compound and could serve as a chamber pot, two wire coat hangers, a small plastic bowl for Man Friday, a pair of faded blue jeans, a pair of socks, and two dark blue T-shirts.

A table with an array of postcards caught his eye. There were cards with pictures of the state capitol in Montgomery, the federal dam at Muscle Shoals, the county courthouse, and other local sights. There were a few with no local connection—Mount Vernon, Niagara Falls, Lookout Mountain, the Great Smoky Mountains, and Churchill Downs. He decided to buy the one showing the Louisville race track. It was only two cents and might be useful.

Just as he was about to leave, he noticed a green-and-white shirt hanging on the clothes rack. It looked almost new, but he spotted a small fleck of blue paint on one sleeve, hardly noticeable. It was obviously a rather expensive shirt, and for that reason it was marked at a dollar and a quarter, more than the other shirts. He debated spending the extra money, but he decided it was easily worth the cost. He would save it for when he wanted to look especially nice like the first day of school.

The lady sitting at a card table acting as cashier added up his bill. It came to three dollars and seven cents. As she handed him his change, she said, "This Gideon Bible hasn't sold, and I thought you might like to have it. It's a nice King James and was marked at fifty cents, but I'll give it to you for free if you'll promise to read it."

"Oh, thank you, ma'am," he said quickly. "I promise."

At that, the lady in charge of the nearby bake table, perhaps as a gesture of acceptance and approval, threw in a package of unsold homemade oatmeal-raisin cookies. He thanked her, then hurried to Banfield's and bought a small box of dry Purina cat food, a roll of toilet paper, a box of laundry soap, a quarter pound of minced ham, and a pint bottle of milk.

At the hardware store next door, he bought a box of matches, a roll of electrical tape, and a small sack of broad head nails. He had noticed a pile of such nails on the workbench in Mrs. Pike's shed, but they looked fairly new. While he could rationalize making use of a piece of rusty baling wire and a piece of spade handle because they were of no use to anyone, his strict upbringing made him draw the line at the nails. Mrs. Pike would have gladly given them to him, he supposed, but the fact of the matter was that she had not. He would just have to buy them himself. That done, he had just three dollars and ten cents left to his name. Next, he went by the army-navy store and bought a battered lantern he had seen there the day before for seventy-five cents. He was glad to find it was full of kerosene.

Carrying most of his purchases in the bucket, he headed through the alleys for Mrs. Pike's shed. Following a routine he'd adopted each day before going home, he stopped at a gas station to use the outdoor privy, avoiding the unpleasant task of emptying the bucket at home.

As he ducked up the alley to the shed, he was taken by surprise by a woman placing a sack of garbage beside the trash barrel, which was full to overflowing. As he got closer, he recognized her as Mrs. Pike's neighbor, Anna Meyer. She stood and watched him as he went by, and he continued on up the alley for another two blocks instead of turning into Mrs. Pike's backyard. He could feel her eyes on his back. He waited ten minutes before retracing his steps, checking first to see that she was no longer there.

At the top of the steps, Man Friday greeted him as if to say, "Welcome home!" He rubbed against Steve's pant leg and darted under his feet as he reached the top step, causing him to stumble.

"Easy, little fella! Don't trip the hand that feeds you." He reached down and gave his friend a little chuck behind the ear, and the kitten preceded him proudly into the room, tail straight up. Steve put his purchases on the table and the kitten bounded up and began to inspect them, pawing at the package of lunch meat.

"Hey, you little heathen! You can't have anything until we say grace." He stroked the kitten's head, and it lay on its back, luxuriating in the boy's attention and flexing its front claws. As Steve poured some of the milk into the bowl he had bought for him, Man Friday flipped over and nosed against the bottle, spilling a little as he did so in his eagerness to get at the milk. The boy opened the box of cat food and poured a handful on the table. The cat finished off the milk before devouring the food without looking up, then he licked up the spilled milk. Apparently satisfied, it retreated to the far corner of the table, doing his ablutions while regarding his new friend with undivided interest. Steve reached over and patted him a couple of times. When the kitten had finished washing up, he jumped down and curled up on the army blanket on the cot and went to sleep. Then Steve realized that he had become so fascinated with the kitten that he had forgotten to say grace himself before eating a minced ham sandwich for his own supper.

When it was almost dark, Steve pulled the tattered curtains shut over the window. Surely the thick cedars outside would prevent the light's being seen from the neighboring houses, but he couldn't be too careful. He struck a match and managed to light the lantern without difficulty. It spit and sputtered and smoked from time to time, exciting the shadows on the dark stains on the walls. Man Friday sat up and tracked the dancing figures with curiosity for several minutes before settling down again, pressing his eyes together and shutting the dreary room out of his own little world. Soon, his whiskers flitted and his paws stuttered as he chased a mouse across a verdant meadow.

Steve ate one of the cookies the woman had given him at the bake sale, watching the kitten with obvious enjoyment before going downstairs into the yard and into the alley to make sure the light couldn't be seen from any angle. Good enough, he decided, but just to be safe, he went back upstairs and hung a gunny sack he had retrieved from a trash can on a couple of nails so that it covered the window.

He wasn't really worried about Mrs. Pike—the dense cedars presented an effective barrier and her poor eyesight and hearing would further ensure against discovery. She was unlikely ever to come into the backyard anyway. Anna Meyer might be a problem, however. She seemed to have an eye on everything.

By the flickering light of the lantern, he read a chapter from the New Testament, something he was to make a habit of doing almost every night when he wasn't too exhausted from work. Sometimes, when he was lonely or depressed, he turned to the Old Testament's psalms for comfort. His thoughts went back again to his mother and the heartache and worry his disappearance had surely caused her. After much thought, he changed his mind and decided to risk sending her the postcard of Churchill Downs he had bought at the rummage sale.

He sat at the table for several minutes, deciding what to say. At first, he addressed the card to "Mrs. John Whitfield, RFD 2, Steadman Falls,

Nebraska." He looked at the address for a long time before he added the words, "Mr. and" in front of it.

Then he began the message,

Louisville, Kentucky
June 23, 1947
Dear Folks,
Don't worry about me. I am doing okay.
Your son,
Joe

He debated whether to close with the word *love*, but he could not bring himself to do so since he had already addressed the card to his father as well as his mother. The word seemed hollow and abstract when applied to him. He sat at the table for a long time, staring at the card. He felt a twinge of conscience. Perhaps his mother's feelings would be hurt, but he decided that she would understand.

He knew he should forgive his father as the Good Book dictated. Probably his father had been treated the same way as a child as he had been. He understood that, but the realization did not erase the hurt. The deep bruises on his arm, chest, and shoulder had only partially healed, and they and the permanent knot on his rib were constant reminders of his father's violence. Perhaps when the bruises had healed and time and distance had softened his relationship with his father, he would be able to use such a word, but not now. He set his jaw, remembering the pain and humiliation of that last evening in the cellar, and he slipped the card into his shirt pocket.

He began to read the book on American history, but in his state of mind, his thoughts kept wandering to home and his father. From time to time he looked over at Man Friday and asked him how he was doing. Each time, the cat looked up, closed his eyes for a moment as if to signify his independence, opened them again to regard his new friend with indifference, and put his head down between his front paws and soon dozed off again. The boy watched him as he slept, his whiskers twitching now and then as he resumed his hunt for his favorite mouse in his private meadow. When Steve's eyes became heavy, he joined his friend on the bed for the night.

* * * * * * * *

The next few days passed uneventfully as Steve occupied his time working at Banfield's and the newspaper and picking up several odd jobs in Mrs. Pike's neighborhood. In the evenings, he continued to work at cleaning up his room in the shed. On Sunday morning, he went back to the Methodist Church and sat outside on the bench again, listening to the hymns floating out through the open windows. They made him homesick, and after a few minutes, he went on back to the shed and read his own Bible. Lunch was two slices of bread, two slices of lunch meat, and two cookies. Nothing like a balanced meal, he smiled to himself. He shared the rest of the milk with Man Friday, who disappeared for most of the afternoon before returning at supper time. Steve wondered where he went, but he knew it was none of his business. Cat Friday would be his own man no matter how close their bond was to become.

He had been thinking about his mother and settled upon a plan to mail the postcard that he hoped would involve a minimum of risk of its being traced. A postmark from Morefield would be a giveaway. He had found a yellowed envelope in the Bible he got at the rummage sale and decided it would be a good idea to put the postcard inside it. He sealed the envelope and addressed it to his parents. When he had finished his Sunday dinner, he walked down to the square and followed the signs pointing toward the main highway. There probably would be more trucks at the stop there than at the gas station on up the highway where he had been left off before. An elderly couple on the way home from eating out after church, dressed in their Sunday best, stopped and gave him a ride.

Steve went inside the gas station and bought a stamp at the counter. Then he walked around the parking lot and looked at the license plates on the semis parked there. He spotted an oil tanker with an Indiana plate, and when the driver, a middle-aged man wearing dark blue coveralls with a bright yellow Shell patch above his shirt pocket, came out of the cafe and got into the cab, Steve tapped on the window on the driver's side.

The man rolled the window down and asked, "What you want, son?"

"Sir. You wouldn't happen to be goin' through Louisville by any chance would you?"

"Yeah, but I don't take no riders. Sorry."

"No, I don't want a ride, sir, but I need a small favor. Would you please take this letter and mail it when you go through Louisville? It's got a stamp on it."

The man took the envelope, turned it over a couple of times, scanning the address. "There's no return address. You in some kind of trouble, boy?"

"No, sir, no trouble. I just don't want my folks to know where I am right now. But I want them to know I'm all right."

The driver regarded him intently, glancing back at the address again, then relented. "Okay, I'll mail it for you. I guess you got your reasons. It's none of my business anyway." He reached up and stuck the envelope behind one of the sun visors with a couple of tattered envelopes and a road map.

"Thanks, mister," said Steve. "I really appreciate it." He hoped the man wouldn't forget to mail the envelope. At least his mother would know he was safe.

It was late afternoon before Steve got back to the shed. Although he tried to avoid using that facility when he could, the gas station near downtown had closed for Sunday and padlocked the privy, and he found it necessary to use the bucket. When he was finished, he set the bucket out on the landing for the night. After supper, he read American history for a couple of hours. When his eyes began to burn, he lay down on the cot beside Man Friday for a few minutes, thinking of home, and drifted off to sleep.

* * * * * * * *

He slept soundly through the night, awakening just before seven. After breakfast with his kitten, he took a spade from the wall downstairs, went outside into the weeds behind the shed, and dug a deep hole. He went back upstairs, retrieved the bucket and emptied its contents into it. He shoveled some of the dirt back into the hole and rinsed the bucket under the hydrant. It wouldn't be hard, he thought with a wry smile, to remember to use the facilities around town before coming home.

That morning, he managed to find a job cleaning out gutters and washing windows farther down the street. Then he went to the library and read about Ohio in an encyclopedia and a history of the state. He studied a map in an atlas intently. He would need to know all he could about the state and his "home town" of Dayton if he were to flesh out his newly assumed background, especially since Mrs. Pike's husband had lived there. Steve also studied a book of legal forms for Alabama certificates that the librarian had found for him. He could use them as models, he thought.

At noon, he sat on a bench in the shade of the trees in front of the library and ate the bread and cheese he had brought with him. In the afternoon, he worked at the grocery for six hours, packing up meat scraps for Friday before heading home. As he walked down the alley behind the stores, he kept an eye out for items that had been thrown away that might be useful to him—perhaps a piece of carpet or a mattress carton. After supper, he settled down to the routine of reading from the textbooks he had borrowed. Man Friday wandered in from his evening rounds, and he jumped up on Steve's lap, pausing only to gather his hind paws beneath him, then make the final thrust onto the table where he ate his evening meal and then lay down in front of the boy, spread-eagled right on top of Durant's *The Story of Philosophy.*

Steve took time out to scratch his friend's back. The kitten splayed his claws at the attention and soon drifted off to sleep, a look of supreme contentment on his face, and continued to preempt Steve's book for his own purposes. It was his due. It seemed to Steve that the cat was entirely self-contained, as if in its warm, sensuous body, it comprised the whole universe. Steve's studies were of no consequence to him, and indeed, Steve's sole purpose of existence apparently was to take care of the cat. He had just been reading about the French philosophers, and he chuckled out loud. "I see it now, Mr. Friday. I exist just for you. I have no identity, no existence without you. It was René de Cat who said, 'I think, therefore *you* are!'"

He laughed to himself, wishing he had someone to share his little joke with.

Steve did not disturb his friend, watching him as he lay there, wondering what he might be dreaming about. After some time, the cat roused up, jumped down from the table onto Steve's knee and then to the floor without so much as a by-your-leave and disappeared again, tail up, into the darkness. Steve continued reading by the dim light of the lantern until his eyes burned from the flickering light and smoke, and shortly before midnight, he lay down on the cot and fell asleep. As was to be his habit, Man Friday returned shortly after midnight to spend the night with him.

CHAPTER 6

Such was the pattern of Steve's life the rest of the summer. Gradually the pieces of his life began to fall into place as he solved problem after problem. He washed his clothes in cold water and Oxydol in the tub he had found downstairs, scrubbing them vigorously. Although there was a clothesline in the backyard, he did not dare hang his clothes there. Instead, he rigged a line inside the shed using some electrical wire he found there. When he could, he put his clothes on while they were still a little damp and smoothed them out on his body as they dried. They looked somewhat presentable, he decided. Mostly, he wore the dark blue T-shirts he had bought at the army-navy store and the rummage sale that could be worn two or three times without laundering and didn't need ironing.

As he went to and from work through the alleys downtown, he continued to keep an eye out for discards he might be able to use in fixing up his room. He found a twelve-foot section of rusty pipe behind a hardware store and installed it in a hole in the north wall of his room. He pushed it on out and across the adjoining roof, reaching to a point above the pit he had dug earlier. Indoor plumbing, he laughed to himself.

The furniture store near Banfield's yielded a continual harvest of empty cardboard mattress boxes, and he lugged them home. There, he opened and flattened them. After covering the holes and cracks in the walls and ceiling with electrician's tape to provide a measure of waterproofing, he secured the boxes there in layers, hammering in the broad-headed nails he had bought earlier. A few days later, when he found a supply of laths at the city dump, he used them to shore up the cardboard more securely. Though cold weather was still a few months off, it was not too early to begin to plan for it. He hoped the thick layers would keep cold drafts out and even provide some insulation against the cold. The brand names and instructions printed on the cardboard provided some measure of relief from the surreal stains the water had left on the walls and ceiling.

He put one of the mattress covers inside the other and stuffed it with cotton bolls he gathered from fencerows along the highway outside of town where the wind had blown them from the fields. He placed the makeshift mattress on top of the carpet, and for a few nights, it shielded him from the discomfort of the springs beneath. However, the weight of his body soon packed the cotton into lumps, robbing it of most of its softness. Still, it was better than sleeping directly on the carpet and springs.

One evening as he lay on the cot, shifting to avoid some of the lumps that poked his body through the mattress, he looked at the ceiling above him and read the advertisement printed in bold letters on the carton he had nailed there that afternoon: "Sleeping on a Sealy is like sleeping on a cloud." He chuckled out loud at the irony. "I don't think I'm in Heaven—not yet."

When he wasn't working his two jobs, he continued to pick up whatever work he could find, hoeing gardens, picking fruit, washing windows, running errands. As word got around the neighborhood that he was a hard worker, it was easier to find jobs to supplement his income. He visited the public library whenever he could and frequented yard sales and the surplus store, buying only what he absolutely needed and saving every penny he could for college. Some days he was able to put a quarter or two aside, some days nothing.

As the work of making the room livable and suitable for winter progressed, he had more time in the evenings to spend studying for the school year and visiting with Man Friday when it suited the cat's schedule. If, as they say, "every dog has his day," Steve decided, "every cat has his night," and Man Friday usually disappeared into the darkness in mid-evening to make his nocturnal rounds.

* * * * * * * *

Steve's life was not entirely bleak, full of hard work, study, homesickness, and bad luck. Despite his problems and desperate situation, he tried to maintain a positive attitude, and his ready smile, flashing blue eyes, and his way of looking people straight in the eyes led most of those who came into contact with him to take a liking to him even though he was from "up north."

Almost every day, he made it a point to stop by Mrs. Pike's front porch to "set a spell," as she termed it, and chat briefly with the lonely old woman. Although he had never known either of his real grandmothers, he decided she was what a grandma ought to be. He liked her very much, and she obviously reciprocated the feeling, taking to calling him "hon."

He understood her loneliness. She had no family nearby, and she had outlived most of her friends. As their friendship grew, she invited him to call her by her first name, Awillah, but as a matter of respect, he continued to call her Mrs. Pike most of the time. However, one afternoon as they bantered back and forth, he playfully called her "Willie."

The old woman's animated response was not slow in coming. "The name's Awillah! When I was a little girl, my older brothers used to call me Willie to tease me. When I got older, I found ways to get even with 'em, if you get my meaning, so you better watch your back, you young scamp!"

Despite her stern tone, he saw that she strove to suppress a smile. She enjoyed the gambit. Humor was the catalyst that drew them together as time went on, and they both relished the repartee that often marked their conversations. Some of her quaint Southern expressions amused and intrigued him, and he teased her about them, referring to her as "y'all," despite her repeated insistence that the expression did not refer to just one person. Sometimes, he even called her "Grandma," something she didn't seem to mind at all—indeed, she seemed to enjoy it—and it was to come in handy for him later, in an unexpected way.

He kept her informed of his work and kept her up-to-date on Aunt Mildred's developing maladies. Sometimes he did little chores around the house for her: climbing up to replace a light bulb, carrying out the garbage, unclogging the sink, opening a reluctant jar of pickles, and running errands downtown for her on occasion. She usually rewarded him with a couple of cookies or a piece of chocolate cake, and sometimes a glass of milk instead of the dreaded pink potable. Sometimes she sewed a button on his shirt and occasionally ironed his best shirt and pants. Theirs was a symbiotic relationship. Perhaps they were drawn together by their separate loneliness. They needed each other.

She was a sympathetic listener too, and he looked forward to their visits as much as she did, although he did not let his guard down, carefully protecting his identity. He enjoyed listening to her talk about her life as a young girl on a cotton farm north of Montgomery. Often, she repeated the same stories he had heard before as older people often do, but he never let on, sensing that she needed to relive the memories of a more pleasant, hopeful time.

Amid the humor, however, there were serious moments. One afternoon, Awillah asked suddenly, "What do you want to do when you finish school, hon?"

"Well," he replied, "when I finish high school, I'll need to go to college if I can swing it. I'm not sure yet what I want to study, but I've been thinking about journalism, or maybe engineering."

"Oh, an engineer!" she replied approvingly. "My nephew in Jacksonville is an engineer. He's done right well for himself down there too."

Encouraged, the boy continued. "I don't know what God wants me to do with my life, but I think maybe that's what would suit me best. Maybe an architect or an engineer. I'd like to make a difference in the world. Maybe the buildings, bridges, and things I could design or build would serve as markers to show that I passed this way—that I was of benefit to mankind, that my life mattered."

"That's aiming pretty high, hon," she commented.

"Maybe it sounds funny. I can't say how things will work out, but I want to aim high, aim for all that I can be, and if I'm to succeed, I can't settle for anything less. If I work hard, maybe things will be within my reach someday."

"I know what you're talking about, hon. I was young once myself, believe it or not," she added with a smile. "I had dreams of a career." A wistful note had crept into her voice. "If a career didn't work out, maybe marrying into wealth and family, living in New York City and traveling in Europe. But I had no money to go beyond high school, no way of going to the city and making my way. I took a job as a clerk in a dry goods store right out of high school, and then I met a young man who had dreams too, and I settled for his dreams. But they were just that, dreams, and he settled for a job as a supervisor in the mill here. We had a son, and he became my life. I opened a beauty shop to make ends meet during hard times, and then one day Wendell and my husband were gone.

"It's all right for a young person to aim for the stars, but sometimes circumstances determine what you will do. You have to play the cards that are dealt you. You realize that your ambitions were dreams, nothing more, and as time goes by, you come to see that it was meant to be—that things worked out the best for you after all. I know you can't see that now—young people can't. But the years will bring it to you, and you'll be content. All in all, I've had a good life, and I have few regrets. Things have a way of working out. You'll see that one day. You will."

Although the hopes and aspirations of her youth had not been fulfilled. She was not bitter; nor was she fatalistic. She spoke with a quiet confidence borne of years of experience and ultimate acceptance. She had embraced her destiny with humility and even gratitude. If the boy, being yet young, could not fully understand her outlook on life, if he had burning ambition and sometimes railed inwardly at his lot, he found her calm acceptance reassuring in a way, and he felt that he gained strength from her. She, on the other hand, understood his youthful impatience and ambition. It was as it should be.

Wanting to please the old woman, he nodded in cautious assent as she presented her point of view, but he had doubts about it. In his present situation and with his life ahead of him, he worried about what the future held for him. His dreams were all he had, and he could not let go of them.

While they both enjoyed their talks there on the front porch, she at her regular post on the swing, he sitting, legs dangling off the edge of the porch, many of the topics of real concern to the boy had to be skirted carefully, as if they were dangerous sinkholes. Too much was at stake for him to venture too near them. Although humor served to draw them together, it also provided a way for Steve to keep her at a safe distance, using it to protect his privacy, his secret. There was always the line he drew between them which kept Awillah at a necessary distance. He carefully rationed his past as well as his present situation to her, and she had no idea that he spent the long, lonely nights out in the old shed on the back of her property.

* * * * * * * *

One evening, when he stopped by to see her, she asked if he would mind carrying some large boxes from the spare bedroom up to the attic. She had finally made up her mind about them. The boxes were heavy and cumbersome, but he managed to get them up the narrow stairway. Awillah, unable to climb the stairs herself, remained at the bottom, cautioning him to be careful and shouting directions as to where to put the boxes.

When he returned to the lower floor, she asked him if he would like a piece of freshly-baked peach pie. He readily assented, knowing what the full menu might include, and he followed her into the kitchen. He sat down at the table, resting his elbows on the red and white checkered oilcloth that covered it. He watched her as she shuffled across the worn linoleum and opened a pie safe, returning with two dessert plates, each with a piece of pie on it.

She placed them on the table and returned in a moment with two forks and two glasses of punch. She sat down heavily with a thump and a grimace in the chair opposite him and cut off a sliver of her pie.

She was about to put it into her mouth when Steve interrupted. "Wait a minute, Willie! Aren't y'all supposed to say grace before you eat?"

"Anybody knows that's only when you eat a full meal, and pie is all you're gettin', especially when you call me Willie. Watch your back, you young scamp!"

"Okay, *Mrs.* Pike! Sounds to me like I'd better say a full prayer!" he said in mock terror. His blue eyes flashed mischievously as he broke out into a grin, and she sought to hide her own by taking an extra-large bite of pie, almost choking on it.

When he had finished eating, he stood up. "Thanks for the pie, Grandma. It tasted all right—guess you didn't have time to put any poison in it. I'd better get on home now. It'll be getting dark pretty soon, and Aunt Mildred will worry. I'll just go on out the back door and through the alley. It's closer."

"You better use the front door, hon," the woman replied with a twinkle in her eye. "The neighbors all saw you come in that way, and they won't see you come out again. They'll think you stayed all night."

"Well, Willie," the boy replied quickly, "it can only do both of our reputations a lot of good." With that, he bolted out the back door, letting the screen door slam with a loud slap, and disappeared in the direction of the back gate.

* * * * * * * *

As Mrs. Pike talked about her life in Morefield one afternoon, she mentioned again that she had been a beautician for many years. Awillah's Beauty Shop had stood on the site near the square where the ice cream stand was now located.

"I don't miss the long hours standing on my feet," she remarked, "but I do miss the people who used to come in. Most all of them gone now, you know. It's been goin' on twenty years now."

"And of course, the gossip," he shot back.

She laughed, her glasses shattering into a thousand shards of light. "Girl talk! You wouldn't understand, hon. I used to cut men's hair too sometimes. I was good at it. You look like you could use a good shearing."

Steve hadn't had a haircut since he left Steadman Falls, postponing the expense. But his hair had grown out over his ears, and he had been wondering if he might be able to cut it himself.

"If you want, I could cut it for you, hon."

"Do y'all have any references?" he asked with an impish grin.

"*Y'all*? You're hallucinating again! There's just one of me here, and I'm fully capable of giving you a proper shearing all by myself. I can trim those big ears of yours too while I'm at it."

"I'll just take the regular haircut if you don't mind, ma'am," he laughed. "Seriously, I sure would appreciate it if you would cut my hair for me."

They went inside to the kitchen, and he sat down on a straight chair beneath the sixty-watt bulb that hung down from the center of the ceiling. Mrs. Pike took the oilcloth off the table and tucked it around his shoulders.

"You hold still now," she admonished, "and I'll do my best not to crop your ears. Not that they don't need it. Would you like a sip of some cranberry punch while I cut? We've got ice today."

He reflected that ice was not likely to make the punch any more potable. "No thanks," he said hastily. "It might make my hair grow out pink."

"Then it'll match the blood," she retorted as she began to snip with the scissors. "I declare! You're a regular wiggle worm! Hold still now!"

But Mrs. Pike did know how to cut hair, and in a few minutes, he emerged unscathed into the daylight with a perfectly respectable haircut. Over the coming months, the haircuts became almost a ritual, each enjoying the taunts and retorts of the other as their bond grew. And the haircuts were free.

CHAPTER 7

Steve's visits with the lonely widow provided a welcome relief from his own loneliness and the daily regimen of hard work, although he enjoyed working at Banfield's and *The Times-Enterprise*. The work at the newspaper was crucial to his plan. He worked hard to finish his assigned tasks so that he could help Howard set type and operate the printing presses.

Howard liked the boy and took him under his wing, showing him how to print documents and occasionally letting him practice on his own. Steve learned quickly, and sometimes Howard left him alone with the press for periods of time while he attended to other tasks.

Working for a few minutes at a time, making sure that Howard did not see what he was doing, Steve managed to design an official-looking birth certificate bearing the name "Steven Joseph Bowman," and the words "issued at the capital in Columbus, Ohio." He used his real first name as a middle name. If he should slip and use Joe as his name, he could explain that his friends at school in Dayton had sometimes called him by his middle name. He printed the necessary information on a piece of heavy stock. Back at the shed, he fashioned a passable seal out of the bottom of a snuff can using a chisel he found on the workbench downstairs to engrave the words "State of Ohio" faintly. He hammered it into the stock and then laminated the document at the shop. The same technique produced a passable learner's permit to replace the one he had left in Nebraska. It would serve as an identification card.

A good job, he thought. Good enough. Maybe, he laughed to himself, he ought to quit working and set up a counterfeiting operation in the old shed.

Next, he designed a transcript from "Orville Wright High School" in Dayton. Surely there was a high school there with a name honoring the native son. He had chosen Orville randomly, hoping the citizenry hadn't chosen to honor his brother instead. Then he realized that he wasn't sure whether Orville had one "l" or two, so he decide to use Wilber's name, certain that it was spelled with only one. Finally, he decided not to play favorites and renamed it "Wright Brothers High School." Not likely anyone would check anyway. He filled in the correct courses and grades he had received at his old high school in Nebraska. He invented legitimate sounding names of the principal and superintendent, and after practicing different styles of handwriting, he signed their names to the transcript using different colors of ink.

Then he tackled a form granting Mrs. Pike, as his grandmother, legal guardianship over him. Back at the shed, he signed it with the fictitious name of an Ohio judge. Who could make up a name like "Elijah W. Pierpont"? He practiced signing Mrs. Pike's name, producing a genuine looking signature of an old woman by jiggling the leg of the table as he wrote. Satisfied, he filled his pen from a bottle of lavender ink he had bought and signed the document, "(Mrs.) Awillah B. Pike" in the proper blank.

That done, he held his handiwork up admiringly and congratulated himself on documenting his new identity so convincingly. But he felt more than a twinge of conscience in doing so, and he slept fitfully for a couple of nights, managing finally to rationalize his deception. He had to finish high school if he was ever to make it on his own. He could not go back home again. That was the irreducible bottom line.

His proficiency in forging necessary documents got its litmus test when it came time to register for the fall semester at the high school. He thought the documents would suffice—they looked official to him anyway. However, he couldn't figure out how he was going to get around bringing an imaginary grandma with him as Miss Edwards said would be required. He couldn't bring Mrs. Pike along. It wouldn't make any sense to her, and she might begin to unravel the secret that he was a runaway and living in the shed behind her house. She seemed like a nice person, a friend, but he couldn't bring himself to trust her completely. Besides, she might accidentally let something slip to the nosey Mrs. Meyer. Too much was at stake. He spent several restless nights trying to figure out a solution. Finally, he invented a story he hoped would work, but no matter how carefully he rehearsed it, he had doubts that Miss Edwards would buy it.

On the first day of registration, he appeared early at the school gym bearing his documents. Already, there were three long lines of students waiting to be registered. He avoided Miss Edwards's line and chose one that led to a young woman sitting at a folding table. When asked, he produced his birth certificate, legal guardianship document, and the transcript from the Ohio high school. The young woman gave them a cursory examination and appeared satisfied. His heart sank, however, when she asked if he had brought his guardian with him.

When he explained that she was unable to come to the school because of health reasons, the young woman referred him to Miss Edwards, who frowned severely when he repeated the explanation to her. He produced a note he had written in Mrs. Pike's shaky, lavender handwriting on a piece of flowered stationery he had found behind a department store saying she was unable to come because of diabetes and severe problems with her feet. She asked the school to register her grandson without having her appear.

When he persisted in his story, the woman, sensing something in his manner—he seemed on the verge of tears—sent him to her office. He sat there for what seemed like half an hour before Miss Edwards came in and closed the door firmly behind her. She questioned him about his grandmother. Apparently unconvinced, she suggested that she call her on the phone. Luckily, Mrs. Pike did not have a phone—a lifesaving fact he did not need to invent. But the woman persisted in demanding an interview of some sort with the grandmother.

Steve was desperate, and he reverted to the last-ditch argument he had fashioned during the long hours lying awake nights. "Please don't contact her, ma'am! She's not really my grandmother. My father died five years ago in an automobile accident coming home from Cincinnati, and my mother remarried two years ago. My stepfather and I don't get along at all. I tried to get along with him, but he slaps me around hard when he gets mad. He has three children of his own and didn't want me around in the first place. My mother only agreed to send me down here because she was afraid he was going to hurt me.

"Mrs. Pike is my stepfather's mother—she's no kin to me at all. She didn't want me either, but she finally agreed to give me a place to stay. She's seventy-seven years old and on Social Security and barely makes it on her own much less with me. She gives me a place to stay, a room in her house, but she doesn't provide anything else—I have to work for food, clothes, school supplies—everything. And she told my mother and stepdad that the first time there was any trouble, anything at all, she was going to send me right back to my stepfather in Ohio. She means it too. She's just looking for an excuse to ship me back there. She's short-tempered and ugly, just like her son. It was all I could do to get her to write that note, and she'll be mad that the school wouldn't accept it. If you even contact her about me, she's going to send me packing. I know she will! I walk a tightrope every day. I can't go back! Please, Miss Edwards, I can't go back to him—I have all of the documents you said I needed and a note from Mrs. Pike. Can't you make an exception, just once? Otherwise, there's no way I can go to school. Please, ma'am," he added softly.

The boy was obviously distraught, and his way of looking her straight in the eye caused her to pause. Mr. Newton, the principal, was a stickler for procedures and regulations, but the impression the boy made on her—his sincerity and his obvious fear of his stepfather—overruled her better judgment. After more than a few anxious moments for the boy, she said, "All right. It's an unusual story, but I guess we can go ahead and let you register without a grandmother, a step-grandmother at that. We've never done that before, but after all, the documents cover all of the bases."

"Thank you, ma'am. I really appreciate it."

He returned to the young woman at the registration table where he was allowed to sign up for the classes for the first semester. He asked her if he could check out a couple of the textbooks that would be used in his classes, and after she consulted with Miss Edwards, who was impressed by his request, he was issued the texts for his science, history, and English classes.

Outside, he sat down on the cement banister by the main entrance to the school and breathed a sigh of relief. "That was a close one," he said aloud, and after a few more minutes to catch his breath, he went on to the newspaper for the afternoon.

* * * * * * * *

As he sat at the table in his room studying late that evening before turning in, he reflected that he had told so many fibs—no, *lies*—that he had to constantly make sure that his stories were consistent. Sometimes he felt that he was really becoming Steven Bowman, a boy from Ohio, but at other times, he felt as if his other self was still inside his body, screaming, "I'm in here, Joseph Whitfield! Can't anyone hear me? It's me, Joe!" He was pushed and pulled two ways, and he had to pay close attention at all times to every detail—who he said he was and what details he had told to whom.

It was difficult to reconcile the two identities, and it seemed that a good bit of the spontaneity had gone out of his life. He had always been friendly and open, quick to accept and to sympathize. Now, he had to be careful about every word that came out of his mouth, crafting a seamless response—one little slip could send his life tumbling down around him like a house of cards, sending him back to his father in Nebraska. Sometimes he felt as if he were peering cautiously out at life through two holes in a skull. They afforded a restricted field of vision, and he often felt a sense of detachment and unreality. And he was constantly preoccupied with money—getting money, spending it carefully only for necessities, and saving what he could for emergencies and college.

Dealing with the two Mrs. Pikes also presented difficulties—one, the kind, pleasant woman in the swing on her front porch, the other his fictitious stepfather's mean, irritable mother.

He thought of home often—thoughts of his mother and his brother, of his girlfriend Barbara, his friends at school, and transiently, of his father. He tried not to think of him. It had not been hard to invent an uncaring stepfather. His own father had been distant, unreasonable, and demanding, and in his violent flights of temper, physically abusive. The violence had seemed to escalate steadily culminating in the violence that last evening in the cellar. The bruises on his chest, shoulder, and arm had been deep, and although they had almost disappeared, there was still some soreness. The knot on his rib and the scar on his leg were permanent, keeping the memory of the beatings fresh. The muscles in his jaw seized, and he said aloud, "No, I *can't* go back!"

He looked over at Man Friday, sprawled as usual on the cot snoozing, the tip of his tail switching back and forth from time to time. Steve went over and scratched him gently behind the ears and rolled onto the cot beside him. The kitten, growing by leaps and bounds it seemed, rolled over, flexed his claws, and gave him a cursory lick on the wrist.

"I don't know what I'd do without my little Man Friday," he said aloud. "You know when I'm blue and need to be cheered up. And you don't even care where I came from or what my real name is." He fell asleep beside the cat, thinking of home.

The next afternoon, when he came into the room, there was a dead mouse on the table where he usually sat. It was the only present his friend could give him.

* * * * * * * *

A few evenings later as he entered the shed, head down, thinking of the afternoon's work at the grocery when he had accidentally short-changed a customer, he looked up suddenly to see a large copperhead coiled on the third step! He sprang back, his heart racing. His first thought after jumping to safety was that the snake might crawl on up the steps into his room, so he carefully circled around to the workbench and tossed a small cogwheel he found lying there at the reptile. It raised its head almost insolently and slowly began to pull its heavy body behind it down the steps, winding sluggishly across the floor like a train switching back from a siding, leaving a twisting trail in the dust. It glided out through the door and disappeared into the weeds beside the path.

When he had recovered from his fright, Steve realized he probably should have killed the snake. It could come back. He resolved never to be out after dark without a flashlight again, and he decided he would rake the floor at the foot of the steps daily when he left so that he could see the snake's telltale track in the dust if the snake had approached the steps again. He found some lumpy garden sulfur that had spilled out of a bag by the workbench and sprinkled it by the threshold in hopes that it would keep the snake away. He felt uneasy, as if his home and safety had been compromised, and he wondered what would happen if the kitten should run into the snake. Perhaps he would try to bring him another present. He shuddered.

Next day, he mentioned his encounter with the copperhead to Mrs. Pike, saying he had met him on the path as he went through to the back alley.

"Oh," she smiled, "I expect that's Old Gus. Wendell called him that. He's been hangin' around back there for years. I almost stepped right on him myself once. I wanted Wendell to kill him, but he wouldn't. He said he caught rats and mice. Gave me the shivers, but he's probably too old to out quick you. Just watch where you step and you'll be all right."

"Well," said Steve, "I expect he'll be long gone when I land back down on earth again."

"Just you don't land on him, hon," she laughed. "Be careful!"

Steve was to see Old Gus from time to time, but fortunately only at a distance. He continued to rake the dust by the steps every morning not wishing to become any more familiar with the old fellow than he had to.

CHAPTER 8

August was oppressively hot and humid, the discomfort seeming to escalate as the month came to a close. The nights in Steve's airless room were almost unbearable, and once in a while he crawled out through the skylight onto a flat part of the roof on the side facing the alley and slept there hidden from view by the watchful cedars. Man Friday had no difficulty climbing up one of the cedars and dropping down onto the roof beside him for the night.

One particularly hot noon when the relentless sun hung overhead, seeming to refuse to move on toward evening, Steve sat down on a bench downtown in the shade and unwrapped a bread and cheese sandwich he had brought from home. He was sweating profusely, and his mouth was so dry he could hardly swallow. Across the street, a huge mock-up of a swirling vanilla ice cream cone atop a Dixie Queen stand beckoned seductively to him. He reached into his pocket and pulled out a handful of coins. He hadn't had an ice cream cone since he left home, and he eyed the stand, weighing the pressing need to save every penny against the promise of icy relief for his parched throat. A sign out front read, "Sweden Creme, Cone 10 Cents." Soft ice cream had just begun to appear at the stands, and he decided to splurge just this one time. It was beastly hot.

When he had finished his sandwich, he crossed the street to the stand. Seeing the two service windows, one with a sign reading "Whites Only" and the other "Colored," he decided he'd better take the white one. He had no particular feeling about black people. He hadn't known any in Nebraska. There were none in Steadman Falls or the whole county for that matter. Although he had read about lynchings and racial prejudice in the South, they had been little more than abstractions in faraway places he never expected to see. Now, whatever his feelings about Negroes, he did not dare draw attention to himself. He stepped up to the white window, ordered a cone, and paid for it with a quarter.

When the clerk held out his fifteen cents change, he was struck by the absurdity of it all. Impetuously, he drew his hand back in mock alarm and exclaimed, "Wait a minute! Did this come from the white cash register or the colored one?"

The clerk stared at him. Instantly, Steve regretted the remark and his momentary loss of control; he quickly accepted his change and headed back across the street, hoping no one had overheard him. *That was really dumb,* he admonished himself.

When he went to sit back down on the bench, he discovered that in his absence a tall Negro boy about his own age had sat down on the ground under a nearby tree. Steve sat down and began to eat his ice cream, savoring its cool caress of his tongue. He looked over at his neighbor, and he was curious about him. He was nice looking, with warm brown skin and even features. Steve had never spoken to a Negro before, but he smiled and said, "Sure is hot today, isn't it."

The boy looked over at him in surprise, and smiled back. "Yes, sir."

"Do you live in this part of town?"

"No, sir, we lives in the south end o' town."

Steve hadn't noticed any Negroes at registration earlier, so he asked, "Where do you go to school?"

"Booker T. Washington." He smiled, displaying a set of even, white teeth, but he looked uncomfortable, and he looked around as if he were expecting someone.

"Where is that?"

"Black neighborhood, 'Niggertown' the whites calls it. South end o' town."

"Oh. My name's J—, er Steve Bowman," he said, holding out his right hand. "I just moved down here."

The boy stood up and accepted his hand briefly. "Taliaferro Davis. I jest goes by Tal," he said, regarding the white boy with a puzzled look. "Where you come from?"

Before Steve could answer, his newfound acquaintance turned away suddenly. "Sorry, got t' go!" He walked away hurriedly without looking around.

Moments later, two white boys who had just crossed the street from the ice cream stand approached Steve. One, a large, muscular youth about a year or so older than Steve stood over him menacingly, his face flushed. He looked down at him and snarled, "Hey, Yankee boy. Down here in Dixie, we don't associate with Niggers!"

The other, his face accented by acne, chimed in, "You a Nigger lover, boy?" Slightly shorter than his friend, he was tubby with baby fat, which gave him a cherubic appearance incongruent with his angry scowl.

Before Steve could answer, the first boy grabbed him by the upper arm and jerked him to his feet, sending the half-eaten cone into the dirt beside the sidewalk. Instinctively, Steve doubled his fist to defend himself, but the boy shoved him roughly back onto the bench, and the other rapped him smartly on the top of his head and gave him a painful Dutch rub.

"Better watch yourself, Yankee boy. We don't take to your kind down here. Why don't you pack up your carpetbag and go back where you come from? C'mon, Tom," he laughed in derision, "let's let him finish his ice cream cone."

As they started to walk away, Steve got to his feet, his fists clenched, and took a step toward them before he thought better of it. He'd just have to watch himself, no matter what his own feelings were. An outsider wouldn't get much support from anyone, especially where race was concerned. They had obviously overheard his remark about the cash register—he should have known better. He looked down ruefully at the remainder of the ice cream melting rapidly into a rivulet that vanished into the dust. Then he went on to the grocery for his afternoon's work.

During the next few days, he found himself thinking about Tal from time to time. He seemed like a nice fellow, someone he'd like to get to know. He was obviously wary of the young toughs, and he wondered what Tal had been doing in the white part of town that day. No doubt there was a lot of hostility there.

While running an errand for Mr. Banfield not long after the incident, Steve happened to walk by Mademoiselle, a women's clothing store on the square. Tal was working outside on the sidewalk, busily washing the display windows that featured manikins dressed in the latest ladies' fashions.

Steve stopped and said, "Hi, Tal. Do you work here regularly?"

"I comes up here sometimes and do odd jobs and chores for a couple of stores here. Right now, I'm cleanin' these windows up so the fancy-dressed ladies inside here can see out to see who's washin' the windows so they can see out."

Steve did a mental double take, then smiled, noting the boy's pixie-like expression. A repressed grin and a slight twitch of his nose seemed to betray a vein of humor hidden beneath. In a moment, several whites came along, and he turned abruptly back to the windows. Taking his cue, Steve hurried on his way.

Late one afternoon about a week later, Steve dumped a load of rotting vegetables into the trash barrel behind Banfield's and headed up the alley toward home. He looked up to see a young man coming down the alley toward him. As he got closer, he squinted against the setting sun and recognized the figure to be Tal.

"Hi, Tal," Steve said cordially. "How ya doin'?"

"Doin' fine, man."

"You working today?"

"I been helpin' out at Patterson's, movin' furniture. Don't come up to this part of town 'lessen I got business here. Guess you knows why."

Steve nodded. "Do they give you a lot of trouble?"

"They beat me up a couple of times when they caught me alone. Cracked one of my teeth once."

"Did you report it to the police?"

"Man, white police ain't goin' to do nothin' to no white boys who beat up black boys, 'specially if the black happens to be in white town. My daddy says that's what happens when you don't know your place."

"I'm sorry," said Steve softly. "I wish there was something I could do to help." He said it sincerely, knowing that in his own situation there was absolutely nothing he could do. He couldn't take on three centuries of ingrained hatred even if he had dared to call attention to himself. Still, he felt a little bit like a hypocrite.

"You about the only white ever acted like he thought I was a human bein'."

"Maybe we could still be friends, sorta on the sly. I guess that's the only way we *can* be friends. What do you think?"

"I think that would be mighty fine. Mighty fine." His broad smile quickly faded, and he mumbled, "Gotta go now. See ya later," and dashed into the shade of the trees across the alley and disappeared.

Steve frowned at the boy's odd behavior and resumed his walk up the alley. A moment later, he looked up to see the two toughs who had roughed him up in the park approaching. He saw them in time to duck into a doorway until they passed. He wondered if Tal had necessarily developed a sort of sixth sense about such things. Perhaps he too would in time. He reflected that both he and Tal had to live in and out of shadows.

Occasionally, as he went to or from the grocery store, he passed Taliaferro on the street. He nodded to him, but he didn't pause to talk, remembering the incidents in the park and the alley. Any public sign of friendship toward the Negro might cause repercussions, getting them both into more trouble.

As he went to the shed one evening after his usual chat with Mrs. Pike, he bounded up the steps and opened the door to his room. He had been deep in thought and hadn't noticed a footprint in the carefully raked dust at the foot of the steps. He opened the door and stepped inside. In the dimming light, he saw a figure sitting on the cot. It stood up and took a step toward him. Steve cocked a fist, ready to defend himself.

"Easy, Bro! What you want t' hit me for?"

The intruder extended his right hand, and Steve unclenched his fist in time to shake hands with Taliaferro.

"I seen you luggin' stuff up the alley from town, and I wondered where you was takin' it to. So I followed you the other day. You *lives* here?" There was a note of incredulity in his voice as he looked around the room at the cardboard walls, the peg-leg chair and the bucket in the far corner.

"Yeah, I live here."

"You ain't got no folks?"

"No. Nobody."

"Well, I knows you don't come from no Alabama. Where you come from?"

"Ohio."

"What you doin' down south, livin' *here*?"

Steve, still taken aback by the unexpected visit, could not think of an answer on the spur of the moment. The grandmother story obviously wouldn't explain why he lived in near squalor in her backyard.

"I ran away from home," he admitted finally. "I couldn't get along with my father. He used to beat the tar out of me when he got mad."

"How long you been livin' here?"

"A couple of months. I've got to keep out of sight of the authorities. If they find out I'm a runaway, they'll send me back to my father."

Tal looked around, trying to digest the incongruity of a white boy living in such conditions. His glance fell on a stack of books on the table. "You goes to school?"

"Yeah. This fall. I've got another couple of years before I can get out on my own. I work two jobs to get enough to eat. I'm not beholdin' to anybody."

"I seen you workin' all the time in town, and I figured you wasn't like most o' the white kids. An' you *speaks!*"

"I'm sorry we can't be friends in public, but you know what happened when I talked to you in the park that time."

"Hey, I been livin' here all my life, man. You don't have to tell me nothin' about that stuff. I know what you has to do. You like me, you jest keeps your mouth shut and tries to get along best you can. But I wisht we could be friends. That's why I followed you, to see where you lives. I thought maybe we could talk now and then. I got a mean daddy jus' like you."

"Well, there's nothing stopping us from being friends in secret. Want to sit down?"

Taliaferro sat down gingerly on the chair, examining the leg wrapped in wire with a clinical curiosity before trusting it with his full weight.

Steve sat down across from him on the cot. "Where'd you get the name Taliaferro? I never heard of that one before."

"My momma wanted to name me that. She read in a book that was Booker T. Washington's middle name. She thought it sounded kinda nice, but my aunt said it was a big name for a bitty baby, and she called me Tal, and that's what I goes by."

"Okay, *Tal*—Steve's not my real name either. It's Joe, Joseph Whitfield. No particular reason I chose Steven. There's not much you can do with it other than Steve."

They talked quietly as the gathering shadows muted white and black into a soft gray. Tal had six older brothers and sisters all out on their own, he said, and things were hard at home. His father was a harsh disciplinarian, not hesitating to give him the back of his hand or apply a belt or a razor strop when he thought the boy needed it, which was often. Both of his parents worked long hours at the local cotton mill, and he had had to grow up pretty much by himself. In the summer, he worked on the county road crew and at the furniture store, and he did odd jobs during the school year while he went to the colored high school on the south edge of town.

"I do all right with the grades, but sometimes I wonder if school will fit me to do anything when I get out. A fella from my end o' town can't aim for much more'n a shoeshine boy at a bus station or fancy hotel in Birmingham or working in the mills like my folks does. My momma says if I want to make somethin' of myself, I'll have t' go somewhere else, maybe up north. Life in the South ain't nothin' for a black man."

"I know what you mean. It must be tough for you ..."

"Beggin' your pardon, man," Tal interrupted with feeling, "but no white man got any idea what it's like to be black! Whenever you runs into a white, you got to wonder how he's goin' to treat you. It don't matter who it is, you has to pay mind to the fact that you're black, and if you forgets, they sets you straight. If they treats you bad, you gotta take it. I been spit at, cursed, beaten up, made to get off the sidewalk and walk in the gutter ..." Long-suppressed anger edged his voice. "It's always right there with you—that you're black, not white. I don't know if it's better up north where you comes from, but I'd sure like to give it a try."

"I'm sorry," was all Steve could say.

The two were silent for a long time. Finally, Tal said, "One thing I noticed about you right away is you talks good English."

"Well, I ought to. My mom was an English teacher before she had me, and she drummed it into me."

"Talkin' right marks you. I know I don't talk good English. Nobody does in my end o' town, not my momma, not even the teachers at school. If I goes up north, I'm gonna need to learn to talk good English. Maybe you could help me—learn me to talk like a proper white man like your momma done you."

"I don't know that I could do that. I don't think you'd like it if I corrected you all of the time."

"What you mean '*all the time*,' man?" Tal exclaimed. "I only makes mistakes *some of the time*." He laughed heartily at his own joke.

Steve joined in the laughter, adding quickly, "You mean that you *make* mistakes some of the time."

"There you go! I *make* mistakes some of the time."

Steve appreciated the boy's humor and sensed that his instincts were good. He had taken an instant liking to him when he first met him in the park and again when they met downtown. Despite their different backgrounds, a bond began to grow between them as they talked of their hopes and aspirations. Being unfamiliar with Negroes, he was not sure at first how he should respond to the boy, but Tal was easy to talk to.

In the dark of the little room, the differences seemed to blur, and he began to relax. The revelation that Steve was a runaway from an abusive father resonated with Tal and seemed to break down final barriers between them. Tal plied him with questions, and as they talked, Steve began to reveal more of his own past—his life in Nebraska and his problems with his father—than he had allowed himself to think about since he came to Morefield.

They sat talking for nearly two hours before Steve felt something rub against his leg.

"Is that you, Friday? Come home to get your supper?" Man Friday responded with a low meow.

"You got a cat?"

"Yes, this is Friday. My Man Friday. He showed up a while back, and we share this place together. Do you like cats?"

"Yeah, I likes cats. Got one that hangs around home for scraps. A big black tomcat. Name's 'Boomer.' Don't know why. My sister's little girl named him that."

"I'm glad you *like* cats," he replied, accenting the proper verb heavily.

"Yeah, I *like* cats," Tal responded with a wide grin that his new friend couldn't see but heard in his voice.

Steve picked Man Friday up and deposited him on Tal's lap, where, after poking his nose around for a few moments, he curled up and began to purr as Tal stroked his back.

"He likes you. They say cats are a good judge of character."

"Don't know about that. But he knows I likes, *like,* him, and he knows I *like* his friend."

It was nearly midnight before Tal took his leave and headed through the encircling shadows of the alley toward the south part of town.

In the succeeding months, Tal dropped by the shed frequently for a chat, always after suppertime when the dark protected him from hostile eyes. Under Steve's somewhat apologetic tutelage, his English began to improve. Although they had become friends, when they met on the street, they continued to acknowledge each other only with a curt nod. However, a simple nod spoke volumes for each of them. It was good to have a friend Steve could confide in, if only on restricted terms.

CHAPTER 9

When school began the first week of September, Mr. Banfield agreed to change Steve's work schedule to allow him to work three evenings a week at the grocery store from five until eight when the store closed. At the newspaper, Mr. Benjamin adjusted Steve's schedule so that he could work from eight until six Saturdays and from six to nine Mondays. He applied for and got a job sweeping and cleaning the school for an hour before school each morning and from five to seven one afternoon a week. That made a total of twenty-nine hours a week. That left him little time for studying or relaxation once school started, and he was glad he had had the foresight to study history and other subjects during the summer. He was gradually training himself in the necessary art of concentration so he could use his time to advantage, but it promised to be a long, hard haul. There was no alternative.

Although the high school was much larger than the one he had left in Nebraska, the routine was not unlike that which he had been used to. He quickly adapted to any variations, trying as always to fit in without calling attention to himself. His primary objective—his only objective—was to get his high school diploma. Once that hurdle was cleared, he would have to find a way to attend college. Somehow. He knew that he would have to work his way through college too, and he needed to save every penny he could now.

It soon became apparent that avoiding attention was easier said than done. As he walked down the hall to his American history class the second morning, he was startled to hear a loud voice behind him. "Hey, Yankee boy! Where's your Nigger buddy?" With that, he was tripped from behind, and he barely managed to avoid crashing headlong into a nearby wall locker.

A second voice snarled, "Better watch your step here, boy!" and he was shoved up against the wall locker. He looked up to see the two boys who had roughed him up in the park the day he talked to the young Negro. As they turned quickly away and walked briskly down the hall as if nothing had happened, he heard one laugh, "Hey, that was a good one, Tom. 'Watch your step!' Ha, ha!"

As he had before, Steve had doubled up his fist but managed to choke down the urge to retaliate in kind. He couldn't afford to get in a fight his first week in school. Later, he learned that the larger of the two was Jack Damon, star tackle on the football team, and the other, Tom Marsh, was a third-string center.

In the next couple of weeks, the incident was repeated several times, but Steve managed to swallow his pride and anger and went on about his business. On several occasions, he observed the two shoving and taunting other students in the halls and on the front steps after school. Stifling his instinctive desire to defend the underdog, he looked the other way. The two were going to be a continuing problem, but he guessed he'd just have to tough it out.

* * * * * * * *

Staying in school and working long hours would be difficult indeed, but Steve had made a start toward saving for college. He had managed to save twenty-three dollars through the summer and had hidden it in a paper sack in the back of the drawer of the table. One afternoon, having finished his job at the school, he trudged wearily home to the shed. As he stepped over the threshold and into the shed, he stopped short. What he saw in the dust he had carefully raked as usual that morning was not the winding imprint of Old Gus. Instead, he saw the familiar outlines of large boots, boots whose heels bore a tread resembling the rays of a rising sun. This time, however, the prints of the intruder did not lead off through the jumble toward the workbench. They went up the steps to his room. Perhaps the intruder had wondered why the dust was being raked and the steps swept and decided to investigate. It appeared that the prints came back down the stairs again, but Steve stood stock still, listening for sounds from above. He heard nothing, and after a few moments, Man Friday came bounding down the steps toward his friend and jumped into his arms from the second step. Steve started cautiously up the steps with the cat, reasoning that if someone were upstairs in the room, the cat would have long since made himself scarce.

The door was wide open, and he entered the room not knowing what to expect. The room was empty, but there was evidence that there had been a visitor. Books and papers he had left on the table lay scattered on the floor, and the blanket on the cot had been tossed into a corner.

With a sinking heart, he saw that the drawer of the table had been pulled open, and the paper bag he'd kept his savings in lay on the floor, torn apart. The money was gone!—his savings from the entire summer of hard work—gone! He sat down on the bed, holding Friday close, and fought back tears. He thought bitterly of the times he had wanted to buy things, even to have an ice cream soda, and had decided to save the money instead. He thought back to the five dollars he had kept in the pocket of his overall jacket. Once again, he was back to square one.

As he sat there, an even more serious problem emerged through his disappointment. Who was the intruder? Tal was the only person who knew he lived there. He immediately dismissed the thought—he had no doubt as to his friend's honesty, and if he had, he had noticed that Tal always wore ragged blue sneakers, not boots. They were probably the only shoes he had. Another thing was sure. The visitor wasn't Mrs. Pike either. The prints were obviously made by a man's boots.

But who could the visitor be? More importantly, would the man give him away? The new existence Steve had so carefully crafted now threatened to come apart at the seams. He looked to the table and the cardboard bulletin board he had constructed—pinned there with a calendar and a couple of lists was the article from the St. Louis paper telling about his disappearance. How could he have been so careless? He hoped that the intruder hadn't spotted it, and he quickly took it down, folded it, and tucked it into his Bible. He considered pulling up stakes and leaving town, but the thought of having to invent himself all over again and to start from scratch after he had put so much work into getting into school and fixing up the room was overwhelming. No, he would just have to stay on and hope for the best.

He felt the loss of his savings keenly. He checked the money in his pocket. Twenty cents—all he had to his name now. That would have to last him until next week when he got paid again. Eight days. He looked in the sack on the desk. Only one orange. Apparently his visitor was hungry and had taken the other two.

Later, as he headed toward the gate to the alley, he glanced down and spotted orange peels thrown down in the weeds beside the path. Judging by the footprints in the dust, the intruder had stood there briefly, peeling and eating the oranges. Steve decided that the intruder was someone from the neighborhood, someone neighbors would not wonder at coming through the alley or even coming into the backyard. A funny thought struck him. Maybe he could seek the assistance of the observant Mrs. Meyer, and she could figure things out for him.

Apparently, the intruder came regularly and was stealing tools and other items, one or two a week, from the lower floor. Steve thought for a moment of lying in wait for the thief and confronting him, but he quickly thought better of it. With his schedule at school and his work, he could hardly spare the time to pop in and out. Besides, if he did succeed in intercepting him, the man probably would figure things out and might turn him in to the authorities. But that was unlikely—the man undoubtedly would not want to attract attention to his visits to the shed. After all, he was stealing things. He had a good thing going, regularly making off with items he could use or maybe sell, and he would want that to continue.

Finally, Steve decided that it might be a good idea for him to leave something for the man to find in the room now and then—maybe an orange or two, maybe a couple of quarters. A payoff, to be sure, but perhaps it would establish a weirdly symbiotic relationship in which there were mutual rewards for silence.

That relationship would have its limits, of course, and Steve decided he'd have to find a safer place for his savings. There were plenty of possibilities downstairs, and he went down to look around. He noticed a Karo syrup bucket among the jumble and decided he could put his savings in it and hide it under a pile of rubble. No need to put the bucket there now—he hadn't any money to put in it.

As Steve lay awake far into the night thinking about the day's events, he realized with a start that the newspaper article he had so carelessly posted offered a reward for information leading to his return. What if the intruder had read it and decided to collect it?

* * * * * * * *

After a fitful night, Steve ate a breakfast of two slices of bread and a small piece of cheese before heading for school. The remaining orange the thief had left him was all he would have to eat for more than a week.

It was hard to concentrate in class that day as he wondered what might come of the mysterious visit of the afternoon before. He pondered what he should spend the twenty cents on. Then in English class, the teacher, Miss Claibourne, announced that students would need to have a workbook containing readings and accompanying exercises. It would not be provided by the school and would cost a dollar and a quarter. She reminded the class that this had been mentioned at registration. Preoccupied with the requirement of having his guardian present, Steve had forgotten about it. His face fell. He simply did not have the money for the book, not until the next week. There were no two ways about it.

The following day, he was the only student in the class who showed up without a book. He tried to look on with the boy sitting next to him, Rollie Chance, who had walked with him part way downtown after school a couple of times and seemed glad enough to help him out. However, the teacher noticed the absence of the book and singled him out in front of the class.

"Steven," she said sternly, "you are the only one who came to class without a workbook. You had plenty of notice that it would be required for this class, and I reminded the class yesterday. Why didn't you bring your book to class?"

Steve scrunched down a little in his seat and made no reply.

"Well, I'll expect you to have your own book when you come to class tomorrow. You can't do the work without one."

Looking on with Rollie, he paid scant attention to the lesson as

Miss Claibourne guided the students through the first exercise in the book, his mind preoccupied as he tried to figure out how he might come up with the necessary money by the next day. Maybe he could ask Mr. Banfield or Mr. Benjamin for an advance on his pay. Being fairly new to both jobs, he decided against that lest he appear to be irresponsible. It would be awkward explaining the circumstances in which his money had been stolen, and how would he explain not having gone to the police? He didn't want to presume on his growing friendship with Mrs. Pike or Rollie. Underneath his reasoning, though he might not have admitted it, was his strong sense of pride.

Trying to find a job that evening in the neighborhood was not an option either since he did not get off work at Banfield's until after dark. When the bell rang ending the class, he was no nearer a solution to the problem, nor did he find one as he worried through the afternoon and evening and well into the night.

He debated whether he should even show up for class the next day. Miss Claibourne projected little personality in class, but she apparently went strictly by the book—a book he didn't have. He finally decided he would go to class. He sat near the back of the room and hoped that she would forget about the previous day and not notice that he didn't have the workbook. Rollie had said he'd be glad to let him look at his book anytime.

However, as soon as she had taken roll, the teacher looked toward the back of the room and walked methodically down the aisle to his desk. "Where is your workbook, Steven?" she asked, her hands on her hips.

He looked down at the desk. "I'm sorry, Miss Claibourne, I don't have one. I'm sorry."

She pounced on the answer, a touch of sarcasm giving edge to her voice. "You will remember, I am sure, that I told you yesterday in no uncertain terms that you were to bring a workbook with you to class. It is essential if you are to do the work. You can't get by using someone else's. All of the other students brought theirs as they were told. Only you did not. Apparently you think you can operate outside of the rules down here. Well, I assure you that that is not going to work. You are dismissed from class, and you will not be readmitted until you show up with the required workbook. Do you understand?"

"Yes, ma'am," he mumbled. He got to his feet and fled the room, his face crimson with embarrassment, and returned to the study hall. Bewildered and stung by the teacher's rigidity, he sat there for a few minutes. *I'd buy the book if I had the money*, he kept saying to himself. It was so unfair. After a few more minutes, he checked himself out to the school library.

Miss Claibourne returned to her desk and proceeded with the class as if nothing had happened, guiding the class firmly through the next exercise in the workbook. When the class bell rang, the students bolted for the door, all except one, Rollie Chance. He approached the teacher's desk haltingly. After a moment, she looked up, her expression indicating that if he had something to say, he should spit it out.

"Miss Claibourne," he began timidly. "It's about Steven Bowman. He didn't have a workbook ..."

"I'm well aware of that," she answered abruptly. "He knew he was to bring it today, and he didn't do so. It's as simple as that."

"Miss Claibourne," he continued hesitatingly, "it's not that he doesn't want to bring a book or forgot. It's that ... well, he just doesn't have the money to buy one."

"It's only a dollar and a quarter."

"Ma'am. He lives with his grandmother. She doesn't provide anything for him except a place to stay. He has to work for everything—food, clothes, school books. She doesn't even take care of his food. He works three jobs, almost thirty hours a week. He told me he had only twenty cents to his name until next week when he gets paid. He *can't* buy a book till then!"

The teacher's expression softened. She was silent for a few moments. "I'm sorry. I didn't know."

"I just didn't think it was fair."

"Thank you for telling me, Rollie. I'll see what can be done about getting him a book."

When the boy had left the room, she sat at her desk for a few minutes and stared at the classroom, her gaze settling on the empty desk at the rear. After a few moments, she went to the study hall and learned that Steve had checked out to the library.

She found him sitting with his head down, cradled in his arms at a reading table in a secluded corner, shielded from view. She sat down quietly opposite from him and said softly, almost apologetically, "Steve."

The boy sat up suddenly, startled. He turned away quickly, but she saw that there were tears in his eyes.

"Why didn't you tell me you didn't have money to buy the workbook?"

The boy did not reply.

"Why didn't you tell me? I would have understood."

"I was … ashamed."

"Ashamed! There's nothing to be ashamed of." She saw that he fought to hold back the tears. "There's nothing to be ashamed of," she repeated.

"Ma'am … you don't know what it's like not to have anything. To have to wear second hand clothes, to …"

"No, I don't guess I do know what it's like. But I do know that being poor is nothing to be ashamed of."

The boy said nothing.

"Is your grandmother your legal guardian? Do you have the paperwork?"

He squirmed uncomfortably in his chair. He hesitated, then replied, "Yes, ma'am."

"Then she has a legal obligation to see that you have the things you need. I understand you are working three jobs to make ends meet. Is that right?"

"Yes, ma'am."

"A boy your age shouldn't have to do that. You're a minor, and the authorities can see that she takes care of her responsibilities. They can straighten that out in a hurry."

The boy looked up in alarm. "Please! … Please don't say anything to her. She's not my real grandmother." He slipped easily into the litany he had used before. "She's my stepfather's mother. No kin to me at all. She just has her Social Security and barely gets by on that. She just gives me a room, and I'm grateful for that, but nothing else. That was the agreement when I came down here. She doesn't want me here. I'm just a bother—she's told me that often enough. If there is any trouble, anything at all, she said she'd send me right back to Dayton to my stepfather. She means it. She's mean, just like he is. I could never go back there. When he gets mad, he … I can't go back there! Please don't bother her, Miss Claibourne. Please! I promise I'll get the book next week when I get paid."

He spoke with such sincerity and emotion that the woman was taken aback. He was almost hysterical.

"Well, we'll have to see what can be done. Maybe we won't have to contact her, at least not now, but it isn't right."

"Thanks, ma'am, thanks a lot."

"What I can do is let you borrow my workbook. I have one extra, and maybe you can do the exercises on a separate sheet of paper and hand them in."

"Yes, ma'am, that would be swell. I'd really appreciate it. I promise I'll have my own book next week."

"You come with me, and I'll get it for you. And we don't need to say anything to anybody. It will be just between you and me."

* * * * * * * *

When Steve's eyes began to burn from the flickering light of the lantern that evening, he went to bed, and around midnight, as usual, Man Friday came bounding up the steps and jumped up on his bed. The two roughhoused briefly, and then the cat curled up in the crook of the boy's arm, kneading him intently, and soon fell asleep, oblivious to human concerns.

But sleep did not come so easily to Steve. He lay there awake for a long time thinking about the afternoon's incident. He felt sorry that he had had to paint Mrs. Pike in such a bad light again, but it seemed the only way to keep things from falling apart. If anyone at the school should contact her, the game would be over. Expediency held a reluctant precedence over conscience, and it made him feel uncomfortable.

As he pondered the situation with his "guardian," a thought struck him. What if the school should send her something in the mail, a report card or an invitation to some school event? Since she was on paper as his legal guardian, it was entirely possible. He decided that it would be necessary for him to intercept her mail every day. That wouldn't be hard. The uneven front walk made footing unsure, and with her foot problems and uncertain balance, walking to the mailbox at the curb and back to the porch was almost impossible. Since the postman came by regularly at about 11:45 each morning, he could make it a practice to drop by when class let out at noon and bring the mail in. It was only five blocks. He had already told her he lived on up the street near the park, so she wouldn't suspect anything and would be grateful to him for doing it. He could go on up the street, circle around the block, come back down the alley, and eat lunch in the shed before returning to school. Lunch in the school cafeteria was out of the question. Saving all he could for college, he did not feel he could afford it.

The problem with the workbook had been solved, but the food problem had not. He had nothing for supper, and he ate the last orange the next morning for breakfast. When he gave Man Friday a handful of cat food for his breakfast, it crossed his mind that it just might be a tasty snack. "No thank you," he said aloud. "There's only enough left in the box for a couple of days, little fella. Better find a plump, juicy mouse till I get money to buy you some more. Maybe you could get one for me too, huh?"

That afternoon at work at Banfield's, he decided to spend his last twenty cents on a box of cat food for his friend.

* * * * * * * *

School that week settled into a groove of sorts. He began to make a few friends with several students besides Rollie, but they were really only acquaintances. He had neither the time nor the money to become a part of their activities. His days were now an unremitting grind of hard work, study, and continuous deception. But having to work so hard not only took time, it sapped his energy, and that sometimes made study difficult.

And then there was the hunger. As the week wore on, attention to his studies became almost impossible as thoughts of food gnawed their way into his every waking moment. When he could, he wrapped up some of the meat scraps at the store to take home to Friday, but they were mostly gristle and fat, and he had no way of cooking them. One noon, when he could stand it no longer, he picked out some of the leaner scraps and ate them. In a few minutes, he dashed down the steps and vomited them into the weeds beside the door.

Next morning, he reported for work as usual at seven, sweeping out the auditorium and gym before classes began at eight. When he finished, he picked up his book for geometry class from his wall locker.

The next thing he remembered, someone was squeezing his hand and calling, "Steve, Steve, wake up! Are you all right? Steve!"

For a moment, he did not recognize the name as his own. When he opened his eyes, pieces of the room revolved and slowly fitted themselves together. He realized that he was lying on a cot with a woman bending over him.

He looked around, trying to make sense of it all.

"You fainted in the hall, Steve. They brought you here—I'm Mrs. Trimble, the school nurse. You gave us all a fright."

"Fainted?"

"Yes, the kids said you just started to sink down and fell to the floor. I don't know if you hit your head or not. You've been out for nearly ten minutes. We've sent for a doctor."

"A doctor? I don't have any …"

"You just lie back down now. Get your strength back," she said kindly, pushing him down gently.

He did not resist. He closed his eyes, wondering what might happen now. He couldn't pay for a doctor. And what if they insisted on contacting Mrs. Pike? He wondered if he had said anything to give himself away while he was unconscious.

In a few minutes, Dr. Travis, who had been summoned from his office downtown, came by, but when Steve tried to get up, he fainted again. He woke to smelling salts hearing the strange name again. "Steve, Steve, can you hear me?"

"Wow, I thought for a minute we'd lost him," he heard the doctor whisper to the nurse. "He's very weak." The doctor opened up the boy's shirt. "Look. You can see his ribs." Then, raising his voice, he asked, "What did you have for breakfast today, Steve?"

"I didn't eat breakfast. … I wasn't hungry."

"A growing boy like you not hungry? How about yesterday? What did you have for supper last night?"

"I didn't have anything," said the boy so softly that the doctor had to strain to hear him.

"Nothing? When was the last time you had anything to eat?"

Steve paused for a long time. "I had an apple Monday."

"And before that?"

"I don't remember. A couple of days, I guess. That's all, just an apple, and some meat I couldn't keep down."

The doctor turned to the nurse and whispered, "No wonder he fainted. He's starving!" He bent over the boy and gave him a shot of something. He covered him with a blanket to keep him warm, then turned to Mrs. Trimble. "Would you run down to the lunch room to get him some food?" He turned back to his patient. "You need to get some nourishment in your stomach, Steve. For now, you just lie back and save your strength till she gets back."

The nurse reappeared in a few minutes with a tray containing a large roast beef sandwich, a bowl of chicken noodle soup, a couple of oatmeal cookies, and a glass of milk. She helped Steve to sit up and put the tray on his lap. The boy attacked the sandwich savagely.

Dr. Travis watched him wolf down a couple of big bites before going into the inner office to confer with the nurse out of earshot. It took no time at all for the sandwich to disappear, washed down by gulps of milk. He had started to take a bite of a cookie when he suddenly fell to his knees beside the cot and vomited it all up. He felt feverish and weak, and the room began to swirl around slowly. Hearing the noise, the doctor and nurse rushed into the room.

"I, I'm sorry," the boy stammered.

Dr. Travis helped him back onto the cot. "You have to take it easy with the food, young fellow. Your stomach isn't used to it. You lie back and keep yourself covered up. We'll get you some more food. This time I'm going to stand over you to make sure you don't gulp it down so it comes right back up again."

When Steve had finished off the new tray of food, this time containing two bowls of soup and a glass of grape juice in addition to a sandwich and milk, he lay back down and slept until mid-afternoon.

At about three, the doctor reappeared to check his pulse and blood pressure. "That's much better," was his verdict. "You stay there until school is out; then I'll have someone drive you home. I've brought you some food to take home with you—a roast beef sandwich, two ham and cheese sandwiches, a couple of bottles of milk, a couple of oranges, some sugar cookies, and a large jar of vegetable beef soup. Surely your grandmother will heat it up for you. And here are bottles of multivitamins, vitamin C, and some calcium. Take one of each every day. I'll leave a supply with Mrs. Trimble. When those run out, come by my office just off the square and get some more."

"I appreciate it, sir, but after I get paid day after tomorrow … I'll be able to take care of myself as soon as I get paid. I don't want any charity."

"Don't let false pride get in the way of good sense, young man," the doctor said sternly. "The salesmen give them to me as samples. They don't cost me anything, and I pass them on to people who need them, and you need them. You're still growing and you need to eat regularly and get proper nourishment. You don't want to get sick, do you?"

"No, sir."

"Then let's hear no more about charity."

Steve's face flushed at the doctor's lecture. "All right, sir, I'll take them. Thanks."

The doctor was not finished. "Miss Claibourne happened to come in this afternoon and told me about the situation with your grandmother. We'll respect your wishes for now, but it's not right. We'll try to work something out, at least until you have money coming in regularly."

"Thanks," said the boy weakly. "I'll be all right as soon as I get paid."

The doctor gave him another shot before he left, and Steve began to feel stronger. He began to worry about the promised ride home. They couldn't let him out in front of Mrs. Pike's house!

Just before school was out, while the nurse was busy in her office, he put on his shirt and shoes, secured the bag of food and vitamins, and slipped out. He felt wobbly, and he knew he wouldn't be able to unload any boxes at Banfield's after school that afternoon, so he walked directly home, pausing twice to sit down to rest. He slipped unnoticed into the backyard and managed with difficulty to climb the steps to the room. He fed the appreciative Man Friday some of the roast beef and milk, drank the rest of one of the bottles of milk, and ate half a sandwich himself. Then he went to bed. His worry as to what the consequences of the day's incident might be was mercifully cut short by the sleep of the weak and exhausted.

* * * * * * * *

The weekly faculty meeting did not fail to bring general attention to the plight of the new student. The principal reported that Dr. Travis had said that the boy could possibly have gone into shock and died that morning, and Miss Claibourne, breaking her promise to Steve, recounted the incident with the workbook.

There were general expressions of dismay and indignation directed at a guardian who would not provide even the basic necessities for the boy. Some suggested that the county authorities be contacted at once, but Miss Claibourne recounted the boy's almost hysterical reaction when she had suggested contacting the grandmother.

"He acted terrified. He says the least little trouble and she'll send him back to Ohio to his stepfather. Apparently, he mistreats him badly. As I said, he was terrified, almost hysterical. He is working and says he'll get paid tomorrow and can provide food for himself. It's a very strange situation. If I had anything to say about it, that old lady would be marched straight to the county jail and locked up for a good while. But I think we need to respect his wishes for now and see if there isn't some way we can help him out. We'll have to avoid any appearance of charity. Despite his circumstances, he's got plenty of pride."

Most of the teachers agreed that this might be the best course of action for the present. Only Mr. Carnahan, the advanced math teacher, a bitter man in his early sixties who delighted in finding the negative in any equation, favored a direct and immediate approach to the grandmother.

"There's something fishy about all this," he remarked darkly.

He was overruled by a majority of the faculty who supported Miss Claibourne's approach, backed solidly by Miss Edwards. If things didn't work out, more drastic, legal measures might be warranted. Finally, Mr. Carnahan acquiesced, but he insisted that the grandmother should be given a short leash and brought before the authorities at the first sign of trouble.

Miss Edwards suggested that instead of sweeping and cleaning the school for an hour five mornings a week before classes, Steve could do janitorial work only two mornings. For the other three hours, he would work in the lunchroom an hour each day on Monday, Wednesday, and Friday. His pay could include a donut and milk, maybe some fruit juice for breakfast and the noon meal as well. Probably he wouldn't be too proud to accept that. And the lunchroom ladies might be able to slip him a sandwich now and then when he worked after school.

Ignoring Mr. Carnahan's continuing scowl, Miss Claibourne spoke up again. "Well, by all appearances, he is a very good student, and he deserves whatever help we can give him. I have just graded the exercises in his workbook, and he does excellent work. More than just excellent—really first rate."

Mr. Davison, one of the science teachers, agreed. "In the test I gave last week, he got the highest grade in the class, and it was a very difficult test if I do say so. His transcript from Ohio shows that he was a straight-A student his first two years of high school. I think he is a decent young man trying to do the right thing, and I move we do whatever we can to help him. I think Miss Edwards's suggestion might be feasible."

After a brief discussion, her suggestion carried the day, and the plan of private philanthropy was put into action. Steve was agreeable to the switch to the lunchroom, although he would continue to clean the classrooms and offices after school. There, he quickly won the friendship of the cooks, especially Jessie Mae Thibidoux, a motherly woman of fifty who had lost her only son, the apple of her eye, nearly six years before at Pearl Harbor. Perhaps she saw her son in him. He was friendly, helpful, and appreciative, and she quickly took him under her wing. As hoped, she frequently had a sandwich or a piece of pie or cake for him when he happened by when he worked after school. Sometimes she sent a few cookies, "leftovers" she called them, and a bottle of milk home with him. If he sensed that charity was involved, he never showed it.

* * * * * * * *

As if to underscore Steve's vulnerability, the mysterious boot prints in the dust greeted him again early the next week as he entered the shed after work at Banfield's. There was the usual evidence of the intruder's visit. The blanket on the cot had been thrown on the floor, and a bag of apples Mrs. Thibidoux had given him had disappeared. The next week, the visit was repeated, and a fountain pen and a package of razor blades were missing. Downstairs the crosscut saw no longer hung on the wall.

Steve had implemented his plan to leave things for the "boot man," as he came to call him. During the weeks and months that were to follow, their tacit "arrangement" seemed to work well enough. Apparently the intruder had not read the *St. Louis Post-Dispatch* article, and Steve's presence was not reported. The man came and went, taking what he wanted downstairs and whatever Steve left for him.

CHAPTER 10

As some of his expenses began to level off, Steve began to bring some sense of order to his new life. Although he continued to watch his pennies carefully, he was not constantly preoccupied with his financial plight. Saving for college was, of course, a priority. However, the problem of his identity was at his elbow day and night. He had to be constantly aware of who he was supposed to be and the need to protect his privacy. He now responded to his new name automatically and felt more comfortable with his adopted identity. Certainly, he was becoming more independent than he had ever been allowed to be at home.

As he began to eat more regularly, the hard work at the grocery and the newspaper complemented the physical work he had done regularly on the farm, and his body began to fill out and his muscles grew stronger. With that, there was a boost in his self-confidence, but he did not swagger or become aggressive. Necessarily, he did his best to keep out of the limelight and kept pretty much to himself.

Sometimes, however, his efforts to keep a low profile broke down in unexpected ways. As he was returning one afternoon from his daily check of Mrs. Pike's mailbox, he went to his wall locker to pick up his textbook for history class. Suddenly, the two boys who had roughed him up in the park and in the hall on several occasions came out of nowhere.

"Well, would'ja look who's here!" a voice snarled.

"Hey, ain't that the Nigger lover?" another voice hissed. "We don't want no white trash here at Morefield."

He whirled and came face to face with Jack Damon. "Yeah, Yankee boy. That's a nice shirt you got on," Jack laughed in derision. With that, he grabbed Steve from behind and gave him a painful Dutch rub.

"You look like a real Bo Brummell. Bet you brought that fancy shirt down all the way from up north."

He shoved Steve roughly on the shoulder, slamming him into the row of wall lockers. Steve winced as his shoulder blade connected with one of the handles.

"Leave me alone!" Steve shouted. "I haven't done anything to you!" He ducked under his tormentors' arms, trying to get away from them. Tom aimed a well-placed fist at Steve's midsection and slapped him across the cheek.

"Yeah, fancy boy," sneered Jack. "All the way down from *North* Fourth Street. That's the shirt my mom dropped off at the rummage sale there last summer. I'd know it anywhere. See the little dot of blue paint on the left sleeve? I got that painting the floor of the back porch. Ha, ha, ha! Hand-me-downs—just what your kind *would* wear. White trash. We threw it away, and now you think you're all the fashion. Ha, ha! You Yankees and your Nigger friends!"

Tom joined in the mocking. "Why don't you go back up north where you come from and take your black buddies with you, all of them?"

"Look!" Steve growled, "I don't want any trouble. I need to get to class. Get out of my way!"

Tom gave him another shove, grabbing hold of one of the sleeves of Steve's shirt and sending him sprawling over his buddy, who had knelt down behind him. As Steve fell, he heard the unmistakable sound of his sleeve ripping. Although he hit the floor with a thud, he bounced to his feet in an instant, his face red as rage.

"Doggone you! You tore my shirt!" he yelled. His voice was a mixture of incredulity and anger. "You tore my shirt!" Then he delivered a blow to Tom's stomach, followed by an uppercut to his jaw. Tom went down like a sack of corn meal, blood gushing from his mouth. He lay there and did not get up. In another second, Jack, who had acted as the fulcrum in their little game, got to his feet and jumped on Steve's back, trying to pin his arms to his side.

Rage and indignation can do wonders, and Steve shook him off as he whirled to deal a haymaker to the boy's nose. Jack dropped to the floor beside his buddy with a loud groan and lay there stunned and bleeding from his nose and mouth. Steve, his fury unspent, dropped down to his knees, straddling Jack, and began pummeling him about the head and shoulders in a hail of hammer-like blows. The sudden force of the onslaught stunned the tormentor, and he lay there unable to collect his thoughts and ward off the furious blows. Blood now gushed from a cut on his forehead and another below his left eye.

After a few moments of unrestrained fury, a couple of boys standing nearby seized Steve by the shoulders, pulled him off Jack and held him back, Steve's arms now flailing into midair.

"You tore my shirt!" he shouted again, struggling to free himself and continuing the onslaught. "Why don't you get up, you big cowards! Had enough? C'mon, get up! Get up! I dare you!"

The two remained on the floor rubbing their faces and spitting blood. Neither took up Steve's invitation.

"I've seen you two and your friends bullying kids in the hallways, kids who can't stick up for themselves. Well, I can take care of myself, and if I ever see either of you doing that again, I'll take care of *you*!" Steve's voice was sharp and hard as forged steel, leaving no doubt as to his intentions.

"Do you understand?"

"Yeah," said Tom, looking at his bloody hands.

"Okay, okay! We got it," Jack mumbled.

By this time a small crowd had gathered around the fight scene, largely silent and shocked at the sight of the well-known toughs, rulers of the halls, who had met their match in the new kid—more than their match. His rage unabated, Steve kept his fists cocked, clearly ready to continue their punishment at the least provocation.

Just then, Mr. Davison, who had seen Steve deliver his final blows to Jack, rushed to the scene and took charge. He pulled Steve back by the shoulders and said, "That's enough of that, Steve! You boys all come with me to the principal's office, and we'll let him sort this out. Right now! We're not going to have this kind of thing going on in the halls. You should be ashamed of yourselves!"

He took Steve by the elbow and steered him firmly down the hall. The two boys got unsteadily to their feet and followed meekly behind, still stunned by the encounter.

When Steve's head had settled a bit and his anger had abated somewhat, he began to consider the consequences of having lost his temper. This certainly wasn't the way to keep out of the spotlight. He wondered what was going to happen to him next. As an outsider, no one was likely to take his side in the quarrel.

The principal, Mr. Newton, was out, and Mr. Davison remained to enforce the peace while the boys cooled their heels in the outer office. Steve pressed his advantage to deliver another warning as to what would happen if he saw the two picking on other students. Tom, who had lost a front tooth and continued to bleed profusely, and Jack, who held a handkerchief over his mouth and nose, blood seeping through in a widening crimson spot, apparently had gotten the message and said nothing.

After a few minutes, Mr. Newton, followed by Miss Edwards, stormed into the room and ordered the three into the inner office, where they stood uncomfortably in a row in front of his desk as if before a sentencing judge.

Motioning to Jack and Tom, the principal demanded to know what had happened. To Steve's dismay, Tom, having had time now to collect his wits, proceeded to blame Steve for the fight.

"I was just walking down the hall to English class minding my own business, when Steve elbowed me in the ribs for no reason at all and pushed me into a wall locker. Then he hit me in the jaw! When Jack went to help me, he hit him the face too!"

Jack quickly backed up his buddy's story. "He came at us out of nowhere and said, 'You think you're so tough just because you're on the football team,' or something like that, and attacked us. He hit me right in the face when I wasn't looking. A sucker punch is what it was. We didn't even have a chance to defend ourselves!"

Tom did not neglect to mention the fact that his father was the county attorney, hinting that there would be repercussions if the school didn't deal severely with Steve.

Without asking Steve for his side of the story, the principal began to lecture him about acceptable behavior at Morefield High, referring obliquely to outsiders who caused trouble. The school simply would not stand for it.

Steve's head whirled at the unexpected turn of events. This was exactly the kind of notoriety he had tried to avoid. And who would believe an outsider against the son of the county attorney? Obviously not Mr. Newton. He would be lucky if he was not expelled from school. Then what?

Fortunately, at that moment Mrs. Trimble and a student named Laura Lee Andrews, who also worked in the lunchroom, knocked on the door and came right on in unbidden. Mr. Newton was highly displeased and opened his mouth to reprimand them for their interruption, but before he could do so, Mrs. Trimble began loudly.

"Mr. Newton, I saw the whole thing, and so did Laura Lee. We were on the third floor landing talking. Steve was walking toward his locker when Tom and Jack came up behind him and began to taunt him about his shirt. Tom grabbed him from behind and messed up his hair, then Jack shoved him hard against the wall lockers. Steve kept telling them to leave him alone and tried to get away, but Tom hit him a couple of times. Then Jack knelt down behind him and Tom shoved him over him. He fell hard on the floor, tearing his shirt. Steve got right up and yelled, 'You tore my shirt!' two or three times, and he hit Tom twice and knocked him flat on the floor. Then Jack jumped on Steve's back. Steve shook him off and hit him in the face, and he fell to the floor too.

"Make no mistake about it, Steve was madder than a wet hen, and he kept yelling, 'You tore my shirt! You tore my shirt!' It wasn't any of his fault. He didn't start the fight ... but he sure did end it," she added with a trace of satisfaction. "About that time, Mr. Davison stepped in and brought all three of them to your office. Laura Lee saw it all and will tell you the same thing. I certainly don't condone fighting, but they had it coming."

Laura Lee had nodded in the affirmative throughout Mrs. Trimble's account of the incident, and then she volunteered, "That's exactly what happened, Mr. Newton. Steve didn't do a thing until they jumped on him and knocked him down. Everybody in the school knows these two—they pick fights in the hall every day and torment the younger kids. They only pick on kids they think they can bully. This time, they picked on the wrong guy, and they got what they deserved."

Mr. Newton's face was stern. He turned to Steve. "Is that what happened?"

"Yes, sir, pretty much. I didn't want to fight, but they jumped me and … and they tore my shirt!"

The shirt seemed to have been the thing that had set him off, and the principal picked up on it. He was aware of Steve's financial plight, and he replied in a softer tone, "Yes, I can see they did. Well, you can be sure that these two and their friends will not be bothering you anymore. They're going to be too busy for a while to get into any trouble."

He cast a quick glance at Tom and added, "And I can assure you, young man, that I don't care what your connections are downtown. And as for your shirt, Steve, you go down to Manchester's on the square and buy yourself the best shirt they've got and bring Miss Edwards the bill. These two will be glad to split it, now won't you, boys?"

"Yes, sir," they replied almost eagerly in one voice.

"You're free to go, Steve. You're in the clear. Mrs. Trimble, would you put a bandage on that cut on Steve's right hand? You two remain here. I have a few things to say to you."

Outside in the hall, Mrs. Trimble and Laura Lee caught up with Steve.

"Looks like you might have recovered from your fainting spell, Steve," the nurse said with a smile.

"I don't think those two will be bothering you anymore," said the girl. "You taught them a lesson they've had coming for a long time. I heard what you said about them picking on other kids. They're always causing trouble in the halls, and I think when the word gets around, you'll be the school hero. *I* think so anyway," she added warmly.

A troubled looked invaded the boy's face. "I don't feel like a hero. I'm a little ashamed of myself."

"Ashamed?" the girl exclaimed. "Why? They deserved what they got, and you should be proud of what you did."

"I'm supposed to be a Christian," he replied almost inaudibly, "and I should have turned the other cheek like the Good Book says. Instead, I lost my temper." He left unspoken the thought that perhaps he wasn't much different, when you got right down to it, from his father and his frequent resort to violence.

"I try hard to follow Christ's teachings too," the girl said, "but I don't think he meant that you couldn't defend yourself. Those two big bullies jumped you and could have hurt you. You shouldn't give it another thought."

"Well," Mrs. Trimble interrupted stoutly, "I think you earned a few stars in your crown for standing up to those two. Where does it say in the Bible that you aren't supposed to stick up for the underdogs? That's what you did. Jack and Tom tease—no, *torment*—younger kids in the halls every day. I see them, and who knows what they do when they're off the school grounds. You did the right thing, and I'm sure even the faculty will agree—even if they won't say so publicly."

Steve paid only partial attention to what the nurse was saying. As she talked, he was captivated by Laura Lee, her quiet way, her gentle smile, and her eyes, sky blue and soft as a May morning. The memory of them lingered on in his imagination into the evening and drifted with him gently into sleep.

* * * * * * * *

Laura Lee had been right about Steve's being a hero in the eyes of most of the students. When the two sheepish bullies slunk into the assembly hall the next morning—Tom with a badly swollen upper lip and a purple bruise the size of an orange on his cheek, Jack with a swollen nose, a cut lip, cuts on his forehead and his cheek, and two black eyes—the whole assembly snickered. When Steve, trying to hide the small bandage on his hand, slipped in quietly and headed for his desk, someone yelled, "Hooray for Jack Dempsey!" and the hall erupted in cheers. Steve blushed bright red, dipped his head, and slid quickly into his seat. For a moment at least, he couldn't help being a little proud of himself, and he thought Joe Whitfield would be too.

The school fairly buzzed about the incident for nearly two weeks, and students in the halls called out Steve's name as he passed. Tom and Jack served detention every day for six weeks, and both were suspended from the football team for three games. When the school, which had hopes for the conference championship, narrowly lost all three, only a few, at least at the school, seemed to really mind.

As Steve was leaving school one afternoon a couple of weeks later, he noticed the two boys sitting on a concrete banister outside the main entrance. Steve walked over to them, and they looked up uneasily.

"How are you guys doing?" he asked evenly.

"We're doin' okay," said Jack. He eyed Steve with a mixture of suspicion and apprehension. Tom nodded in affirmation.

"Good," said Steve. "I don't hold any hard feelings against you two. I hope we can manage to get along."

Jack squirmed uncomfortably, and after a couple of moments he said, "Yeah, I guess so." Tom looked down at the ground and said nothing.

A guarded truce ensued. While the boys did not become friends by any means, they treated each other civilly, if warily, when they met in the halls and on the street, and Steve hoped that was the end of the trouble.

Not long after that, Miss Edwards stopped Steve as he was sweeping down the hall after school. "Steve," she said with a flicker of a smile, "you haven't given me the receipt for that new shirt. I intend to hold those two to paying for a new one. Why haven't you given it to me?"

Steve didn't answer, looking uncomfortable.

"Why haven't you given me the receipt? You did buy a new shirt, didn't you?"

"No, ma'am, I didn't buy one. I don't have the money just now, and you can't get a receipt unless you pay for it."

Miss Edwards rummaged in her purse and handed him a ten-dollar bill. "Now you bring me the receipt … and the change," she said. "I'm anxious to see you in that shirt."

Steve accepted the money and started down the hall.

"And remember, Steve—you get the most expensive shirt in the store," she called after him with a smile. "You've earned it," she added under her breath.

That afternoon, he bought a very nice looking Arrow, a dark maroon with two vertical blue stripes. He remarked to Rollie that he wished they had torn his pants too. He wore the shirt to school on special occasions and came to regard it as sort of a badge of honor.

* * * * * * * *

The remainder of the first six weeks of classes passed quickly, and when the first report card was mailed out, Steve was successful in intercepting it in Mrs. Pike's mailbox. He took it to his room and was pleased to see that he had received an A in every subject. In the comments section, Miss Claibourne had written, "A hard worker and a very fine student. You can be proud of him."

He looked at the back of the card. There was a space for Mrs. Pike to comment as his guardian and a place for her signature. He got out the bottle of lavender ink again and jiggled the rickety table with his knee as he practiced the shaky signature he had written on the guardianship paper. After a few attempts, he was able to produce a signature that looked authentic. Then he wrote in the blank, "Hope he continues to do well," and signed "(Mrs.) Awillah B. Pike."

He looked at his handiwork approvingly and said to himself, *A fine job, Steven. You get an A in penmanship. Keep up the good work!* Next morning, he returned the card to the principal's office.

His system of collecting Mrs. Pike's mail, however, broke down one day that fall, threatening for a moment to give him away. As he prepared to make his daily trip to Mrs. Pike's mailbox, Mr. Davison, his science teacher, intercepted him in the hall, wanting to discuss his class project with him. When Steve arrived at the mailbox nearly an hour late, he discovered that Anna Meyer had brought the morning mail to her.

Mrs. Pike sat in the swing as usual, sipping from a tumbler. "Steve," she said, "this came for you in today's mail." She handed him a white envelope with the return address of the public library. He realized with a start that he had carelessly forgotten to return a book, and an overdue notice had been sent to the address he had given when he first got his library card.

"I wondered why they sent it here. Are you using my address for your mail instead of your aunt's?"

He flushed but recovered quickly. "Oh," he replied as nonchalantly as he could, "I got the library card the day after I arrived in Morefield. I needed to give them an address to get a card, but I couldn't remember Aunt Mildred's exact address, being brand new and all. For some reason, I remembered seeing your address on an envelope when I brought your mail, so I used that. I hope you don't mind. I didn't imagine you'd ever get any mail from them, but I forgot to return a book. Guess this means you'll have to pay the fine," he added with a twinkle in his eye.

Mrs. Pike was immediately disarmed and she chuckled. She had grown very fond of the boy. "Oh, no harm done, hon. I just wondered, and Mrs. Meyer thought it was a little strange. It isn't one of those books 'banned in Boston,' is it?"

"Sure is, Willie! Pretty steamy. If you want to read it, I can hang onto it for a couple of weeks longer." His eyes flashed with amusement.

The old woman broke into laughter, spilling a little of the pink onto her yellow dress. "Keep it longer, and maybe they'll lock you up for a while."

He breathed a sigh of relief, although the suspicious Mrs. Meyer's part in the matter made him a little uneasy. He gave himself a silent lecture about the need to be more careful in the future—the least little mistake ...

* * * * * * * *

Man Friday was a pure delight, an intriguing animal whose antics and companionship helped to fill the lonely hours. Although perhaps an animal cannot fully take the place of another human being, Steve was thankful for his little friend. He looked forward to his nocturnal visits and his playful ways. He knew he could never fully understand the cat, but he came to appreciate his mysterious ways and the independence of his personality.

Late one afternoon, Steve picked up a piece of string he had saved from a wrapping and began to play with the cat, teasing him with sudden jerks and stops of the string. When he pulled it around corners, making it disappear and reappear, it seemed to heighten the cat's curiosity and sense of the hunt. Friday's eyes widened and his pupils dilated; he switched his tail and did a little jig with his hind quarters before pouncing. The boy marveled at the animal's quickness. Sometimes he swung the string above the cat, just out of his reach, and he enjoyed the cat's acrobatic flip-flops as he tried to catch it.

"Get it, boy! Get it! Whoooeee!" he shouted gleefully, his delight growing with each of the cat's manic attempts to snare his prey. "Hey you, let go of that! That was a cheap shot, 'tiger pup!' Ha, ha, ha, ha! Wheeeee, wheeeee!" He broke into gales of laughter at the cat's antics. "Good one, old cat! Loop the loop! Wheeee—whooee, wheeee ..."

Suddenly, Steve stopped short, leaving Man Friday in midair. He dashed to the window and cautiously pulled the curtain aside. There in the alley below, staring up at the window, stood Mrs. Meyer, frowning as she shielded her eyes against the setting sun. She had brought some trash to the can in the alley and had heard the ruckus above.

What now? he wondered to himself. *What if she comes upstairs to see what is going on? Suppose she mentions it to Mrs. Pike? How could I have been so careless*?

His heart pounded wildly. He stood peeking out of the window for some minutes until the woman at last dumped the bag of refuse in the trash can and went back through the gate into her yard, casting a last glance over her shoulder as she went.

The incident troubled him for days afterward, and although nothing seemed to come of it, he was careful not to make any noise when he played with Man Friday. The cat responded to the string with his usual wide-eyed gusto and frantic acrobatics, but it wasn't the same. Steve reflected that this was yet another of the restrictions that had come to circumscribe his life. His was a somewhat voluntary prison to be sure, but a prison nonetheless. He had just passed his birthday without any fanfare, but at sixteen when the whole world lay before most young people, life seemed to be closing in on him.

CHAPTER 11

When you live on the edge of poverty, your needs are constant, but you learn to adjust your wants. Steve had learned to do without many things he had once considered necessary by lowering his expectations, but one of the things he missed most was not material at all. It was singing. Back home on the farm, he had enjoyed singing, and when his frequent run-ins with his father didn't spoil his muse, he sang as he worked in the fields and around the house. His mother liked to hear him and gave him what encouragement she could. He sang frequently at church, and at the high school's spring concert his sophomore year, he had won enthusiastic applause for his rendition of "The Minstrel Boy." That seemed a long time ago.

How he had enjoyed walking out to the far side of the farm to bring the cows in for milking in the late afternoon as the sun was going down! He loved to look up at the billowing thunderheads that loomed against the western sky, watching the flaming red ball of the sun disappear below the darkening horizon, the colors of the clouds softening to pink and lavender, then darkening to purple and gray, the upper reaches tinged with rose, silver, and salmon against the teal blue sky—the clouds caught in updrafts, the colors swirling up toward the boundless universe.

The clouds were, as he imagined them, his mountains, towering over the Nebraska plains, more grand than any mountains could ever be. In a way, they represented something indefinable—perhaps the future—something distant and as yet unattainable. The world beyond seemed fresh with expectation. He was buoyed by their majesty and beauty, and he sang all the way out and all the way back, everything from popular songs to hymns and what little classical music he knew from school and the radio. He had a warm, baritone voice, and he liked to imagine singing on a concert stage in some distant city before large, appreciative audiences, their applause echoing now in his memory. But in his room in the shed, singing or even whistling was out of the question except when a nearby power mower or other noise masked the sound. But this was not often.

Sometimes, he whistled or sang softly as he worked after school when the building was deserted except for the front offices. Working later than usual one afternoon, he went into the auditorium just off the music instructor's office to sweep, dust, and empty waste baskets.

He finished dusting the piano and moved on to a record player nearby. As he worked, he noticed the record on the turntable was a Boston Pops instrumental version of Grieg's "I Love Thee," conducted by Arthur Fiedler. The song was a favorite of his that he had sung at his cousin's wedding a year before. Steve looked around. The school janitor had warned him explicitly that Miss Mountford, the music teacher, was adamant that no one was to play the instruments or equipment in the auditorium without her permission. "There'll be Hell to pay if she catches anyone monkeying around with them," was the way he put it, and Steve had never disturbed any of the things there—except to give them a light dusting.

On this particular afternoon, however, he was in an especially melancholy mood, and he impulsively turned the machine on and set the needle down on the groove. He put the feather duster down on the piano, and in his imagination, the world famous conductor raised, then lowered his baton. As the music began to swell, Steve forgot himself, enchanted by its beauty. He was standing center stage at Symphony Hall. Awed by the audience, he began to sing timidly, but soon he was lost in his fantasy and his voice filled the great hall, clear and strong.

He was no longer Steven Bowman or even Joseph Whitfield. He was a famous singer whose voice could stir the hearts of thousands.

As the last strains of the music died away into the shadowy reaches of the concert hall, swallowed up in thunderous applause, Arthur Fiedler put his baton down, and after a moment, Steve reluctantly picked up his duster and resumed his work.

Suddenly, out of the corner of his eye, he caught the figure of someone sitting near the back of the auditorium. He stopped short, his face white. It was Miss Mountford!

"Oh! I didn't know anybody was around!" he blurted out. "I'm sorry, ma'am. I know I wasn't supposed to turn on your record player. I guess I just got carried away. I know that's no excuse, and I promise it won't happen again. I'm really sorry, ma'am."

What if she reported him to the principal? He could lose his job.

Miss Mountford got up and walked quickly up the center aisle to the stage. The boy watched her with mounting apprehension.

"You have a beautiful voice, young man. I mean it! You have real talent! Why aren't you out for music? With a voice like yours, you should be singing in the glee club and chorus, and you should be singing solos."

Steve swallowed hard but said nothing.

"What's your name?"

"Steve, Steven Bowman, ma'am."

"I'm serious, Steve. I've been looking for someone to sing 'O Holy Night' with the chorus at the winter program. I'd like you to do it. I could work with you to get ready, although I don't think you'd need much help from me. How about it?"

Steve was secretly pleased with the offer, more than pleased. He would have liked nothing better than to sing for audiences at school programs, and he had dreamed of singing "O Holy Night," but he said, "I'm sorry, ma'am, I can't. I don't have time to go out for extracurricular activities. I need to concentrate on my classes, and I have to work. I wish I could, but I just don't have any time to spare. I'm sorry, ma'am."

"Surely you could carve out two or three hours a week to practice. You probably wouldn't even need that much time to get ready. You really have a talent."

When Miss Mountford persisted briefly, Steve held his ground, and she decided to drop the subject, at least for the time being.

"All right, Steve, but won't you think about it and let me know if you change your mind?" she said as she picked up her purse to go. At the door, she turned and said, "And don't you worry about playing my records or singing in here—any time."

* * * * * * * *

The incident drew considerable interest and comment when Miss Mountford mentioned it at the faculty meeting the following afternoon. Steve was already building a reputation among the faculty as a top-notch student, and Miss Mountford's glowing report served to enhance it.

"It's a shame to waste talent like that," frowned Miss Edwards, a sentiment shared by everyone except Mr. Carnahan, ever the brooding dissenter, who again voiced the opinion that there was something that didn't quite jibe about the boy's situation—that "business" with his grandmother.

However, Miss Edwards, now solidly in Steve's corner, lent her imprimatur to his story. "We have to respect the boy's wishes. He has a lot on his plate for a boy his age, maybe more than we know."

The subject wasn't so easily dropped by Steve. He thought about the incident all evening as he tried to study. He wanted badly to sing. It was true that he had little time for such things, but he realized that he could make the time when it came right down to it. He could not admit to Miss Mountford the real reason he could not sing. Lying in bed that evening, tears came to his eyes, and he reflected bitterly that when you are poor, everything has a price tag, and the price is usually too high to pay.

His thoughts turned again to his mother. He missed her, and he wished he could sing for her again. His sanctuary had never seemed so confining and lonely, and for the first time since he had run away, he began to consider returning to Steadman Falls and trying to make the best of it with his father. He quickly abandoned the idea—it was out of the question. His father's fits of temper and physical violence had been increasing, and he knew there was no way of reaching any accommodation with him. He reached up and felt the knot on his rib. It was a constant reminder of the real danger his father posed. "I *can't* go home," he said aloud. He would simply have to adjust to his circumstances, giving up things he wanted and things he liked to do. Singing was one of them.

After midnight, Friday jumped up on the cot, walked across Steve's chest, and curled up beside him, kneading his right elbow and purring loudly, but it wasn't enough.

Next morning, as the advancing sun announced another busy day, he tried to put thoughts of singing out of his mind. It would have been nice, but he had to keep focused on the course he had set and his ultimate goals of graduation and perhaps college.

* * * * * * * *

His was a solitary existence. When Steve wasn't working, he was studying. As time went on, the near slips about his real identity had become fewer and farther between. Nevertheless, the need to keep the details of his new identity straight and to present a seamless front was wearing. He wished he could relax now and then, and he wished he could confide in someone. Many times in their frequent conversations, he was on the verge of revealing something of his past to the grandmotherly Awillah Pike, but he could never quite take the first step in trusting her. Although several of the teachers including Miss Edwards had become friendly and supportive, he could not bring himself to trust any of them to any degree. This was no doubt a function of his situation, but it was more than that. It was in part the legacy of his father—and of the truck driver, Marvin.

While Steve valued his friendship with Mrs. Pike, he felt keenly the need for friends his own age. His situation and necessary isolation made it hard to build relationships with other students. Rollie Chance was an exception. Despite the differences in their circumstances, their friendship grew steadily. They sat beside each other in two classes, and their almost daily walk downtown after school afforded opportunities to get to know each other. Although they never lacked for topics of conversation—school, sports, and girls, even religion, as with Mrs. Pike, Steve carefully guided the conversation away from dangerous topics, especially where he lived and his background in Nebraska. He would have liked to be able to confide in his friend, but Rollie liked to talk, and he did not feel he could rely on him to keep a confidence.

As far as Rollie knew, his friend was a boy from Ohio sent down to live with his stepfather's uncaring mother. Thus their friendship was partly based on fiction, and it was an unlikely one in the first place. Rollie was the son of a prominent local banker, and his mother was a bona fide member of the Daughters of the American Revolution and the United Daughters of the Confederacy. Rollie was a solid member of the upper crust at school. While he could not have half-guessed at his friend's private life and the near squalor he lived in, it could not have escaped him that Steve, besides being a northerner, was an outsider and did not belong. The town, and thus the school, was built on social class—old families, old money—highly structured and unforgiving.

Rollie played on the football and basketball teams, participated in dramatics and music, and was actively involved in the school's social life, dating, though not seriously, some of the prettiest and most popular girls in school, including one of the cheerleaders. He was affable, nice looking, and he had a set of graceful southern manners. In short, he was everything the scion of one of the town's most influential families should be. He was a good student, and it was expected that he would go into either law or medicine when he finished college, perhaps his father's alma mater, William and Mary.

From the beginning of their relationship, Rollie sensed something of quality in his new friend, a strength of character, and he cultivated their friendship, trying to get to know him better and to draw him out.

One afternoon, as they walked downtown after school, Rollie said, "Steve, I don't mean to butt into your personal life, but I think you ought to know that Miss Mountford came up to me after mixed-chorus practice yesterday. She told me you've got a great voice, and she wants you to sing at the Christmas program! She knows you have a tough schedule, but she said you are good enough so you wouldn't have to practice much. Since you and I are friends, she asked me to see if I couldn't get you to change your mind. How about it? She said you are really good, and it's a shame to waste your talent. You really ought to do it, you know."

Rollie watched earnestly as his friend's expression changed. It was as though Steve retreated into a distant, previously established location where Rollie could not follow. But there was an expression of hurt in Steve's eyes that made him seem, despite his remoteness, somehow vulnerable. Steve stammered, looking uneasy and nervous, and finally launched into his patented excuse of having to work and study.

Sensing that these were not the real reasons for his refusal, Rollie persisted, his friend looking more and more uncomfortable by the minute.

Steve wanted so much to sing, and he wanted badly to be able to confide in his friend. The issue of trust gnawed persistently.

"Steve, I think you could find time to practice and sing if you really wanted to. Work and studying aren't the reasons you won't sing, are they? And I think I know what the real reason is."

Steve looked at him uncomfortably but made no comment.

"Wally Henderson told me he sees you sitting on the bench across from the Methodist Church almost every Sunday morning listening to the music. He says you never go in, and I'll bet I know why."

Steve's guarded expression scarcely hid the struggle going on inside. Rollie obviously was near the mark, and he waited patiently for the outcome.

"No, those aren't the real reasons I can't sing," Steve said at last. "I guess I could find the time for practice, when you get right down to it. I didn't want to tell Miss Mountford because I'd be embarrassed. I guess maybe you'll understand ..." He paused for a moment. "You've got to promise not to tell her or anyone else."

"Cross my heart," he said, making the necessary gesture.

"The fact is I'd need a nice, dark suit to be in the program, and I don't have one, and I just don't have the money to buy one. It's out of the question."

"I thought so!" exclaimed his friend. "That's a piece of cake! I'd lend you one of mine, but you're taller than I am and it wouldn't fit you. But Miss Mountford could find one easy; someone could lend you his just for the program. There! Problem solved."

He had not reckoned with his friend's sense of pride.

"No, Rollie," he said sadly, "I'm sure she could, but I'd be ashamed to have to wear someone else's, and I wouldn't want anyone to know, not even Miss Mountford."

"C'mon, Steve. There's nothing to be ashamed of. She'd understand, and nobody else would have to know anyway."

"*I'd* know, and right now I just couldn't handle it. Sorry, but I just couldn't. You have no idea how much I'd like to sing in the program, but it's something I'll just have to give up."

"Steve, that's just foolish pride. There isn't anybody who wouldn't want to help you out, anybody who would think any less of you."

The look of inscrutable hurt had returned. "No, Rollie, I just couldn't handle charity. I'll have to ask you to understand that for now."

Rollie knew a wall when he saw it, and he said with feeling, "Steve, you've got to swallow your pride and trust someone! Just remember, I'd like to be that someone whenever you're ready. For now I guess I'll have to respect your feelings. Don't worry, I won't tell Miss Mountford the reason, but I wish you'd think about what I said."

Steve nodded, and turned and walked quickly into Banfield's.

Years later, Rollie would remark that although he was Steve's friend, he felt that he never really knew him.

* * * * * * * *

Rollie did not give up in seeking to draw Steve out of his isolation. One afternoon as they walked downtown, he and Steve were sparring, enjoying the give-and-take that had become part of their friendship.

Steve teased him about being the idol of the cheerleading corps. "Every one of those girls turns cartwheels when they see you, Don Juan."

Rollie grinned. "If you play your cards right, Stevie, I might put in a good word for you with one of the jayvee cheerleaders. You're not ready for the varsity yet."

"Hey! I'll remember that if I ever need you."

Steve hesitated, then asked, "Seriously ... what do you think of Laura Lee Andrews? She took up for me when I had that fight with Tom and Jack. She sure is pretty and seems awfully nice—we work together in the lunchroom and she's friendly, not stuck up like some of the girls."

"Laura Lee? I dated her three or four times last summer. Very nice girl. Really nice!"

"Just three or four times?"

"Yeah. We had a good time, and I liked her a lot. A lot! We're still very good friends, but she didn't want to go steady. I wanted to. She doesn't date very much, not that she doesn't have plenty of chances. Her parents are pretty strict, though. A real nice girl. Why? You interested in her?"

"Interested, yes. But you know I couldn't take her any place. For now, it'll have to be just interested."

"I think she'd go out with you. In fact, I know she would. She's mentioned you to me a couple of times—what a nice guy she thinks you are. She's real down to earth, and she wouldn't expect you to spend anything much on her. Why don't you ask her?—maybe just walk her home from school. I suppose she's gotten over me by now," he laughed.

"Probably not too hard getting over dumping you," Steve retorted, punching his friend on the shoulder and bursting out laughing.

Rollie grinned. "Take your chances—ask her out."

"Maybe I will."

Chapter 12

Steve hardly noticed when Thanksgiving came. School let out Wednesday noon, and he used the free time to advantage, lining up several jobs raking leaves on Decatur Street. When his friend Rollie asked him what he was going to do on Thanksgiving, he replied truthfully that he would eat dinner "at his grandmother's place." At noon, he sat in his room and ate a minced ham sandwich, drank a half pint of milk minus a saucer for Man Friday, and ate an orange and a piece of pumpkin pie Jessie Mae Thibidoux had slipped him when he stopped by the lunchroom Wednesday afternoon. He dropped by to see Mrs. Pike, who was sitting in the swing enjoying the unseasonably warm weather. She gave him a couple of pieces of cold chicken and a glass of iced tea.

Iced tea? he laughed to himself. Surely some of her patented cranberry punch would have been more appropriate to the holiday. He reflected that he truly had something to be thankful for—her friendship and the friendship of Man Friday. He wrapped the pieces of chicken in a paper napkin and took them back to his room for the cat's Thanksgiving dinner.

On impulse, he decided to walk down to the west edge of town to the banks of the Coosa River. He had never gone there before, but he longed for an hour or two in the country for its feeling of freedom and oneness with nature. The walk down to the flood plain was a pleasant one. He swung his arms wildly in wide arcs, breathing deeply, unwinding from the constant need to be watchful that dominated his daily lot. In the western sky, huge thunderheads billowed, sweeping majestically upward to their crowned heads, carrying his spirits upward with them.

He walked down to the edge of the river, the muddy water indolent in the afternoon sun as it slowly wound its way southward toward the Gulf of Mexico. The current gurgled against the driftwood, sounding like the soft murmuring of distant doves. It had piled debris high in the bend of the river and left a dirty, reddish-brown foam clinging to the mud banks there. He watched the water eddying away and soon became lost in thought. He hadn't been this close to nature and the feeling of wholeness it gave him since those quiet evenings back on the farm when he brought the cattle in from the far pasture. It seemed so long ago. He feasted on the towering silver-white clouds in the west.

He climbed up on a large pine log that had lodged on the driftwood and looked down at the swirling water. It was peaceful and soothing. He thought of home and those long, quiet walks, and he began to sing.

Suddenly, something hit him full force in the back, and he went rocketing out into the water below! He barely had time to catch his breath before he was swallowed up in its churning, murky depths. It seemed to him that he was under the water for a long time. His lungs bursting, he flailed desperately in the darkness to save himself, and he came shooting up to the surface at last, coughing and gasping for air. When he regained his wits and had control of himself, he began to swim toward shore. Suddenly, he felt strong hands grab him by the wrist, pulling him to safety on the bank. He stumbled to his feet and fell again headlong to the muddy earth. When he had regained his feet and pressed the grimy water from his eyes, there on the bank dripping wet and looking concerned stood Taliaferro.

Steve was livid. "Tal!" he sputtered. "D-doggone you! What in the h-heck did you do that f-for? You almost got me d-drowned! Look at my clothes! I'm soaked—mud clear through!"

"Sorry, bro," said his friend, "but you was standin' on that log not two feet from a big cottonmouth that was coilin' up, gettin' ready to strike. I didn't have time to say nuthin' to you. I was up on the bank there, and I just give a flyin' leap so's to knock you off before he could get you. See over there, he's crawlin' onto that pile of driftwood. He's a big'n!"

"Wow, I didn't even see him! Look at him! Gosh! Thanks a lot!"

"Wasn't nuthin,'" the boy shrugged. "I'm wet through too, but you looks like somethin' the dog done drug in," he laughed.

"I *look* like something the dog drug in," Steve corrected him with a smile.

"You got that right," laughed Tal, and Steve joined in the little joke.

"C'mon to my house with me. My momma'll wash your clothes for ya an' put 'em out to dry while you eats yourself some supper. Won't be much, but we can follow the river on down to the south end o' town and cut on over to my place. Nobody'll see us, and my ol' man won't be home from the mill till almost midnight."

"That'd be fine," Steve said. The sun was almost down, and the rapidly dropping temperature made him shiver in his wet clothes. He gladly followed Tal as he headed down the bank toward the colored part of town. "Man alive!" he exclaimed again. "I didn't even see that snake. I owe you one! Maybe I can pay you back some day."

Steve did not know what to expect when they reached Tal's house, a gray, unpainted frame shanty with a rusting tin roof. It stood precariously on stilts made of cinder blocks. A thin column of gray smoke rose almost proudly straight up from the chimney until it joined those of the neighboring houses, all of a pattern. The floorboards of the sagging front porch responded uncertainly to his tread.

He took an immediate liking to Tal's mother, a large woman whose pleasure in fussing over them was obvious. She wore a perpetually hopeful smile that somehow made him glad just to be around her. When she saw that their clothes were dripping wet, she exclaimed, "I declare, if you'uns don't look like somethin' jest crawled up out o' the swamp! Better shuck them wet clothes and get into some dry before you takes your death o' cold."

Without waiting for a word of explanation, she shooed the boys into a bedroom, and as instructed, Steve handed his wet clothes through the door to her and received a green chenille bedspread in exchange. He wrapped himself in it and spent the next couple of hours looking, as he imagined, like a refugee from some far-off, war-torn country.

When they emerged into the kitchen a few minutes later, Mrs. Davis was busying herself at the big cook stove. The fire hissed and popped as it devoured wood cut green. As she bustled about, wiping her forehead from time to time on her apron, she turned to talk with her white guest. The sound of clattering pans and dishes formed an accompaniment to her chatter.

To Steve's amusement, she pulled a large pan of piping hot biscuits from the oven, dumped them into a bowl on the table, and put his clothes, which she had already washed in a big tub on the front porch, into the pan and popped them into the oven. After a few minutes, she took them out, steam rising from them, and hung them on the front porch railing to finish drying.

"The wind's comin' up and they'll be dry in no time," she said, returning to her post at the stove.

As she worked, Steve recounted Tal's actions at the river, crediting him with saving his life. Mrs. Davis reveled in her son's heroism and insisted on all of the details. "That was somethin', Steve. You coulda died from the snakebite—or even drownded! Did Tal have to give you artificial restitution?" she asked.

"Naw," said her son. "He was breathin' by hisself. Wasn't no big deal, Momma. I jest pushed him in and pulled him out, that's all."

"Well, you can thank Prominence that Tal was there to save you, Steve. The Good Lawd takes care o' his own."

Steve suppressed a smile. She was a perfect Mrs. Malaprop! Her tendency to misuse words was engaging, and as she fussed about and got supper ready, she kept up a running chatter spiced with comments put forth as aphorisms about daily life and local government, which seemed to him to go slightly wide of the mark. Still, he couldn't be sure that they didn't contain more than a few kernels of wisdom, insight into life, points of view he hadn't given much thought to before. He bit down hard on his lip when she spoke of George Washington Carver's "promiscuous" accomplishments. To Carver's benefit, Steve charitably assumed that she meant to say "prodigious." His amusement was entirely sympathetic, however. He sensed that she was a good person, a woman of kindness and character, and her lack of formal education did not really matter to him. The time passed quickly and pleasantly.

Steve ate supper wrapped in the chenille bedspread, which was a source of merriment as the boys devoured a meal of hot biscuits and molasses, hominy grits, fried okra, and fatty bacon under the watchful eye of Mrs. Davis. As her son had said, it wasn't much, but the warmth the three shared at the table made the meal one of the best he had ever eaten.

"Who's that man up there?" Steve asked suddenly, pointing at a large charcoal portrait of a severe, rather mean-looking man hanging on the wall above the table. He had noticed that the old man's piercing black eyes had seemed to follow him as he walked around the room.

"Oh," replied Tal, "that's Granpa Davis, my daddy's pa. Died of a heart attack one mornin' over a big bowl o' oatmeal and raisins with brown sugar sprinkled on it, settin' right there where you're a'settin'. I sees him sometimes in the night standin' over my bed, moanin', chains clankin' ..."

Steve didn't think Tal was serious. Nevertheless, he felt a shiver run up his spine. There was something creepy about the portrait.

"Lawd o' mercy!" protested his mother. "You knows none o' that ain't so. Ain't no ghost been 'round here. That's jest a fragment o' your imagination!"

Her son paid her no heed and continued right on, taking some pleasure in her irritation. "He was some kind o' mean! So mean, he'd cut your backbone out the front side, but he takes a shine to anybody who sits in that chair he died in. Wouldn't surprise me none if he followed you on home tonight, but don't worry, he won't never go into the white section. Family knows its place."

"Well, it gets lonesome walking these dark streets at night—I'll be glad for the company," Steve replied lightly, but he had to admit that Tal's little joke, if that's all it was, made him a little uncomfortable.

Suddenly, Steve let out a bloodcurdling scream. "Yeeowww!" Something had come out of nowhere and landed in his lap! Recovering his wits after a moment or two, he looked down into the penetrating green eyes of a large black cat staring up at him.

"Forgot to mention, Granpa sometimes comes back as a black cat. Don't move!" Tal chuckled.

"Boomer! How'd you get in here? You git on outta here now!" In a single motion, Mrs. Davis swooped down on the animal, scooped it up, and deposited it out on the front porch. "That's Boomer. I declare, Tal, what you want to make things up like that for?"

Tal continued to chuckle, and in a moment Steve burst into laughter. "You got me, Tal!"

Mrs. Davis, hiding a grin herself, shook her head in disapproval and changed the subject. "Tal says you're helpin' him learn to talk good English, but I ain't heard you correctin' him tonight. Keep after him, Steve, and maybe he won't have time for all this foolishness."

"Oh, he done it to me this afternoon right after I pulled him up on the river bank."

"*Did*."

The boys burst into laughter, giving each other little jabs on the shoulder. Mrs. Davis looked on approvingly, and after a few moments, she said, "The wind's come up and I expect your clothes'll be dry by now." She quickly retrieved them from the porch and insisted on ironing them for him, using the flatirons she had placed on the back of the stove to heat.

It was half past eight when Steve traded the chenille for his own clothes and started home. Mrs. Davis patted him on the back. "You come back and see us anytime now, Steve. 'Bye now."

Tal flashed his patented, mischievous grin as he shook his friend's hand. "G'bye Steve. G'bye Granpa. See ya later!"

"Hush!" his mother cried and boxed him on the ear.

The temperature had dropped sharply, and the north wind made Steve bend against it as he hurried along the darkened streets. Tal's story about his grandfather's ghost stayed in his mind. There was something about the picture that made him wonder, and he caught himself looking over his shoulder a time or two. While he had no anxiety about being seen in this part of town by its black residents, the living ones anyway, he worried that someone from the white section might happen to see him. He was glad that he was well into the main business section before he encountered the policeman, leaning as usual against the drugstore.

"Say, how's that there bunny rabbit of yours gettin' along, young fella?" he asked with a patronizing smile.

"Oh, I don't see much o' 'im anymore. Spends most o' his time over in Mr. McGregor's garden, I reckon. Prob'ly shouldn'ta taught 'im to like carrots."

"McGregor? Don't guess I know him. Town's gettin' too big. Lots of new people movin' in all the time."

Steve hurried on, again giving himself a stern lecture about being too clever for his own good. *Don't be a wise guy*, he said to himself. *What if he'd caught on*?

He was thoroughly chilled when he reached the shed, and he went straight to bed. It had been an exciting day for him, and he basked in the warmth of his new friends as he drifted off to sleep.

He awoke to a noise shortly after midnight and quickly flipped his flashlight on to find Man Friday pawing at the chicken that Mrs. Pike had given him.

"Sorry about the cold chicken, old cat," he laughed. "I would've warmed it up for you in the oven, but I keep my clothes in there now."

Man Friday cocked his head to one side and regarded him strangely while he finished off his Thanksgiving dinner. Satisfied, he sprang down from the table, disappeared out the door, and bounded down the steps as if he had another important engagement elsewhere in his neighborhood.

Now wide awake, Steve lay on the cot for some time, remembering the Thanksgivings he had known at home in Nebraska. Thanksgiving was not a particularly big day for his family. If the weather was nice, his dad made him and David husk corn until noon, but no work was scheduled for the afternoon. His Aunt Mary and Uncle Robert and his cousin Larry, a bachelor, usually came over, and Edna Lockhart, a widow down the road, joined them. He had warm memories of them all sitting around the dining room table, his mother and aunt bringing in bowl after bowl of fried chicken, mashed potatoes, giblet gravy, cranberry sauce, creamed peas, sweet potatoes with walnuts and marshmallows on top, scalloped corn with oysters, homemade bread with churned butter, and pumpkin pie with whipped cream. Aunt Mary usually brought her specialty, mince pie, and Mrs. Lockhart, a cheese and pimento salad.

His mother was the best cook for miles around, and that wasn't just his opinion. She often did nice little things for him as if to make up for his father's hostility, and he knew what he had done had caused her much pain and sorrow. He wished he could explain his running away to her, but he decided after a few moments that she understood.

She certainly had witnessed enough of his father's flights of temper. At least she knew from the postcard that he was safe.

After dinner, the women would clear the table and adjourn to the kitchen for the traditional washing of dishes and exchange of neighborhood information. The men would adjourn to the living room and talk crops and tease David and Larry about getting married. David had been engaged to the same girl for nearly eight years, and Larry had been through a series of brief attachments. There would be much laughter, and they would all have a good time, including his father. Holidays with company present were one of the few times he could unwind. The afternoon would pass quickly and pleasantly, Uncle Robert's clouds of cigar smoke giving the room an eerie blue tint as the afternoon sun slanted through the west windows.

Toward five, Steve's dad would announce, "Time to chore, boys," and the guests would head homeward. Then there would be the usual round of bringing the cattle in, throwing down hay from the mow for the cows and horses, feeding and watering the hogs, milking the cows, and feeding the calves. Steve usually had to milk two cows, Whitey, a Holstein that gave milk so low in butterfat that it had a blue tinge, and Babe, a Jersey that gave rich milk. His mother saved most of Babe's milk for the family's use, and the rest of the milk was taken to the cellar where his parents operated the separator. When the cream had been extracted, it was then poured into cans to be sold to the local creamery. It was Steve's job to take the buckets of skim milk out to the barn to feed the calves.

He scowled. That's where it all began or rather, where it all ended that last night. As he lay on the cot, the events of that evening came back clearly as if from yesterday. He dreaded working with his father, who could blow sky high at the least little thing. His whole life, as far back as he could remember, his father had criticized and belittled him at every turn. He had never praised a single thing Steve had ever done except for a few times when he used praise to try to get more work out of him. Steve especially resented that, and even those times were few and far between.

That evening there had been a problem with the separator, making things later than usual. He had a date at half past seven for the free picture show in town with his girlfriend Barbara, and when his dad had asked, or rather ordered him to take the milk out to the calves, he ...

The memory was interrupted suddenly as Man Friday returned from his customary rounds and bounded up on Steve's chest, butting his head against the boy's chin, bidding insistently for his undivided attention and providing a welcome relief from the recollection of the unpleasant events of that evening. Steve clutched him to his chest and held him close, stroking his head tenderly until he at last followed his little friend into the realm of sleep and forgetfulness.

CHAPTER 13

Winter came early to the Nebraska plains in all its impartial fury, sweeping down from the wastes of western Canada and in from the Dakotas with a sudden vengeance, lashing the prairies with its biting winds and drifting snow.

John Whitfield and his son David had long since planted the winter wheat, and since it had been a dry fall, they had finished husking the corn by Thanksgiving. If John felt his son Joe's absence keenly, he kept it pretty much to himself. Joe's mother, Edith, thought of him many times in a day, wondering if he had enough to eat, if he was warm, if he was hurt somewhere, even if he was alive at all. Sometimes David would find her at the window watching the school bus go by at four, crying to herself.

One evening about two weeks before Christmas when the three were sitting at the kitchen table after supper, there was a knock at the front door. When David answered it, the county sheriff Andy Petracek and a deputy asked if they could come in. They followed David to the kitchen and stood uneasily in the doorway.

The expression on the sheriff's usually jovial face was grim, and the three eyed him uneasily, guessing that he bore bad news.

"I suppose you haven't heard anything from your boy Joe since he disappeared."

"No, not a word," John said matter-of-factly. "It's almost six months now."

"Well, I thought I'd ought to come out to tell you before you heard it from someplace else." After a long moment in which the family braced themselves for what might come, the sheriff continued. "A couple of coyote hunters down east of Sioux Valley ran across a human skeleton in a hedgerow this afternoon. I'm not sayin' it's your boy. We don't know who it is. Animals scattered it some, and we haven't found anything to identify it yet. It could be someone else we don't even know is missin'."

At the word "skeleton," Edith put her hand to her mouth, and in a moment she got up and went over to the sink, turning her back, hiding the tears that began to gather in her eyes.

"Didn't they find any clothes?" asked her husband. "What was he wearin'?"

"Haven't found any yet. Like I said, the animals could've drug 'em off. I believe you told us Joe was wearin' a blue plaid shirt, blue jeans, and a blue overall jacket. We're searchin' the entire area to see what we can find, but it's hard with the snow deep on the ground. We need your permission to get Joe's dental records."

"All right. Dr. Morrison over in Norcross has 'em."

"Do you think it might be Joe?" asked David.

"We don't know who it is. I just thought you'd want to know. There'll be a lot of talk, and I thought it would be best if you heard it direct from us first."

"You don't know if anybody else is missing?" David wanted to know.

"We're callin' all around, contactin' authorities to see. I'm sorry to have to upset you folks—might not be your boy at all. Probably isn't. We just don't know. It's best not to jump to any conclusions."

With that, he and the deputy headed for the front door. "We'll let you know as soon as we know anything for sure. Sorry to spoil your evenin' like this." Then they were gone.

The three sat silently at the table for a long time. Finally, Edith said, "You don't know whether to hope it's him or not. It's the not knowing, wondering if he's all right or if he is suffering somewhere. Maybe he'd be better off ..."

This last was delivered as a half sob, and David got up and went to her and put his arms around her. His father sat at the table, silent, apparently lost in his own thoughts.

The discovery of the skeleton grabbed the headlines of the county newspaper, and speculation as to its identity dominated all conversation at school, in church, and on the streets of the town. A few friends called the Whitfields to say they were praying for them, but most did not, not knowing what to say. The hours seemed as frozen as the winter landscape while the family waited for word. It was three long days before the phone rang just after lunchtime. Mr. Whitfield had just gone out the back door to bring in a box of firewood when his wife called after him, "John, it's the sheriff. You'd better talk to him."

While her husband went to the phone, she sat down and put her head down on the dining room table. In a couple of minutes he returned.

"The sheriff says it ain't the boy. It's a young man been missin' from out by Grand Island. Hit and run—dragged hisself to the hedgerow and died. Says he's probably been there more'n a year."

His wife sat at the table for a long time, her face a kaleidoscope of conflicting emotions. Finally, she said simply, "If only he'd just call or write so we'd know he's all right."

* * * * * * * *

While winter in Alabama was not so cold and windy as on the Great Plains, a couple of times the temperatures flirted with the lower teens and there were a couple of light snows, just enough to dust the ground. Awillah was driven by the cold from her customary place on the front porch and spent the long winter afternoons sitting in her rocking chair in the bay window watching for the boy.

When the leaves had started to turn in mid-October and there was the first touch of fall in the air, Steve considered asking Awillah if he could move into her spare bedroom in return for doing chores around the house. He rejected the idea. It would be awkward explaining moving from his aunt's house, and she might begin to figure things out. While he didn't think she would turn him in to the police, he couldn't be sure, and the real danger was that she might let something slip to the suspicious and watchful Anna Meyer. She would sort it all out, and he had no doubt that she would report him to the police! He couldn't risk that.

Steve had begun to search the want ads in the local newspaper, hoping to find a room for rent at a price he could afford. Possibly, he thought, he could offer to work for the rent. But only a few rooms were available, and his inquiries were somewhat handicapped by the need to avoid attention. It would be awkward, he decided, to explain abandoning his fanciful but free lodgings with his grandmother, Awillah Pike. His guarded inquiries around town produced nothing, and, although he continued to keep an eye out for suitable rooms, he finally decided that his only option was to continue to fix up the room in the shed as best he could.

Although the layers of cardboard provided some protection from the cold, keeping drafts out, when the temperatures dipped well below freezing it was bone-rattling cold in the room. There was no stove, and Steve could not have used one anyway. The smoke would be a giveaway. Moreover, there was a high probability that a stove would catch the building on fire. Of course, there was no electricity. He redoubled his efforts to make the room tight, covering the walls with yet another thickness of cardboard. He found a piece of carpet that had been discarded in an alley and covered the bare floor with it. At the army-navy store, he bought another surplus army blanket. On the coldest evenings, Steve put on two pairs of socks, both pairs of long johns, and his navy pea coat, but the cold was distracting as he attempted to study and do his homework. The army blankets were little protection against the penetrating cold, and it was difficult to get a good night's sleep when he was shivering. The nights seemed to have no end.

He went back to the army-navy store and bought two more blankets, which made the nights only slightly more bearable. After a couple more uncomfortable nights, he took three dollars from the Karo bucket downstairs and went back to the store again where he had seen a surplus sleeping bag on sale. With the blankets on top and the bag zipped up, he was able to survive the frigid nights, although he was hardly comfortable.

When Man Friday came home from his romantic forays after bedtime, he would walk across Steve's chest and butt his head against the boy's chin or tap his paw on his nose, the cat's "open sesame." Steve would unzip the bag far enough to admit him, and he would inch his way down Steve's body and spend the night curled up snugly on his feet. Steve reflected that they were the only parts of his body that were really comfortable on cold nights.

"Hey, my Man Friday," he said one especially cold night, "I'm freezing! Why don't you bring your girlfriend home for a sleepover some night?"

As he lay there shivering, he amused himself with the thought that instead of measuring the cold by degrees Fahrenheit, perhaps it could be measured as a one-cat night, a two-cat night, a three-cat night, and so on. It was nothing he could mention in science class, however.

Some mornings when the water bucket was frozen over and he was unable to brush his teeth or wash his face, he went to school a little early and ducked into the locker room at the gym for a quick brush and a hot shower before going to class. He was reluctant to do so since it might cause someone to wonder about his situation. One morning, when Henry Jackson, the black janitor, popped into the room unexpectedly while he was drying off, Steve explained that the pipes in the bathroom at home were frozen.

"Just clean up after yourself, sir," he said respectfully and walked out.

Steve reflected on the irony of being the beneficiary of an ingrained system in which blacks didn't tend to question whites.

* * * * * * * *

Unlike Thanksgiving, Christmas was a special occasion for the Whitfields. There was always the Christmas Eve service at church, the exchange of gifts early the next morning, and a big dinner with plenty of relatives invited. But this year, the opening of gifts was restrained and awkward, and dinner was a quiet, solemn affair with no guests. Edith had set a place at the table for her missing son, and his absence dominated the family's mood. They were all secretly relieved when John's announcement that it was time to do chores signified the end of the day.

Steve's holiday was no more joyous. He did not attend the school's Christmas concert, knowing it would only depress him. Since he did not have a good suit, he didn't feel comfortable attending the Christmas Eve services at the church either. He sat alone on the bench across the street and listened to the joyous carols until the unrelenting cold drove him back to his room. Next morning, he slept past ten.

Mrs. Pike had invited him to have Christmas dinner with her, but he knew the day would be depressing for him. Although the meal would probably have been marked with the usual exchange of humor, he didn't feel he could enter wholeheartedly into the spirit. He wouldn't be good company. Perhaps there was an element of self-pity involved, but he decided he'd rather spend the day in the solitude of his room. He told the widow that his Aunt Mildred expected him to be with her on the holiday, and she understood, of course, giving him a plate of homemade sugar cookies cut into shapes of Santas, stars, bells, lambs, and camels, and sprinkled with colored bits of sugar to take back to his room. He gave her a small, framed Currier and Ives print of a snowy New England scene.

He had bought himself a one-pound box of cherry cordials at the drug store, wrapped it in Christmas paper, and tied it with a red ribbon, planning to open it with ceremony on Christmas morning. At least he'd have a present. However, the thief had made his rounds, and his present had disappeared along with the fountain pen and apple he had left out for him.

Steve gave Man Friday his present, a can of tuna festively tied with a long, red ribbon and wished him a Merry Christmas. When the cat had finished off the tuna, Steve enjoyed a noiseless romp with the cat, who pounced upon the ribbon as he pulled it, doing flip-flops and barrel rolls around the room in his manic attempts to subdue it. He was grateful for the homemade cookies Mrs. Pike had sent with him, and he ate the Santas and bells for breakfast and saved the rest for an afternoon snack.

The celebration over, he studied history and mathematics all afternoon and most of the evening. It helped keep him from thinking of home. When he tired of his studies in the evening, he read the Christmas story from the book of Luke by the light of the lantern and sat at the table for a long time, thinking of home.

He had few memories of his father at Christmas, but his mother always went to great lengths to make the holiday special for him. Perhaps she tried to make up for his father's lack of feeling. He remembered vividly sitting on his mother's lap when he was only three or so as she sang "Jolly Old Saint Nicholas" and "Up on the Housetop." Thinking back at her sprightly rendition, he realized that she got at least as much enjoyment out of it as he did.

It was not long after he had started going to school that a classmate told him that there was no Santa Claus. Nevertheless, he hadn't let on, playing along with his mother's charade of thumbing through the toy section of the Montgomery Ward catalog with him, noting his reaction to various toys, some of which showed up under the tree on Christmas morning. He showed no obvious interest when he saw her putting wrapped packages into the closet in the spare bedroom and locking the door. Later, when he was seven or eight, she caught on to his little game, and they both gave up the pretense. She supplemented their new relationship with little homilies on the meaning of giving and receiving.

Thinking about it, he realized that the thing he missed most of all about Christmas was, of course, the continuing love of his mother. The presents—progressing from tricycles through sleds, an erector set, a bicycle, to scarves, gloves, and ties—were important only as they represented her love for him, and it was almost midnight before he realized that for the first time in his life, he had not received a real Christmas present.

The thought only intensified his feeling of emptiness and loneliness, and, like his faraway family, he was glad when the day was over. Lying in bed that night, he cradled Man Friday in his arms and held him tight. "Friday, my little man, you're the best Christmas present I ever had—even if you did arrive last summer." After a while, the two fell asleep.

CHAPTER 14

As Steve's public friendship with Rollie continued to grow as the second semester progressed, so did his secret friendship with the other end of the socio-economic spectrum in Morefield, Taliaferro Davis. Steve went to the south end of town on a couple of occasions, enjoying his visit with Mrs. Davis, but usually Tal came to visit him in the old shed, slipping unseen up the darkened alley. One evening in late January, when Steve stumbled into his room exhausted from an afternoon of unloading a truckload of newsprint at the newspaper office, he was not at all surprised to recognize the figure sitting on his cot as his black friend. His nocturnal visits had become routine, something both of them looked forward to.

"Tal! How ya doin'?"

His friend rose to his feet and extended his hand, letting out an involuntary groan as he did so. "Ooooooh! Ouch!"

"What's the matter, Tal? Are you all right?"

"The boys got to me good as I was leavin' work at the store this evening," he grimaced. "A couple of friends of Tom and Jack jumped me in the alley. I usually can outrun 'em, but they surprised me and punched me and kicked me, and left me layin' on the ground. They ran off when they heard somebody comin'."

"A bunch of cowards," Steve said with feeling. "Did they hurt you bad?"

"Nah. The usual bumps and bruises, and I got a cut on my lip. They told me there'd be more if I didn't keep to my own end of town."

"Can I do anything for you?—some cold water to put on the bruises? I've got some rubbing alcohol for the cut."

"Nah. I'll be okay. It isn't the first time."

"I wish there was something I could do to stop them from jumping you like that."

Tal cut him off quickly. "Hey, you and me both knows—er, *know*—you can't do nothing—"

"*Anything*," Steve corrected.

"Anything. There's too many of 'em, and the police ain't gonna take up for any black man or his northern friend. Besides, they might find out you're a runaway and send you right back to your pa. You can't risk that. I'll be okay. My momma says it's jest the way things are, and you do what you can do, and when you can't, you jest turn the other cheek and make the best of it."

"I guess you're right, but you saved my life that day down on the river, and you know I'd do anything I could for you. Someday maybe I can pay you back."

Despite the reality of his situation, Steve felt like a hypocrite, and perhaps as a way of expressing his sympathy, he suspended the usual informal grammar lesson, overlooking Tal's mistakes as they talked in the darkness.

"Between them boys and my pa, been lots o' times I've wanted to take out like you done—er, *did*—but didn't have any idea where to go. I didn't have the courage to take the first step, but I been thinkin' about it a lot lately. How'd you manage it? What set you off? Tell me all about it."

Spurred on by his friend's interest and his need to unburden himself of the repressed memories, Steve began to recount the events of that last evening and the flight to Alabama, the words tumbling out effortlessly as he relived the events and feelings in detail. However, the memory of the quarrel with his father in the cellar that last evening, the immediate stimulus that led to his break, was still too painful and unresolved, and he described it only briefly, leaving out most of the details.

"We had just finished separating the milk in the cellar, and I was supposed to feed some of the skim milk to the calves. As usual, my dad lost his temper over nothing and slapped me around good and started beating me around the head and shoulders with a hoe handle. I thought he was gonna kill me! Last spring, he hit me with a two by four—I think he broke a rib. Here, feel the knot."

"Man, that was some kind of lick!" said the boy, withdrawing his hand.

"I was almost sixteen, and I didn't have to take that any more. He was getting more and more violent all of the time, and I decided it was time to clear out before he really hurt me. I didn't go back for anything—not even to say good-bye to my mom. I just lit out with nothing but the clothes on my back."

"Can't say as I blame you none for goin' like you done. Wisht I had your gumption!"

"It was something I'd been thinking about for a long time. Whenever I have any doubts about it, I just rub the knot on my rib. It still hurts when I press on it." The bruises on his arm and chest had completely disappeared, but the emotional hurt of that last evening remained undiminished. He bit down on his lip at the memory, and he reflected that the incident that evening represented the end of the life he had known and the exact beginning of a new life, heading somewhere, somewhere into the unknown. The final curtain had rung down.

Tal's appetite for the details of his flight was insatiable. "How'd you get clear down here to Alabama? Is that where you aimed to go? Did you catch rides? Tell me everything you done."

The memory of the details of his flight seemed to have a cathartic effect as Steve recounted them as if reading them from a diary: "When I finished feeding the milk to the calves out at the barn, I headed up the cattle lane to the back side of the farm where the federal highway was. I stuck out my thumb for a ride. It was almost dark, but it was only a few minutes until a truck slammed on its brakes and stopped about fifty yards on up the highway. I ran to catch up and climbed into the cab.

"The driver asked me where I was headed. I really hadn't given it any thought. All I could think of was getting away from my father, so I just told him I was going to Des Moines.

"He asked me if that's where I come from, and I told him no, that we had just got word that my grandma had a fall and broke her hip, and I was going to stay with her for a few days until she could get up and around, that she was almost eighty and needed someone to take care of her for a while. I wasn't used to telling lies, and I made things up as I went along, never dreaming they'd lead me to Alabama and this place."

He paused for a moment before continuing. "The driver said he was taking a load of lumber up to South Sioux City, and I could ride as far as Omaha. When we got to South Omaha, he let me out in front of a roadside diner. It was dark then, and I was hungry. I'd taken off before supper, but the only money I had was a five-dollar bill in the upper left pocket of my overall jacket. I thought I'd better save it for later, so I didn't go into the diner.

"I stood out there in the dark for nearly an hour before another trucker stopped and gave me a ride as far as Des Moines. I told him the same story about my grandma being hurt. It was past midnight when he let me out, when he turned north to Ames. I had no idea where to go, but I could make out a barn in the distance, so I climbed a fence and walked to it. I climbed into the hayloft and slept until almost nine the next morning.

"All I had for breakfast was some cool water at a windmill pumping water into a stock tank.

"Then I caught a ride with a slow-moving truckload of squawking chickens and got as far as Charleston, Illinois." He smiled at the memory. "I spent the night in an abandoned gas station, and next morning this guy hauling a big load of furniture to Pittsburgh gave me a ride as far as Dayton, Ohio. By that time, my grandma had moved all of the way to Columbus. Not too bad for an old woman with a bad hip!" He laughed, and Tal joined in.

The memory of the incident with Marvin was still too painful for Steve to relate the details to his friend, and he glossed it over and brought his saga to an end by saying that after he was let out at Dayton, he caught rides with a book salesman and another trucker to the gas station on the main highway north of Morefield.

"I had thought I'd go on down maybe to Jacksonville or Miami, but I hadn't had much of anything to eat for about six days, only a hamburger, so I decided to head into town to find work to earn some money and rest up a bit before going on. I happened to meet Mrs. Pike, found this place, and decided to stay here. I've been here since June."

Tal had listened to every word, soaking up every detail of his friend's journey vicariously. "Man, that was some kind o' trip!" he said in admiration.

They sat talking in the darkness for some time, Steve filling in additional details about his flight in response to Tal's questions. It was nearly midnight when Tal started for home, and Steve walked him through the shadowy alley down to the well-lit street at the end and watched him until he disappeared toward his end of town.

* * * * * * * *

Steve had passed his sixteenth birthday in October, and despite his somewhat haphazard eating habits and nutrition, he had grown to a little over six feet. His body, thanks to his daily regimen of hard work and heavy lifting, was becoming hard, lean, and muscular. With his light brown hair and deep blue eyes and a smile that often lit up his serious demeanor, he attracted glances from many of the young ladies at school. Not a few were disappointed when their interest was not returned, though it was not that he was not interested. He was attracted to several of them, in fact, but any serious relationship was out of the question. He could not spare the money even for a soda at the drugstore nor the time or money for a movie. His existence continued to be defined by his need to provide the bare necessities for survival, to get a high school diploma, and to save money for college, all the while maintaining a carefully constructed façade.

Perhaps it was a blessing that he was preoccupied with these immediate concerns from dawn to dusk, but often as he lay in bed with Man Friday before dozing off to sleep, his thoughts drifted to home—his mother and his brother Dave. He missed his friends back at Steadman Falls. He thought too of his father, trying to reach some sort of distant accommodation with him, but at these times, he quickly shut him out and tried to think of something else. The wound was still deep.

Sometimes he thought of his girlfriend back home, Barbara. They had dated only a few weeks, and whether she was serious about him he didn't know. He thought so, and he wished he could have at least said good-bye, or that he could let her know that he was all right. No doubt his mother had shared the postcard he had asked the trucker to mail when he passed through Louisville. Probably Barbara was dating somebody else by now. She certainly was pretty enough.

In those times, however, his thoughts increasingly strayed to Laura Lee Andrews, who had defended him after his fight in the hall with the school bullies. As they worked together in the school lunchroom, he found himself contriving reasons to speak to her. She seemed to welcome these rather transparent overtures and was always pleasant—and she was pretty too. Very pretty! Her soft blue eyes and brown hair had a freshness about them, and she always had a smile or a flippant greeting when he came in, sometimes teasing him a bit. She had asked him questions about his life in Ohio, not prying but interested, and about where he lived in Morefield. At those times he had to adhere strictly to his well-rehearsed persona and to try to change the subject without causing suspicion. He enjoyed their talks, and he appreciated the interest that she showed in him.

He wanted to take her to a movie or for a Coke date, but that was out of the question on a regular basis. At least back home in Steadman Falls, in the summer, they had free picture shows shown twice a week on the wall of the drug store.

No doubt Tennyson was right when he wrote, "In the spring, a young man's fancy lightly turns to thoughts of love." At any rate, as the winter cold gave way to early spring, he found that Laura Lee was almost constantly on his mind. It wasn't only that she was pretty. As they got to know each other, he was drawn to her honesty and her lack of pretense. It didn't seem to matter to her that he didn't dress up for school—the usual pair of faded blue jeans or khakis and a dark blue T-shirt or a somewhat wrinkled sports shirt seemed to make no difference to her. And they seemed to look at things in much the same way, whether the subject was events at school, ambitions, or even religion and values.

Rollie had said he was sure Laura Lee would go out with Steve, and acting on a sudden impulse at work one particularly bright spring afternoon, Steve asked her if she would like to take a walk with him after school. She readily agreed as if she had been expecting the invitation, and at four-thirty, she was waiting for him at the front entrance of the school. They walked along together toward a nearby park, much as two old acquaintances would—walking and talking, nothing more. But once inside the relative privacy where the trees shaded the path and the awakening azaleas and tulips brightened the dappled shadows, he reached down to take her hand. They walked down to the statue of General Beauregard in the center of the park and sat down on a nearby bench, half hidden by the large rhododendrons that promised to bloom any day. There, they sat and talked for more than an hour, and it seemed that they had always known each other. Their exchange of ideas and opinions was spiced with good humor and ready accommodation, and the time passed quickly.

When the lengthening shadows reminded them of the passing time, they walked together toward her house, which was only a few blocks east of the town square. When they came within sight of it, he released her hand, then impulsively grasped it again, led her gently into a thicket that shielded them from view and kissed her—not a passionate kiss, but a lingering one. Then he stepped back quickly, color coming to his cheeks, and said with a shy smile, "I've been thinking of that all afternoon."

Before she could reply, he was gone, trotting up the street toward the town square. She watched him out of sight, then stood there in the thicket for a while, savoring the warmth of his embrace before heading into the house.

His sudden show of affection surprised her. She had thought of him often in the preceding weeks, despairing that he would ever ask her out. She was very much attracted by his good looks, quick wit, and engaging smile, and she looked forward to working with him each afternoon in the lunchroom. As others had, she sensed in him an inner strength, as well as honesty and decency. There was something strong and enduring about him.

As spring progressed into summer, she accepted without hesitation his almost daily invitations for walks in the park. He was warm and caring and by nature open, even impulsive at times. Their first kiss was not entirely out of character. But his new life demanded that he keep a tight rein on his emotions—as the lapse at the Dixie Queen ice cream stand the preceding summer and its violent aftermath in the park had amply demonstrated.

Although their dates included holding hands and warm embraces and kisses, for the most part they just talked, being careful that their physical affection did not go too far. Their discussions were frank and lively, and there was often no need to fill silences—they seemed to communicate without words.

Nevertheless, Laura Lee sensed that there was something very private, almost distant, about him—about his life and family in Ohio and even where he lived in Morefield. She sometimes felt that he held her at arm's length, and she wondered how far such a relationship could develop.

Steve, too, was not entirely confident in their relationship for some time. Laura Lee was a very pretty girl—the prettiest in the whole school to his way of thinking, and he knew of several boys who continued to ask her out. He could offer her nothing but conversation and walks in the park. He was no competition for them. Sensing this, Laura Lee took care to let him know that none of those things mattered to her, and eventually he began to feel more secure in their relationship. Accordingly, he was able to relax and invest more of himself emotionally, although a certain distance continued to be implicit in their situation.

Chapter 15

Although life continued to be a serious proposition for Steve, demanding a maturity unusual for a boy his age, as the end of the school term neared, Steve was able to provide for his needs, if not for luxuries. Managing his pennies carefully, he was able to put aside a little money regularly toward his college education. It was clear, however, that he would have to work his way through college even if he managed to win some sort of academic scholarship.

Several of his teachers, familiar with his situation and his desire to attend college, gave him lists for summer reading, and when he had a moment, he stopped by the public library to read materials that might be useful in competitive exams. In mid-summer, he landed a part-time job at the library, working eight hours a week at the desk, which allowed him to read a little when there were few patrons. For Steve, school was a year-round activity.

With the advent of summer, there were no report cards to intercept, but Steve continued to check Mrs. Pike's mail. With the warm weather, the old woman had resumed her post on the front porch, and he visited her almost every day. However, when he came by one noon in late May, not long after school let out, she was not at her usual station, and there was no answer to his knock. He knocked loudly several times, but still there was no response.

That's odd, he said to himself. *She never goes anywhere.* He put the mail on the porch swing and left, needing to get back to work at Banfield's. That evening, again there was no answer to his insistent knocking. *Where could she be?* he wondered. He was sure she didn't have any relatives or close friends around Morefield she would stay with overnight. He went around to the window where her bedroom was and tapped on it without results. The next day, she was almost constantly in his thoughts, and when he finished sweeping up at work, he went back to the house, knocking repeatedly on the door and the bedroom window. Then he went next door to Mrs. Meyer's, hoping that she might know where the old woman was, but she was not at home.

Something was wrong. He went back to the shed, found a putty knife on the workbench that thus far had escaped the intruder's notice and returned to the front porch. Slipping the flat blade between the lock and the doorjamb, he managed to open the door and went inside, calling Mrs. Pike's name loudly, his concern mounting. "Mrs. Pike! Awillah! Awillah!"

There was no answer.

The weather that week had turned cold, unseasonably cold, and the house was chilly. There was no fire in the heating stove in the front room. He went quickly to Mrs. Pike's bedroom. She lay under a mountain of blankets and a comforter on the bed, breathing in long, rasping drafts. She answered her name with a low moan.

Steve called to her, worry gripping his voice. "Awillah! Are you all right?"

The woman coughed loudly, her whole body shaking violently, sending the mountain of covers into rippling convulsions.

He put his hand to her forehead. "Oh, Awillah!" he exclaimed. "You're burning up! You're really sick; let me call a doctor."

"No, Steve," she gasped faintly, raising up slightly. "I'll be all right. There's some aspirin in the kitchen cupboard and a jar of Vicks in the medicine cabinet in the bathroom—would you bring them to me?"

"I'll get them." He rushed to retrieve them and drew a glass of water at the sink. He was back in a minute and gave her two aspirins which she managed to swallow after a couple of attempts. She dabbed the Vicks on her chest and lay back weakly.

"Grandma, you're really sick. You ought to have a doctor."

"No, no, Steve. I'll be all right."

"Well," he replied, "I still think you ought to have a doctor. I'm going to stay here all night, and if you're not better by morning, I'm going to get one for you whether you want me to or not."

She did not reply, and he went to the kitchen where he found a can of Campbell's vegetable beef soup, which he poured into a saucepan and heated on the gas stove. In a few minutes, he reappeared at the woman's bedside with a bowl of steaming soup. With some effort, she managed to eat it all and soon fell back exhausted on her pillow and went to sleep. Her rasping breathing and coughing seemed to find every corner of the house.

He quickly got a fire burning in the wood stove in the front room. Then he sat by her bedside for more than an hour anxiously monitoring her labored breathing and debating whether to disobey her wishes and go for a doctor when she seemed no better. When she awoke again after midnight, he gave her a small glass of juice he had squeezed from a couple of oranges he found on the kitchen table. He gave her another aspirin, making sure she drank two full glasses of water. When she drifted off to sleep again, he went into the spare bedroom, took his clothes off, and slipped under the covers. He stretched out, luxuriating at the feel of the cool, smooth sheets. He had almost forgotten the feeling. It was the first time he had slept in a regular bed with clean sheets in almost a year. He was exhausted from the worry and soon fell asleep, but he awoke twice during the night, attended to the old woman, and stoked the fire.

By morning, she seemed no better. She was seventy-eight now, and he was genuinely worried about her. He made a breakfast of a slice of toast, scrambled eggs, some sausage, and the pulp of the oranges he had squeezed the night before. She ate most of the eggs and orange pulp but refused the toast and sausage, saying she wouldn't be able to swallow them. When she fell asleep again, he left the house and hurried downtown to Dr. Travis's office.

When the nurse told him the doctor was busy, he sat down anxiously in the waiting room. In a few minutes, the doctor appeared. He remembered Steve from his collapse from hunger at school the preceding fall and greeted him warmly. Heeding Steve's urgent request, he hurried with the boy to the house on Decatur Street and was soon at Mrs. Pike's bedside. Steve waited in the front parlor while the doctor examined her thoroughly. When at last he stepped back into the parlor, his expression was grave.

"She's a very sick woman, Steve. Very sick. She has the flu, and at her age that can be very serious. I'm glad you came for me. I don't think she would have made it through another night without proper medicine. I've given her a shot and some tablets. I've left the tablets on the bureau. Give her two of them every four hours until I come back tomorrow afternoon. Be sure she drinks plenty of water and lots of fruit juice. If she takes a turn for the worse, come get me right away. As I say, she is a very sick woman."

"Thank you, sir. I'll come by your office tomorrow and pay you."

"No need for that," the doctor said, remembering Steve's straitened finances. "I know Social Security is about all she has, and I'll take care of it. You've done your good deed. If she makes it, it'll be because of you."

Steve didn't mention that there was no fruit juice in the house—not even any cranberry juice. After the doctor had gone and he had checked back with Awillah, he walked down to Banfield's and bought several cans of orange juice and some lemons, as well as half a dozen cans of chicken soup. He remembered that his mother had given it to him when he had the flu.

Mr. Banfield was sympathetic when he told him he needed to care for his grandmother and would have to miss work. For the next four days, Steve stayed at Awillah's bedside watching her closely and making sure that she took her medicine regularly and drank plenty of water and fruit juice. The chicken soup seemed to give her a little added strength. He continued to spend the night in the guest room, getting up several times in the night to check on his patient.

Doc Travis came by once a day, and when her fever had broken, she began to recover rapidly. Reluctantly, Steve moved back into the shed when she was able to get out of bed and move about the house.

Her recovery was remarkable for someone her age, and she was quick to heap praise upon the boy. "Bless your heart, if it hadn't been for you, I'd be in my grave now," she said. "I really appreciate what you did for me, hon."

"Shucks, ma'am, it warn't hardly nuthin,'" he said with affected modesty, masking the lump that had risen in his throat. "I didn't want the cranberry market to collapse," he added with a twinkle in his eye. Then he added seriously, "I know you'd do the same for me."

However, when he came down with a sore throat, a high fever, aching muscles, and an upset stomach himself the next morning, he lay in bed alone in the room in the shed. There was no one to go for medicine or fruit juice, no one to check on him in the night. After several miserable days, his hardy constitution and a regimen of water and aspirin began at last to pull him through. The only assistance he could trust Awillah to give him was the note to Mr. Benjamin at the newspaper he forged in shaky lavender to explain his absence.

Man Friday, of course, came and went at will during his illness, making his customary rounds in the neighborhood. Late one evening as Steve lay resting on the cot, the cat, tired of his mysterious pursuits, bounded up on the cot and curled up heavily on his friend's chest.

"Thanks a lot, old friend," the boy growled. "You're a bit late. I could have used a furry poultice like you on my chest last week."

* * * * * * * *

After he recovered from his illness and returned to work, the summer settled quickly into a familiar routine. Hard work at Banfield's and the printing office and the temporary job at the public library occupied his daylight hours, although he was able to find time several times a week for a walk down to see General Beauregard with Laura Lee. His evenings, as usual, were taken up with his studies with regular time-outs with the faithful Man Friday.

He had completed his first full year in Morefield and was now well settled into his new identity. The protection of his privacy had become a way of life. If he had had a tendency to let his guard down, however, the need for constant vigilance was brought back into sharp focus by three incidents of near discovery that followed one upon the other within two weeks in late summer, causing him to wonder if they might somehow be omens of things to come.

One Sunday after returning from his usual private service across the street from the Methodist Church, he read his Bible for more than an hour and then lay down on the cot for an afternoon nap. He had scarcely settled into a languid snooze when he felt a presence, call it ESP, and he opened his eyes to see a little girl about four years old standing not three feet away staring down at him! She looked like something out of a fairy tale, long golden locks, bright blue eyes, and rosy cheeks. Standing in the sunlight flooding in through the window in her Sunday-best yellow chiffon dress, she looked like she might have descended daintily from Heaven on a sunbeam.

"Where did the kitty go?" she asked, continuing to stare steadily at the boy.

Steve was taken aback by the vision presented to him so suddenly, and it took a moment for him to process the question, groping for a response. He sat up, secured the top two buttons of his shirt, and smiled at her kindly. "Did you follow the kitty up here?"

"Uh huh."

He searched frantically for an explanation for his presence to the little girl, who continued to scrutinize him doubtfully. Stalling for time, he asked, "Was it an orange cat?"

"Uh huh."

"Orange with stripes, like a tiger?"

"Uh huh."

Finally, he said, "Well, he is a magic cat, and sometimes he just disappears into thin air. One moment you see him, and the next moment he's gone." He was not entirely sure what this remark might lead to. Perhaps it would buy him a little more time to come up with something she would believe.

"A magic cat? What's his name?"

"Friday," he answered quickly. "What's your name?"

"Anna Lucinda."

"Anna Lucinda? That's a pretty name," he said, reflecting momentarily on the Southern penchant for giving big, double names to little children. "Do you live near here?"

"No. Mama and Papa and I came to see my grandma."

"Your grandma? What's her name?"

"Nana."

"Where does Nana live?"

The little girl pointed toward the window, south toward Anna Meyer's.

"Is her name Anna?"

The girl nodded and after a moment said brightly, "Today's her birthday. We had ice cream."

"Mmmm! I like ice cream too. Do you live in Morefield?"

"No. Magomy."

"Montgomery?"

Another nod confirmed his guess.

"How long are you going to stay with Nana?" he asked, fearing the worst. The ever watchful, ever curious Mrs. Meyer wouldn't require too many clues from her granddaughter to figure things out.

"Just today. We're going home pretty soon. I don't think my daddy likes to come up here. Just once ever so often."

That's a break, he thought, but he needed to come up with something that would keep the little girl from betraying his secret. Maybe a secret. A secret might appeal to a little girl.

"Well, you've come to the Magic Hideaway …"

"What's your name?"

"Steve," he replied, then added, "Prince Steven." Trying to avoid more questions, he quickly preempted her train of thought. "Anna Lucinda is a very nice name, but you need a special, a secret name. May I call you Sunbeam? In your yellow dress, you look like a little sunbeam come floating in through the window for an afternoon visit. Better yet, Princess Sunbeam of the Kingdom of Secrets."

The little girl seemed to find some humor in this, and she broke into a giggle and nodded, returning nevertheless to her questioning.

"Do you live here, Prince Steven?" she asked, looking around at the Spartan furniture and cardboard walls.

"No, Princess, this is the Magic Hideaway," he said, avoiding her question. "My father, the Wizard, built it many years ago. I just stay here sometimes when I need to talk to Friday. The only people who get to visit the Magic Hideaway are those the fairies and magic cats bring here, and they don't bring anyone here unless they think they can trust them to keep our secrets. You are the first little girl Friday has ever brought to visit me, so that means he thinks you are a very special little girl. You can keep a secret, can't you?"

She nodded vigorously, inwardly pleased at the compliment that Friday had bestowed upon her.

"You must promise me that you won't tell mama and papa and your nana about me and this place. If you keep our secret, maybe next time you come up from Montgomery, Friday will appear out of thin air and lead you here again. Maybe we could have a tea party, and I'll ask him to sit with us for a while. He never stays long before he disappears again. But you must promise not to tell anyone that you saw me here. Can you do that, Princess Sunbeam?"

He smiled kindly at his little friend, the privileged initiate, hoping to mask the anxiety that underlay his words. One word from the princess to Mrs. Meyer and the Magic Hideaway would disappear in a puff of smoke—and he with it.

"Uh-huh, cross my heart and hope to die," she said solemnly, making the necessary motions with her hand.

Further discussion was interrupted suddenly by a voice calling loudly from the neighboring yard, the voice of a young woman. "Anna Lucinda! Anna Lucinda! Come on—we're going to be leaving for home in a few minutes."

Without a word, Princess Sunbeam turned and ran quickly out through the door of the Magic Hideaway and vanished down the stairs, her patent leather shoes tick-tacking lightly on the wooden steps as she flew away as quickly as she had come.

Although Steve was anxious for quite some time about what might come of her visit, the little girl never reappeared. He reflected that she was probably right that her father didn't like to come up for visits. Mrs. Meyer was his mother-in-law.

* * * * * * * *

Steve had scarcely time to recover from the visit when the second in the series of close calls occurred late one afternoon as he again lay half-dozing on his bunk, tired from an unusually taxing day unloading trucks at the newspaper office. The unrelenting Alabama sun had made the room an oven, and he had stripped down to his shorts. He lay there, sweat pouring off his body. Man Friday lay snoozing with his friend, sprawled across the boy's left arm.

Suddenly, the boy sat bolt upright, dumping his friend to the floor. The sound of voices below came up the stairway, the voices of young boys at play.

"Hey, Mitch! Let's see what's up there."

"Up where?"

"Up them steps. C'mon, let's go see."

"Okay. Wait a minute till I get a drink of water. I'm thirsty."

Steve panicked. If the boys came upstairs and found him, he wouldn't be able to explain his presence, and in no time his secret would be all over the neighborhood. He glanced frantically around the room, but he knew already there was no place to hide. And even if he could hide, the boys would wonder at the cardboard on the walls and the books and papers on the table. Perhaps, he thought, he could step out on the stairs and confront the boys, putting up a front and telling them sternly that they had no business in the shed. But what if they were boys from the neighborhood who knew he had no business there either? They were sure to talk. No, that wouldn't work. Besides, how could he explain why he was stripped down to his shorts?

As he cast about wildly in his mind for a course of action, grabbing for his clothes, he heard one of them say, "Let's go! C'mon! Let's see what's up here!" He heard the sound of a footstep on the stairs.

Suddenly, Friday trotted to the door and disappeared from view.

"Look! A kitty! Let's catch him!"

Steve listened breathlessly to the sound of the thumping of shoes on the steps, a wild meowwwww, and excited cries of "Get him!" "Head him off at the door!" "Ouch! He scratched me!" "Don't let him get away!" "There he goes—grab him! Grab him!" He listened with relief as the hue and cry headed up the path toward Mrs. Pike's house, around the corner, and out of earshot.

He gave little thought to the possibility that the boys could overtake his friend. It was strictly no contest. "That means a special can of tuna for you tonight, old boy," he said aloud.

He sat down weakly on the cot again. It was possible that the boys might come back, if not that afternoon, some other time. However, he hadn't noticed any small boys in the immediate neighborhood. Perhaps they didn't belong there. Maybe, like Anna Lucinda, they were only visiting. Nevertheless, it was a worry, and he felt as if a new sharp sword hung by a thread over his head.

* * * * * * * *

Steve had little time to worry about this latest threat before a new one cropped up unexpectedly. Dropping by Mrs. Pike's one noon to take her mail in, he was surprised to see a fiftyish man and a teenage boy sitting in the swing with her. He couldn't remember having seen them before. Most of the few people who stopped to sit with her were elderly neighbors.

"Steve, I want you to meet my son Wendell and my grandson Michael Dean. They dropped in a few minutes ago from Memphis for a surprise visit. How long has it been, son?"

Wendell grimaced, replying reluctantly, "Four years now, I think, last month."

"I hardly knew my grandson. He's grown a bunch. A young man now," she said proudly.

Michael Dean fidgeted under the unwanted attention of the older generation and said nothing. Neither paid much attention to Steve, responding mechanically to his outstretched hand.

"You know we'd come oftener if we could, Mom. It's a long ways down from Memphis, and gas has gone up to almost a quarter," said her son a bit defensively.

"Are you going to stay a while?" Steve asked only partly to make polite conversation. He did not welcome the idea of long-term visitors poking around the property, specifically the backyard.

"Leavin' in an hour or so," said Wendell. "We want to have a good visit with Grandma. We're headed for the beach at Panama City for a few days in the sun."

Steve breathed a sigh of relief. He noticed that the grandmother gave no sign that she found that leg of the trip incongruent with Wendell's assertion that the trip from Memphis was too expensive.

"Things don't seem to have changed much since we were here last. One thing I wanted to do while we're here was show Michael Dean my old hideout back there in the shed. Me and my buddies used to have a club when we were kids, no girls allowed of course, and we practically lived back there. Snuck a cigarette now and then too," he added with an amused glance at his mother. "Sometimes I slept back there when it wasn't too hot."

"Not much back there anymore," Steve said quickly, trying to be as nonchalant as he could. "The place is about to fall in. Lots of mice and rats and snakes. Old Gus hangs around the steps ready to strike if you're not careful." He hoped the threat of the lurking copperhead might dissuade the grandson from an inspection trip. The boy said nothing.

"Must be Old Gus's great-grandson—that's more'n thirty years ago.

It'll be old home week," said the father, apparently trying to impress his son. "Maybe he'll slither out and say, 'Hey, Michael!'"

Michael Dean didn't react one way or another.

Steve fought desperately to come up with something that would discourage them. At that moment, the screen door banged open, sending the resident flies swarming in all directions, and a middle-aged woman with bleached blonde hair, a deep tan, and sunglasses stepped out onto the porch, filling it with her presence. Steve guessed that she was Wendell's wife. He scarcely had time to take in the heavy rouge, lipstick, mascara, the pink blouse, chartreuse slacks, and sandals that effectively displayed ten nails painted Flamingo pink before she announced loudly that they needed to get on their way if they were to be in Panama City before dark.

The next few minutes were a frenzied confusion as her husband and son, galvanized into action, sprang to their feet, located a misplaced camera, took a couple of family photos, grabbed a cooler and a sack of ham sandwiches from the kitchen, hugged the old woman, promising to visit again "real soon," and packed themselves into an overloaded station wagon out front. The vehicle slowed at the end of the street, the cloud of dust almost catching up with them. Three tanned left arms waved good-bye out the windows, and Wendell gave a last, affectionate toot on the horn as they turned onto Market Street and disappeared in the direction of the Gulf of Mexico.

Steve wondered what had hit him, finally managing to sort through the whirlwind to the fact that he had once again dodged a bullet aimed directly at his very existence. *Looks likes Old Gus and I are safe from Wendell for at least another four years,* he thought with a wry smile.

He looked over at the old woman, sitting in her usual place, looking down the street and beginning to push the swing back and forth with her foot. She said nothing, but he knew what she must be feeling, and he sat talking to her as long as he possibly could before heading for Banfield's. He hoped God would forgive him for wishing that the cooler they had loaded in the station wagon was filled with gallons of her famous cranberry punch.

Chapter 16

While Morefield was hardly on the main street of American tourism, Steve was glad when school resumed in September and the flow of out-of-town visitors diminished to a tiny trickle. His life pretty much followed the routine established the previous terms, working the two jobs downtown and the one at school and studying at home far into the night. Mrs. Pike's lavender signatures again marked the completion of each six weeks period, and the beginning of another. After the early encounter with the two bullies at school the preceding fall, Steve had scrupulously avoided getting into any sort of trouble. Nevertheless, serious trouble found him again.

Superintendent Ford was a man of strict integrity, and he had instituted a no-nonsense policy regarding cheating on academic exams. Those accused of misconduct were referred to an honors board consisting of three faculty members who heard the charges, investigated them, and handed out punishments. Mr. Ford backed the board unquestioningly in their decisions, and there was no appeal. In the most flagrant cases, students convicted of cheating were expelled from school.

Although Steve had attracted favorable attention from a number of members of the faculty through his fine academic record and his exemplary conduct, Mr. Carnahan continued to have reservations about him, making it abundantly clear in faculty meetings that he did not join Myra Edwards in Steve's corner. He was often short and cutting to Steve in class and less than cordial when they met in the halls outside of class.

Steve put extra effort into studying math, wanting to prove himself to the teacher, but their relationship did not improve. The six-week exam Mr. Carnahan gave on Monday afternoon proved to be a difficult one, but Steve felt he had done it justice and anxiously awaited the results of his teacher's strict grading. When Mr. Carnahan announced that the grades would not be posted as promised on Tuesday, he attached no special significance to it.

Steve paid no particular attention to the rumor that a special meeting of the honors board had been called for that afternoon after school. Had he known that the meeting had been convened at Mr. Carnahan's request he would perhaps have given it more thought.

* * * * * * * *

Mr. Carnahan's face was grim as he met the members of the board, which included Miss Edwards, Miss Fontaine, who taught shorthand and typing, and Mr. Sproul, the American literature teacher.

"I appreciate your convening the board on short notice," Mr. Carnahan began. "I would not have requested the meeting if I didn't think the matter was a very serious one indeed. It involves a student in my advanced algebra class, Steve Bowman. I know he has an excellent reputation around the school, and he has done well in my class. However, I am certain that he cheated on the exam I gave Monday afternoon."

"It is hard to believe that Steve would be dishonest in anything," said Miss Edwards. "He's bright enough that he doesn't need to cheat. However, I'm sure that you don't make these charges lightly, Mr. Carnahan. What makes you think that he has cheated on the exam? Do you have any proof?"

Mr. Carnahan's tone was firm and righteous. "Monday morning I discovered the master copy of a test I was going to give to the class was missing from the center drawer of my desk where I had locked it Friday morning. The only person besides Mr. Newton and myself who has a key to my office is Steve. He sweeps up after school. He undoubtedly found the key to the drawer where I hide it in a filing cabinet, unlocked the drawer, and took the test."

"Are you certain it is missing?" Miss Fontaine asked.

"Of course I'm sure!" he retorted angrily. "I've looked through the drawer carefully three times now, and it definitely is not there. And there's more. The test is one of a set of standardized tests put out by Princeton. It is comprehensive and very, very difficult. It has been eight years since I gave this particular one. It was not long before class time, and I didn't have time to prepare a different test. In thirty-six years of teaching mathematics at Morefield High School, I have had only one student, Roger Oliver, whom you all remember—probably the finest student we've ever had here—who got above 90 percent on the exam. He got a 91, and Steve got a 92 on the very same exam. It's highly suspicious."

"Well," said Miss Edwards, "you yourself said he is a very good student. Isn't it possible that he got a good grade on his own? It's hardly proof."

"I locked the test in the drawer before noon on Friday," he said, ignoring her question, "and Steve was in the room when I came in later, unexpectedly. No one else other than Mr. Newton could have entered the office after I locked it in my desk drawer. The room was locked all weekend. Steve undoubtedly found the key and took the exam and the answer sheet."

"It does sound serious. We'll have to hear from the boy, of course," said Miss Edwards, disappointment edging her voice. "The board will meet again tomorrow at noon. Would you notify Steve that he is to appear before us then? Of course you'll need to be here too, Mr. Carnahan."

"Oh, I'll be here! You can bank on it!"

* * * * * * * *

Steve got his first inkling that something was wrong when he joined a knot of students outside Mr. Carnahan's classroom. The grades from the math class had been posted on the bulletin board there, but next to his name was an "Inc.," meaning that he had received an incomplete grade.

As he stood there trying to make something of the grade, Mr.

Carnahan stepped out of his classroom and spoke to him, his voice cold as steel. "Steve, you are to appear before the honors board tomorrow at noon."

Steve could not believe his ears. "What's wrong, sir?" he asked. "Why am I to go before ...?"

Mr. Carnahan cut him off sharply. "Just be there at twelve o'clock! Don't be late. They'll inform you of the charges."

"Charges! What kind of charges?"

The teacher did not reply, leaving the boy standing bewildered in the hall, leaving him to wonder about the summons through a sleepless night.

* * * * * * * *

Steve's appearance before the board was a nightmare for him. He took a seat across a table from the three board members and Mr. Carnahan.

Miss Edwards began the inquiry. "Steve, Mr. Carnahan is missing the master copy of the test given last Monday in his advanced math class, and he thinks you might have taken it."

Steve was taken by surprise, and before he could say a word of denial, Mr. Carnahan jumped in quickly to assume the role of prosecuting attorney.

"There's no use denying it, Steve. The test and answer sheet were locked in the center drawer of my desk, and you are the only one aside from myself and Mr. Newton who had access to my office. I usually go directly home after class, but I had some things I needed to work on in my office for next week's classes, and when I came in just before four Friday afternoon, you were cleaning my office. I asked you to leave so I could concentrate. I worked until about eight, then went home."

"Did you lock the office door when you left? What about your desk drawer?" asked Miss Fontaine.

"Yes to both. Well, actually I hadn't opened the center drawer since I locked it before noon, so I didn't need to lock it. Anyway, Steve would have locked it back up after he took the exam."

"Was it locked when you came into the office, Steve?" Mr. Sproul asked.

"I don't know, sir. I just dust and straighten up, empty wastebaskets and sweep out. I don't open drawers. I didn't check it, and I certainly did not take any test," he said emphatically, "I …"

His accuser cut him short. "Apparently you found the key to the drawer where I keep it hidden in my filing cabinet, unlocked the desk, and took the exam. I missed it when I came in at about seven-thirty Monday morning. I hadn't finished my work Friday afternoon, so I came in an hour early. When I unlocked the drawer I noticed the test was gone. There's no use denying it—it's an open-and-shut case, Steve."

"But I didn't take it!" Steve said indignantly, his face turning crimson. "I didn't take it!"

Mr. Carnahan pressed his advantage. "No one else could have done it. Only you had the opportunity, and your exceptionally high grade on the exam would seem to confirm your guilt."

Miss Edwards stepped into the argument, seeking to regain control of the discussion. "Do you have any idea how the exam could have turned up missing, Steve?"

Steve shook his head. "No, ma'am, I don't have any idea. But I didn't take it, and that's for sure! I would never do anything like that!"

"It's as plain as day …" Mr. Carnahan began, but Miss Edwards interrupted. "Is there anything else you want to say in your defense, Steve? Now is the time to speak up."

Still reeling from the surprise accusation, Steve could only say, "I've never been accused of anything like that in my life—I didn't take it!"

Miss Edwards, looking very disturbed, brought the hearing to a close. "Well, the board will consider all of the facts. We'll let you know our decision. You are both excused."

Steve left the room, and hurried down the hall, not wishing to have any more contact with his accuser. The hearing had been short and ominous. All he could do was proclaim his innocence. Things looked very bad indeed.

* * * * * * * *

When the two had left the room, the members of the board met immediately to discuss Mr. Carnahan's accusations.

"Well," Miss Edwards began, "Steve certainly is adamant in

denying the charges. He says he didn't take the test, and Mr. Carnahan is equally certain that he did. Whom can we believe? Steve certainly has demonstrated in all of his classes, including Mr. Carnahan's, that he is an excellent student, and a top grade, even one better than Roger Oliver's, is not beyond the realm of ..."

"But he could have got hold of the exam," Miss Fontaine interrupted. "He certainly had the opportunity."

"But why wouldn't he return it to the drawer after he got a good look at it and the answers?" asked Mr. Sproul.

"Mr. Carnahan says he returned unexpectedly to his office Friday afternoon and worked most of the evening, finishing some reports," Miss Fontaine replied. "Steve was cleaning the office when he arrived, and he told him to leave without finishing since he needed to concentrate on his work. So Steve could have taken the master copy from the drawer and been unable to return it when Mr. Carnahan came in unexpectedly. More likely, he planned to take the test home over the weekend, and locked the drawer up before Mr. Carnahan came in. And Monday morning, Mr. Carnahan arrived at school early, needing to finish grading some exams before school, so Steve may not have been able to return it to the drawer before Mr. Carnahan discovered that it was missing."

"I suppose that's a possibility," said Mr. Sproul.

"Yes," admitted Miss Edwards, "but I can't help thinking that Steve is fully capable of making a top grade all by himself on such an exam."

The board was silent for a minute or two. Then Miss Edwards continued. "Mr. Carnahan says the exam is one of a set of eight exams put out by Princeton. It is several years before he repeats administering the same exam. Why not give Steve the benefit of the doubt? Mr. Carnahan says the exams are all about the same difficulty. Why not let Steve take one of the other exams? If he gets a top grade, then I think it is plausible that he got his grade fair and square. If he doesn't make a top grade, we have good reason to believe the charges. We can give him the second exam first thing in the morning so he won't have extra time to study for it."

The board, not anxious to convict the boy of wrongdoing and expel him from school even on the word of a teacher, decided on this course of action. When he was informed of the plan, the suspicious

Mr. Carnahan was so sure of the alternate exam's difficulty that he agreed to the plan. No one had ever gotten more than an 87 on that particular exam.

* * * * * * * *

Shortly after he arrived at school the next morning, Steve was summoned to Miss Edwards's office. Without any notice, an alternate exam, retrieved from the vault in the principal's office, was administered under the sharp-eyed surveillance of Mr. Carnahan, who insisted on being present.

Although he felt he did well on the exam, Steve could not help feeling anxious, and he found it difficult to concentrate as he attended his classes that afternoon. As he went to his wall locker after his last class, he ran into his friend Rollie.

Rollie's expression was serious. "Steve, I just want you to know that I don't believe those charges—not one bit! I know you wouldn't do that."

Steve stiffened. "Charges? ... How did you hear about them?"

"They're all over school! Wally Henderson told me about them during glee club practice this morning, and a couple of others mentioned them at noon."

Steve's expression darkened. "I guess that explains why those kids passed me in the hall without speaking to me. I wonder how the word got out."

"Mr. Carnahan probably leaked it. He's mean enough. Or could be that one of the students who works in the office overheard something. The cat's out of the bag, that's for certain."

As they talked, Laura Lee stopped on the way to her wall locker. "Oh Steve, some of the kids just told me," she said, tears gathering in her eyes. "I'm so sorry! I know you'd never do anything like that!" She gave him a quick hug. "I'm so sorry," she repeated. Then she hurried on, trying to hide the tears that were now threatening to cascade down her cheeks.

After school, Steve went on to Banfield's and then plodded home through the gathering darkness, despondent and defeated. Throughout the evening and a fitful night, he mulled over the charges. He was innocent, but now his good name had been besmirched and spread out for everyone in the school to judge. Moreover, he could be expelled! All he had worked so hard for—lost! And even if he could prove his innocence, he could never recall the rumors that were circulating around the school and the suspicions that they would implant in the minds of those who heard them—people who did not know him and some of those who did. There would always be the lingering suspicion that he was guilty after all, but that the board had just not been able to prove it. It was only human nature.

* * * * * * * *

The next morning he was met at the front door of the school by a beaming Miss Edwards. "Steve, I have good news for you! You got a 93, an even higher grade, on the alternate exam. In my mind, and I'm sure the board and maybe even Mr. Carnahan will agree, it exonerates you from the cheating charge. I'm so glad for you!"

Steve was only momentarily buoyed by the news. He had doubts that the results would remove the blot on his reputation from many minds. He hung his head as he brushed past students now silent who usually greeted him.

When news of his sterling performance on the alternate test circulated around the halls, several of his friends and acquaintances came up to him to tell him, belatedly, that they had never believed the accusations in the first place. *Where had they been when my honor was on the line?* he thought bitterly. Only Rollie and Laura had come to him to express their faith in him.

* * * * * * * *

One morning a few days later, Mr. Ford intercepted him in the hall and asked him to accompany him to his office. *What now?* Steve wondered. He was surprised to find Mr. Carnahan sitting on the sofa there. He nodded uncomfortably to him and sat down at the superintendent's invitation. Perhaps he had come up with some new charge against him.

"Steve," Mr. Ford began awkwardly, "we have something to tell you." He glanced pointedly toward Mr. Carnahan as if he expected him to say something and paused to clear his throat before continuing.

"Mr. Carnahan has come to me and told me that in looking through a stack of papers at his home last evening, he came across the missing copy of the mathematics exam. He had taken it home one night and it just slipped his mind. It goes without saying that this completely puts you in the clear with regard to the cheating charge. Of course, your performance on the alternate test had already done that."

Steve did not reply.

"We're all very sorry about the mistake."

Steve turned to look directly at his accuser, who fidgeted with a fountain pen he held in his hand and finally muttered, "Yes, sorry."

There was a long silence. Mr. Ford looked at Steve expectantly, then quizzically. "I thought this would be good news, Steve."

"Yes, it's good news," Steve said, turning again to Mr. Carnahan, "but who is going to give me back my reputation? Who is going to take back the rumors that have buzzed around the school? Who's going to erase the charges from the minds of those who heard and repeated them? Even after the second exam supposedly cleared me, some of the kids still look the other way and whisper when they see me in the halls. The truth never catches up with the lie!" he exclaimed passionately.

Mr. Carnahan shifted uncomfortably in his chair, his face flushed, and the superintendent said at length, "Well, I'm sure your splendid record here and your continued fine example will convince them in the end. What's done is done, and we have to move on. I'm sorry for what happened. Now can you two shake hands?"

The two got to their feet. Steve stared angrily at the outstretched hand of his accuser without responding. After a few awkward moments, he broke the silence. "I suppose I should forgive you, Mr. Carnahan," he said hotly, "but you've made me out a liar and a cheat before the whole school. How are you going to give me back my reputation? Maybe I'll be able to put this behind me someday, but not now!"

With that, his face flushed, he turned and stalked out of the office.

As he headed briskly toward his wall locker, he reflected that Mr. Carnahan had only grudgingly said that he was sorry. His good name, no matter which name he was using at the moment, was important to him. He bit his lower lip in anger and frustration.

* * * * * * * *

During the ordeal, Laura had tried to keep up his spirits. "I don't see how anyone can possibly doubt your honesty," she told him. "Everybody knows what a sour old grouch Mr. Carnahan is—everything will come out all right in the end. I promise." It was an opinion worthy of the philosophical Awillah Pike, he thought, but he appreciated Laura's faith in him and her efforts to cheer him up.

They had continued to grow closer as spring had given way to summer, then to fall. That their dates, if that is what you could call them, continued to consist of little more than walks in the park or nearby neighborhoods made no difference to her. The warm embraces and kisses they shared there made their time together special. Moreover, they shared values and interests. In retrospect, it was often difficult to remember who had first voiced a particular opinion.

In their times together, Steve felt that their souls had become one, and he could not imagine life without her, even on the restricted terms his situation imposed.

Although she did not understand the reserve that kept her from sharing much of his background, she had accepted it at last, deciding that the thing that counted most was character. And she had no doubts about that.

* * * * * * * *

Despite his best intentions, trouble found Steve again a few weeks later. With his gesture of conciliation to Jack and Tom following the fight at school the preceding autumn, Steve had assumed that the matter between them was closed. There had been no further trouble between them since, but he was to find out that he was wrong about that. Apparently the pair waited to settle scores until their senior football season was over.

Not more than a week after the final game, he was walking up the alley leading to the shed one afternoon when he caught a glimpse over his shoulder of a couple of male figures dodging out of sight behind a projection in the fence.

It struck him as strange, and he quickly dived into an opening under the privet hedge. Lying there concealed from view, he waited, and in a minute Tom and Jack passed by his hiding place. To his dismay, he saw that Tom was carrying a baseball bat.

"Where'd he get to?" he heard Tom ask.

"He must have ducked into his grandma's place," his friend replied. "We'll get him some other time, and when we do, he's gonna get what's comin' to him."

The two hastened on up the alley on past Mrs. Pike's gate, and when he was sure they were out of sight, Steve quickly slipped into the yard and raced up the steps to his room. He sat down on the cot in the dim light of early evening to collect his wits. No doubt about it, the quarrel was not over. He'd have to be doubly careful about being caught out alone and be sure that he was not being followed to his hiding place—those two would like nothing better than to sic the police on him.

However, as he was returning from delivering an order of groceries to an elderly woman on the east side of town a few days later, he let his guard down. As he walked along, he was counting the money the woman had given him as payment when he looked up to find the two toughs standing abreast across the sidewalk, barring his way.

Suddenly Jack threw himself at him, striking him a glancing blow to the left side of his head. So furious was his onslaught that Jack got his feet tangled up and pitched headlong to the sidewalk. Tom took over the attack and began to pummel Steve with punches to his chest and shoulders, some of which Steve was able to ward off, managing to avenge himself with a couple of blows to his assailant's stomach that caused him to double over and back away for a moment.

Jack, however, had regained his feet and wrapped his arms around him, holding him while Tom began to beat him about the face and shoulders. Steve winced as the boy connected with his nose, and he felt hot blood begin to gush down his face. In another moment, he fell to the sidewalk, scraping his right elbow badly. Jack jumped astride him and began to deliver blows of his own. Steve struggled to throw him off, but the boy's weight held him pinned to the sidewalk and the beating continued.

"All right, you boys! Stop that right now!" a familiar voice said, and Steve looked up to see the policeman who had finished his usual vigil near the drugstore and was on his way home. The policeman grabbed Jack by the collar and pulled him to his feet.

"He jumped us first," said Tom.

"Yeah," began his buddy. "He came up behind ..."

"None of that, boys!" interrupted the officer. "I saw exactly what happened from half a block away. I saw the whole thing. All three of you—come with me. We're goin' on down to the station."

Steve's heart sank. The police station was the last place he wanted to go. He had carefully avoided the place for a year and a half now. Even if he was quickly exonerated, they were bound to ask him questions—questions that could be dangerous. Nevertheless, he had no choice but to obey the officer, and he fell in behind the three as they headed for the station just off the town square.

Things at the station turned out far better than Steve could have hoped. When asked for identification, he produced the Alabama driver's license Mr. Banfield had suggested he get so he could pick up supplies at the railroad station. It listed the address on Decatur Street as his residence. Although the sergeant made a note of it, apparently it wasn't important enough to check since he wasn't the one being charged. It was the policeman's eyewitness account that settled the matter, and after a few questions concerning the fight, Steve was allowed to leave—leaving the two toughs to spend the night in the city jail.

Tom's father came to retrieve him in about an hour, using his influence as county attorney to persuade the sergeant to release his son based on the latter's contention that he was not actively involved in the fracas and that Jack was solely to blame. Jack's father, a section hand on the railroad, did not arrive to bail him out until nearly midnight the next day, leaving his son fuming in his cell.

Steve's punishment was more severe. His left wrist was sprained, and he had multiple scrapes, cuts and bruises on his arms, neck, and face. When his injuries had healed, the memory of the beating lingered, underlining his continuing need to be vigilant and careful. He doubted that their run-in with the authorities had done much to convince the two of the folly of further confrontations since the charges against Tom were dismissed a couple of days later and Jack was sentenced to having to sweep out the jail every evening for a month. Position and connections were preeminent in Morefield's structured society.

Although Steve remained on his guard, there were no further incidents. Not long afterward, Tom, who had been absent from school all week, came to school limping noticeably and bearing a shiner, a split lip, and cuts and bruises on his arms.

Steve was puzzled, and as he was walking downtown after school with Rollie, he remarked that he hadn't imagined that he had been so successful in the fight.

Rollie laughed. "Don't flatter yourself, Stevie. It was nothing you did. The way I heard it, Jack was furious with Tom when he got the blame for the fight, and Tom's dad got his son out of jail and let Jack rot in there for almost a day and a half. Jack caught Tom in the park about a week ago and beat the tar out of him. Tom's father had him arrested and he spent three days in jail. I don't think you'll have to worry about you being their target anymore. I think they're going to be busy with each other for quite a while."

* * * * * * * *

With that problem apparently settled, there was another unexpected resolution of a problem that had troubled Steve for many months—a tragic resolution. As Steve was bringing the mail to Mrs. Pike one noon less than a week before Christmas, he heard some sort of commotion coming from the direction of the backyard. Making an excuse that he had to hurry on to his Aunt Mildred's house, he walked up Decatur Avenue and circled back down the alley toward the shed. Halfway down, the alley was blocked by a garbage truck and an ambulance, its red lights flashing insistently. On the other side of the truck, he could see Dr. Travis bending over a man lying on the ground.

"What's going on?" he asked one of the bystanders.

"Gabe Windle, the trash man. He's been hurt real bad. I think he may be dead!"

"How did it happen?"

Mrs. Meyer, standing in her gateway, chimed in. "The truck rolled and pinned him up against the fence. Crushed his chest, I reckon. I guess he forgot to set the brake when he got out to empty the trash can. Doesn't surprise me—not the brightest guy in the world—couldn't even read and write. Never could depend on him," she added sourly. "Made his rounds whenever he felt like it."

Steve edged on past the truck in time to see the victim being loaded into the ambulance.

"He's dead," one of the ambulance crew announced to the knot of onlookers, and Steve glanced down at the man's boots hanging limply over the end of the stretcher. He drew in a quick breath as he recognized the unmistakable pattern of a rising sun on the heels of his boots!

There could be little doubt that Gabe Windle was the thief who had visited the shed for many months. While collecting the trash, he probably had looked around the shed for something to swipe each week and had happened upon the room upstairs and found Steve's money.

While Steve felt sorry for the unfortunate man, wondering if he had a family to support, wondering if he had children who would miss their father at Christmas, he could not help feeling relief that the threat of the recurring visits and the possible disclosure of his secret no longer existed. If further proof of the man's involvement in the thefts was needed, the footprints never appeared again. However, Steve continued to rake the dust at the foot of the steps each morning. Old Gus—or his great-great-grandson—was still around.

* * * * * * * *

As Christmas approached, Steve had been thinking about finding some way to tell Laura how much she meant to him. He decided the holiday would afford an ideal opportunity to do so, and he took some of his college savings out of the Karo syrup bucket to buy her an expensive present. He wanted to be sure it was a nice one, an appropriate one, and he enlisted the help of his friend Rollie in choosing it.

One afternoon after school, they went to a jewelry store near the courthouse, Danielsons, and looked at the array of rings, bracelets, and pendants under the shiny glass of the display cases, the fluorescent lights adding an exciting sparkle to the items. Steve had taken fifteen dollars from the cache in the shed, and with Rollie's help, he selected a silver bracelet, had her name engraved on it, and had it wrapped with Christmas paper topped by a festive red and green bow.

The next afternoon after school, the last day of school before Christmas vacation, was unseasonably mild and bright, and he and Laura walked down to the statue in the park and sat in their customary place on the stone bench, the stern old general looking on.

Something in Steve's manner caused Laura to pause. He seemed to be preoccupied and nervous about something, and she sought to diffuse the uneasy feeling it engendered by recounting a humorous incident that had occurred in the food line that noon when she was distracted and delivered a ladle full of green beans into a bowl of tomato soup on a student's tray.

"Pretty Christmassy!" Steve laughed.

The two fell silent again. After several awkward moments, he cleared his throat and began, "Hon, I think you know that you mean a lot to me. I think you are the nicest person I've ever met. Well … more than nice. When I'm not with you, I think about you all of the time. What I'm trying to say is … that I care for you … very much. I, I've fallen in love with you."

Laura was silent, looking intently into his eyes as he spoke. In another moment, she had put her arms around him and kissed him, a long, lingering kiss that needed no interpretation.

"Oh, Steve! I love you too! I don't know what I'd do without you. I think about you all of the time."

They held each other close for several minutes, communicating without words. Then Steve remembered the bracelet and took the package out of his jacket pocket and said, "I'm not good enough with words to tell you how I feel, and I hope maybe this says them for me. Merry Christmas, honey."

She unwrapped the package slowly, careful not to tear the wrapping paper. Her eyes lit up as she parted the tissue paper, and she exclaimed, "Oh! It's beautiful! Oh, Steve … thank you … I love it!"

"Put it on," he said.

Laura clasped the bracelet on her left wrist and held it up in rapt admiration. "It's beautiful! Every time I wear it, I'll think of how much I love you."

Her expression darkened. "You know I won't be able to wear it at home. My folks are very strict, and they don't want me to go steady with *anyone.* They won't approve of such an expensive present. They know I sometimes take walks with you, but that's all. I'll just wear it when I come to school—and it will make our times together even more special."

"I understand. But someday though—soon, I hope—things will be so we can drop the secrecy, and I can meet your folks myself and let them know how much you mean to me."

"I hope so too, but till then, it will have to be our secret," she said wistfully, taking the bracelet off her wrist and putting it into her pocket.

* * * * * * * *

Laura Lee, of course, would be spending Christmas day at home with her parents, and Steve reflected that she would not be wearing the silver bracelet he had given her. Like their relationship, it must be kept secret. He spent the day alone in his room. His celebration included putting on the light gray wool pullover sweater decorated with green Christmas trees, her present to him, hoping that it would give him a feeling of nearness to her. From time to time as the day wore on, he looked down at the band of green trees that encircled his wrists and waist, but the pattern only served to remind him that they could not be together. He had unwrapped it shortly after he got up that morning and then spent some time frolicking with Man Friday, who pounced on the wrappings and swatted at the red ribbon as Steve swiped it back and forth above his head. Mid-morning, he stopped briefly to visit with Awillah, who was spending the day alone. He gave her a silk kerchief, and she reciprocated with a pearl-handled pocketknife and a plate of gingerbread cookies cut in seasonal shapes. She also wrapped up a piece of fruitcake to take to his Aunt Mildred. Steve ate it later that day for supper, feeling a twinge of guilt in having appropriated it.

After a brief afternoon nap curled up with the cat, he sat at the table reading *A Tale of Two Cities*, which would be an assigned novel in his senior English Literature class in the spring semester. He found the reading tough going as his thoughts strayed continually to Laura Lee and to home in Nebraska. The gingerbread cookies reminded him of Christmas with his mother—helping her bake gingerbread Santas and snowmen for the school Christmas party, spreading the cookies with white frosting. He could hear her singing carols as she worked, and he warmed to her obvious joy as she watched him unwrap his presents on Christmas morning.

* * * * * * * *

His thoughts found a distant echo in Nebraska. Late Christmas evening after her husband and David had turned in for the night, Edith Whitfield sat in the dark at the front window looking at the snow-covered landscape now bathed in moonlight and shadows, her thoughts reaching out to her missing son.

The day had been as joyless and bleak as the frozen landscape that now presented itself as she sat by the window. There had been no festive dinner, no guests to liven the holiday. Scenes of earlier Christmases when Steve was a boy came to mind from time to time—the gusto with which he licked the frosting pan, the playful give-and-take with his brother David, his furtive shaking of the wrapped presents in the days leading up to Christmas, his flashing smile as he unwrapped them and thanked her wordlessly from across the room. She found little comfort in these images. The passage of another year, another Christmas, had not lessened the hurt and anxiety that filled the hours of each day and each night. What had become of her son? Why didn't he write to say he was alive? What was he doing at this moment—was he thinking of her? If only she could send her thoughts and wishes, her love, across the miles. Was he warm on such a cold night? Was he hurt? …

She stopped short of completing the thought, but as she sat there as the hours ticked slowly toward morning light, the thought returned unbidden again and again. Each passing day seemed to diminish her hope, but she could not let go of it. How long she sat there reliving the cherished memories of her boy and the troubling thoughts that accompanied them she could not have said. At length, she drifted off into troubled sleep.

Before seven, she awoke with a start, hearing her husband and David returning from the morning milking, and she rushed to the kitchen to begin preparing their breakfast.

Chapter 17

Toward the end of February, Steve's physics teacher, Mr. Crofton, called him to his office, motioning for him to sit down. "Steve," he began, "you are one of our best students—on track, I would assume, to be in the top two or three or so in the class academically this spring."

Steve modestly expressed surprise, and the teacher continued, "I know your personal situation isn't such that you can go to a really good college without a scholarship. Because of your record, you probably can easily get a scholarship to one of the smaller teachers or liberal arts colleges around here, but you have the ability to do well at a first-rate school.

"As you may know, the absolute top scholarship that is available in the state of Alabama is the Drew Memorial at Tuscaloosa—the University of Alabama. It offers almost a free ride—books, tuition, board, room—almost everything—for four years if you keep your grades up. Only one scholarship is given for the whole state each year, and there have been a few years when they didn't give one at all. We've had some wonderfully gifted students here at Morefield, students who have done well later in college. I'm sure you've heard Roger Oliver's name mentioned a time or two—Class of '39. Roger was a splendid student, the best we've had since I've been here and that's eighteen years now, but even he didn't win a Drew. He was a finalist.

"The competition is stiff, but I think you might have a chance at it. It wouldn't hurt to apply—won't cost you anything. All you have to do is get the recommendation of three faculty members and take a four-hour written exam. I know you won't have any trouble getting the recommendations, and I think you've got a shot at doing very well on the exam. What do you say? Want to give it a try?"

Steve was at a loss for words. The Drew Scholarship! He'd certainly heard of it, and he'd heard Roger Oliver's name mentioned with awe ever since he first came to the school. In a school better known for its all-state football players, Roger was an academic legend. But Steve certainly had never considered applying for the scholarship himself. He sat for a few moments, thinking it over. He was tempted to play the modest bit, but something inside of him, a competitive spirit and a self-assertion engendered by the past two years of coping on his own against the odds, caused him to say, "Well, sir, if you think I've got a chance, I'd like to take the test."

"Fine," said Mr. Crofton. "Here is a brochure that describes the exam and gives some indication as to what sort of things are emphasized on it. I'll give you further particulars as I get them. I do know that it will be given in Birmingham on the third of April, and I'm sure we can find a ride down there for you. I have a lot of confidence in you, and I know the rest of the faculty do too. You've earned, and I mean *earned*, a lot of respect in this school, and I know you'll make us proud even if you don't get the scholarship. It's no disgrace to aim high and fall short, and a good score might stand you in good stead for getting a scholarship at another school."

Steve went back to his room that night walking on a cloud, determined to do the very best he could on the exam. There was no use vowing to redouble his efforts to learn as much as he could—he had been doing that for nearly two years. He could only continue on the difficult course he had set for himself when he came to Morefield and hope for the best. Still, he did study the brochure Mr. Crofton had given him. He tried to focus his extra reading in the directions indicated, but he hardly dared hope to succeed when even the celebrated Roger Oliver had not. Oliver, he had heard, had graduated from Vanderbilt with high honors, finished medical school at Duke, and was currently a vascular surgeon at one of the hospitals in Nashville.

* * * * * * *

As busy as he was, especially with the Drew examination and final exams looming, he was always pleased when Tal dropped by in the evenings for a chat, Tal still insisting that Steve correct any mistakes in grammar he might make. Tal picked things up quickly, and both were pleased with the progress he made despite hearing the Negro dialect day and night in his own environment. They had developed a strong friendship, and Steve reflected that his social life was rigidly compartmentalized into two distinct areas, black and white. There could be no gray area, and he regretted that very much.

Late one Saturday afternoon when a delivery for Banfield's took him near the south side of town, Steve decided to drop in to see his friend Tal. His knock was answered by Tal's mother, who did not work at the mill on Saturdays. She invited him to come in although Tal had picked up a job unpacking crates at a hardware store downtown and would not be home until late. He gladly accepted the invitation, welcoming the chance to get to know her better. She was a good person, warm and caring, qualities she had passed on down to her son.

She greeted him warmly and motioned toward a chair at the kitchen table, offering him a glass of tea, tepid as it turned out. Steve cast a quick glance upward at the glowering portrait on the wall as if he were asking for permission, and then sat down gingerly in Grandpa Davis's favorite chair.

By way of opening the conversation, Mrs. Davis said, "If I remember right, Tal said you was from up north somewhere."

"Yes, ma'am," he replied. "I'm from Ohio." Apparently Tal hadn't told her about his real background, and he thought it best not to trust her unnecessarily with extra information.

"I got a brother in South Bend, Indiana. Guess that's not too far from Ohio."

"No, ma'am, not far."

"He went up there to work in the Studebaker plant right out of the army after the war. Said there was nothin' here to keep him, and I guess that was about right."

"He like it there?"

"It's okay, I guess, but the only job he could get was sweepin' up in the plant—about what he'd a got here. Him bein' a sergeant in the war, I'd a thought he'd a got somethin' better."

"You'd think so."

"He married a nice girl he met up there. She's got a year of college and works as an arsonist at the library there at Notre Dame."

"An arsonist?"

"Um, you know, she has somethin' to do with filing papers and things. They got a baby on the way now, so I expect she'll have to quit soon. I tell Tal that he needs to go up there somewhere when he finishes high school. Nothin' much here for him exceptin' the mill, and that's no future. He couldn't work his way up here, bein' colored, you know. I don't want him to have to buck the system around here like my other chil'ren have to. My brother don't have no education past the seventh grade, and maybe that holds him back up there. Tal's got ambition, and he's smart. He wants to be a doctor. I'm not gonna say he's a child progeny, but he does real good in school and picks things up right quick. We both appreciate you helpin' him learn good grammar."

"Yes, ma'am, he's doing real well with the English lessons."

Tal's mother went on, "He's a good boy, and I think he could make somethin' of hisself up there. You come from Ohio. Maybe you could give him some idea about where to go."

"Tal's my friend, ma'am, and I'll do anything I can to help him," he replied vaguely, finishing his tea. He glanced at his watch. "Ma'am, I gotta go now. I'm workin' at Banfield's this afternoon; I just thought I'd stop by for a minute to say hi on my way back downtown. Thanks for the tea, ma'am."

"You come back any time, Steve. G'bye."

Chapter 18

If the fragile façade Steve had carefully built, his life defined by the need for deception and secrecy, was to remain intact, two of the people who had come to mean the most to him, Laura Lee and Mrs. Pike, could not meet. He purposely kept them apart, making sure that his afternoon walks with his girlfriend through the park and quiet neighborhoods nearby avoided Decatur Street.

However, one evening as he and Laura Lee were deep in conversation discussing an incident that had occurred in the lunchroom that noon, he looked up in surprise to discover that their walk was taking them past Mrs. Pike's house. She was sitting in her customary place in the swing, and there was no avoiding her. When she waved to them and invited them to come sit down for a while, he reluctantly led Laura Lee to his usual place on the edge of the porch.

"Grandma," he said, glad that he had often called her that, "I'd like you to meet my girlfriend, Laura Lee Andrews."

"Pleased to meet you, Laura Lee. I guess you two go to school together. I'll bet she's the prettiest girl in the whole school, hon."

"We-l-l-l," Steve replied slowly with a twinkle in his eye, "at least a tie for first."

"You!" exclaimed the girl, giving him a sharp poke in the ribs. "Who's the other one? Sounds like you have an eye out for other things than books."

"Ha, ha, ha!" laughed Mrs. Pike. "You're on your own, Stevie. You can get yourself out of the doghouse just the way you got yourself in."

With that, she got up suddenly, went inside, and reappeared in a few moments through the usual cloud of flies with a double dose of the dreaded fruit of the bog. Steve had warned Laura about the traditional treat, and he muttered under his breath, "Serves you right for punching me in the ribs."

Laura Lee ventured a sip of the drink. Struggling to avoid any facial expression, she whispered, "I think I've been properly punished."

The trio talked about school, Mrs. Pike's early days on the farm, and changes she had seen in the town in the last fifty years. The time passed quickly and pleasantly, and as the light began to fail, Steve said, "I need to get my girl home before dark."

"You come back anytime, hon," Mrs. Pike said, beaming at her new visitor. "I'll try to teach him how to treat a southern lady before next time."

"I'd appreciate that, Mrs. Pike, and I'll work on finding out just who that other girl is."

The walk to her home was done for the most part in silence, Laura Lee seeming to be troubled about something.

"You aren't upset with me about my joke about the tie for prettiest girl in school, are you? You know how I feel about you."

"Of course not," she replied, and as they reached the thicket near her home, she put her arms around him and assented readily to a warm kiss.

* * * * * * * *

Laura Lee had been quite taken with Mrs. Pike, and from time to time she insisted that their walks include a visit with her. Mrs. Pike obviously looked forward to their visits. The visits, however, were a danger, and Steve was careful to steer the conversation away from sensitive topics. He was grateful that Mrs. Pike had never happened to mention his Aunt Mildred. He had no idea as to how he might explain his other imaginary relative to Laura.

On one of those visits when Mrs. Pike wasn't looking, he poured what was left of his cranberry punch into Laura Lee's empty glass. The girl took immediate revenge, however, exclaiming, "Steve, have you finished your drink already? You must really be thirsty!"

The faithful Mrs. Pike got to her feet immediately, appropriated the empty tumbler, and in what seemed to him like a single motion reappeared with it filled to the brim with the her specialty.

"She must have a vat of that stuff in the basement, ready to go," he growled under his breath.

Steve was pleased that the visits seemed to be going well, but one afternoon as they sat on the bench in the park, Laura Lee turned toward him with a troubled look and said, "I've been wanting to ask you something, Steve."

"What, hon?"

"When you first came to work in the kitchen, you told me that you lived with your grandmother, only she didn't want you around, barely tolerated you. Always threatening to send you back to your stepfather if there was any trouble."

"Yes, I did." Steve shifted his gaze away, dreading where the conversation seemed to be heading. He looked up at General Beauregard, whose solemn expression gave him no comfort.

"She's not like that at all, Steve. She's not mean. She's ever so sweet and kind—gives you a big glass of cranberry juice every time we come." She giggled, then grew serious again as she returned to her train of thought. "And she obviously adores you. I don't understand why you would say something like that. It isn't like you. She wouldn't send you away—I'm sure she'd do anything she could for you. I just don't understand it, Steve. Why would you say such things?"

The boy was silent for a long time, Laura Lee beside him biding her time. Her question had obviously disturbed him, and she waited patiently for him to respond. Surely there was an explanation for his behavior.

Steve weighed his relationship with Laura Lee on the one hand against the protective façade, the tissue of lies he had so painstakingly constructed and preserved for almost two years. His whole existence had been based on lack of trust, and it had served him well. Although he had opened up to his friend Tal, that was different. He did not belong to his daily life—their friendship was separate—had to be.

Now, the first crack in the wall of secrecy and deception had opened up. If his relationship with Laura Lee was to continue to develop, he realized that it must now be based upon trust. It was hard to let go, but it was becoming obvious that he had no other choice.

Finally, Steve said in little more than a whisper, obviously upset, "I never meant to speak unkindly of Mrs. Pike. She has always been nice to me, and I love her as much as I could ever love a real grandmother."

"A real grandmother?"

"Yes, I thought I told you she's not really my grandmother. And she's not my stepfather's mother either. I don't even have a stepfather. The fact is that I don't even live with her."

"Don't live with her? I thought ... Where *do* you live? I don't understand. What's this all about?" She felt as if she were talking to a stranger.

"I always try to tell the truth, and you know I've always been honest with you, as honest as I *could* be anyway. But I guess it's time to be completely honest—I guess you've got a right to know everything."

"Everything?" A sense of dread welled up in Laura Lee's throat.

"Steve isn't my real name, and I'm not even from Ohio. My real name is Joseph Whitfield, and I grew up on a farm in Nebraska, at least until just before my sixteenth birthday." The words came out rapidly in clusters, riding emotions coming to the surface at last.

"My dad and mom are farmers, and I have a brother David fifteen years older than me. My father isn't dead. I ran away from him."

"Ran away? Why?"

"My dad ... he's ... let's just say he and I never could get along. I tried to be a good son, really I did, but I could never do anything right for him. He was on me all of the time. When he'd get mad, he'd blow sky high. Sometimes a hard slap or two right across the face was good enough for him, but sometimes he'd grab the first thing he could get his hands on and start in on me. I've been hit with everything from the tug of a horse harness, a hoe handle, and a razor strop to a two by four and even a board with a nail in it once."

"Oh, Steve, I'm sorry!"

Encouraged, he continued. The stopper was out of the bottle. The words bubbled out. "It was getting worse. Here, put your finger on my rib. Feel that bump? That's from when he hit me with the two by four about two years ago. The bruises across my arm and chest have disappeared, but the bump stays. I think he broke the bone."

She reached up and felt the bump gingerly with her forefinger.

"Don't worry, hon, it doesn't hurt much anymore," he said reassuringly, almost in a whisper. "Bad as they were, the beatings weren't the worst of it. It was the personal abuse I couldn't take."

"Oh Steve. Weren't there any good times at all?"

"I can't remember ever sitting on his lap as a little boy, and I can't remember that he ever wanted to do anything with me, like play ball or go fishing like some fathers do. All he wanted was to get all of the work he could out of me on the farm.

"You know," he said almost with a sense of wonder, "I went all though grade school and the first two years of high school with an A in every class, and he never once said I had done a good job or that he was proud of me. He just grunted when I told him I'd made starting quarterback on the football team as a freshman. There was always the yelling and the threatening. He'd get mad and he'd say, 'I wish you'd never been born,' or 'If you don't behave, I'll call the sheriff and he'll send you off to the reform school at Kearney. That's where they put boys like you!'"

Steve cleared his throat a couple of times and continued. "Looking back, I really can't tell you what set him off most of the time. I think I tried to get along with him, I really did, but it just kept getting worse. My older brother David was from his first marriage, and there were four besides him. I just think he didn't want me in the first place."

She saw that he was on the verge of tears. "What happened that last night, the night you ran away? And how did you get to Morefield?"

"It wasn't a sudden decision. I suppose I'd been deciding to leave almost all my life. Even as a small boy, I fantasized about running away to the 'big city,' whatever that was. A couple of times when it got bad, I headed up the road, but I had no idea where I was going to go, and when the dark came, I decided I'd better go back home and try to make the best of it. My mother sometimes tried to take up for me when my dad got mad, but there was no stopping him when he lost his temper. As I got older the abuse kept getting worse. That last night was the final straw. I just couldn't take it any longer. That night I thought I saw murder in his eyes."

Steve no longer seemed to see Laura Lee. He was transfixed,

transported to the night in the cellar, reliving the details of the scene there and the subsequent flight to Morefield. Wisely, she listened and did not interrupt as the memories poured out.

"My folks and I were running the milk through the cream separator in the cellar like we did every evening after the cows were milked. I was to take a bucket of the skim milk back out to the barn to feed the calves as I always did, and I was going to do it. But we had trouble with the separator, and we were later than usual. I said I wanted to call my girlfriend first to tell her I'd be a little late to take her to the free picture show in town. It wouldn't have taken very long, but things always had to be done just the way my dad wanted—right when he wanted.

"He flew off the handle and yelled, 'You do what I tell you to!'

"I said, 'It won't take me two minutes to call her, and then I'll feed the calves like I always do.'

"He exploded. 'It's always something with you, Joe! You do it right now, like I told you, and don't you give me any back talk!' Then he slapped me hard right across the face a couple of times, bloodying my nose, and grabbed a hoe handle that was leaning against the wall and struck me twice, as hard as he could, across the chest and shoulder. His face turned a dull red and I could see the veins in his neck standing out. He bit down on his lower lip and yelled, 'Now Git! Git!' I had already turned and started up the steps, but he gave me a kick and goosed me with the hoe handle all the way to the top of the steps. He *goosed* me!"

Steve choked as he spoke. Sometimes his words became almost inaudible, and there was anger in his voice. "I took the bucket on out and fed the calves at the barn, then I brought it back to the well, and I just took off. It wasn't so much being hit—he'd done that more times than I could count. It was the *goosing* with the hoe handle—almost as if he'd found a new way to humiliate me. I couldn't take it anymore. I didn't go back for anything, not even my billfold, not even to tell my mom good-bye. I just headed up the cattle lane to the back side of the farm to the highway.

"I caught the first ride I could, and I didn't stop till I reached Alabama. I stopped here because I was too tired and hungry to go on. When I got here, I didn't have anything but the clothes on my back. I've worked hard and I've done okay—I had no other choice.

"When I got here, I had to hide out and invent a background, a new identity to explain why I was here so the authorities wouldn't send me back to my father. And I had to find a way to get into the high school. I made up Mrs. Pike as my mean grandmother who'd send me back to an abusive stepfather in Ohio at the first provocation so they wouldn't check with her. I got the job at the printing company and printed up a birth certificate, guardianship papers, and school records so I could get into school. I've been forging her name on the report cards. It's all been a pack of lies, and I really hate that. And I hate having to make Mrs. Pike out to be a mean old woman when she's always been a good friend."

"Kind. Except for the cranberry punch!" said Laura in an effort to relieve the tension.

He flashed a grin that disappeared as quickly as it had come. "I *can't* go back to my father! I just can't. I've managed to work to support myself till I can graduate, and I'm almost there. Just a couple more weeks. Mrs. Pike doesn't know anything about my real identity. She thinks I live with an 'Aunt Mildred' I invented who lives up by Thomason Park. Maybe I should have trusted her and told her who I was, but I never could quite bring myself to do that. There was too much at stake. She's been awful good to me, but I've never asked her for any support or anything. If I can just hang on until I'm twenty-one, I'll be okay, but until I'm of age, I'll have to keep out of sight. If they find me, they'll send me back to my father. All he wants is an unpaid farmhand. I'm afraid to go back!"

Laura Lee had listened intently, fighting to hold back the tears as Steve's past had unfolded before her. "Oh, Steve, I'm so sorry. I had no idea you've had it so rough. I didn't mean to stir up all of the bad memories."

"Oh, that's okay; they never go away."

They sat without speaking for several minutes before Laura broke the silence. "But if you don't live with your aunt or Mrs. Pike, where do you live?"

He hesitated. "C'mon, I'll show you."

She took his hand, brushing tears from her eyes as they walked up the street toward Mrs. Pike's house. They slipped up the alley unnoticed and turned in at the back gate. He led the way up the wooden steps, pushed open the door, and they entered the room. "Home sweet home," he said dryly.

Laura stood still, shocked by the walls lined with mattress boxes, the rickety chair, the cot with its moth-eaten army blankets, the battered lantern on the desk, the bucket in the corner. "This is where you live? No electricity? ... No plumbing? No stove? ... How do you manage to keep warm in the winter?"

"I found this place, fixed it up with what I could find, and I've lived here for almost two years now. It's not so bad. You get used to things."

"Not so bad! Oh, Steve!" With that, she sat down on the old cot, covered her eyes with her hands, and began to cry. "I'm so sorry, Steve. So very sorry."

Steve sat down beside her and put his arm around her shoulders. "It'll be all right. Don't cry, hon. As soon as I turn twenty-one, I won't have to live the lie anymore. I just need to keep out of sight of the authorities like I've been doing for two years now. Then I'll be of age under Nebraska law and they can't send me back to my father. It'll be all right. I'm okay as long as I have you. You're the best thing that's ever happened to me, Laura. Please don't cry," he said tenderly and kissed her tears away. After a while, he guided her head and shoulders down onto the bed and lay down beside her and held her tight. They lay there long after the sun went down and fell asleep in each other's arms.

The moon, a pale silver sliver, had long since passed the window on its westward journey when Steve awoke suddenly with a start as Man Friday returned from his nocturnal rounds and walked across his bare chest and nuzzled against his chin.

"Wake up, Laura Lee! It's way past midnight. Your folks will be wondering where you are."

In a few moments, they stumbled down the steps, not bothering even to get a flashlight, and hurried through the darkened streets and alleyways toward Laura Lee's home. After the usual goodnight kiss in the thicket, he watched as she walked up on the front porch, put her key in the lock, and slowly pushed the front door open.

Almost instantaneously, a light went on in an upstairs window.

* * * * * * * *

The next day when he went to work in the lunchroom, he sought

Laura Lee out. She had taken some trash out to the barrel behind the lunchroom, and he followed her, greeting her cautiously.

"Hi, Laura Lee. You okay, honey?" The color came up in his cheeks unbidden. He looked away.

"Yes, I'm okay, Steve. I'm fine."

"Can we meet after school to talk?"

"I can't."

"What did your folks have to say about you getting home so late?"

"That's just it. They were really angry. Furious! I wouldn't tell them where I'd been. I told them I was just talking to some friends and the time got away from me. They didn't believe me, and now I've been grounded for the next month. I have to go straight home when I get out of school. I really want to see you, but I don't know how we can work it out. They were really mad!"

He saw that she was wearing the silver bracelet. "Look, hon, I'm sorry about last night."

"Don't be sorry," she said quickly.

"You know you're very special. I love you," he said warmly.

"I love you too, Steve," she said, "but I don't know how we're going to work things out. Look, I've got to go now. Mrs. Tyndall has an errand she wants me to run right away. See you later, hon," she said, giving his hand a pat. Then she hurried back into the kitchen.

CHAPTER 19

It was only two weeks now until commencement, and graduation activities were a busy time for seniors. There was the senior prom, but Laura understood that Steve couldn't have taken her anyway even if she could have gone. Several times, he was able to use the noon hour to talk with her a few minutes, sharing a kiss when no one was around, and once he took her to see Mrs. Pike for a few minutes. By tacit agreement, they did not visit his room again. Although their feelings for each other had not diminished, it was best to be more circumspect.

What little time they could manage together pretty much consisted of the usual walk to the park and stolen kisses on the bench under the general's watchful eye or in the protective thicket outside Laura's home.

Final exams were sandwiched in between the flurry of graduation activities. One afternoon, Miss Edwards called Steve into her office. "Steve, I have good news for you, although I wouldn't think you'd be too surprised by them. Based on your grades here and those you transferred from your first two years in Ohio, you have the number one spot academically in the class at this time. I don't expect the exam results to change that. You are almost certain to be class valedictorian! I want to be the first to offer you my congratulations."

"Oh, thank you, Miss Edwards."

"I'll admit I wasn't too sure about you when I ran into you in the front hall two summers ago, but you've been a fine student and have a wonderful record here. I'm very proud of you," she added, shaking his hand. "I look forward to your graduation speech."

"I'll do my best, ma'am," he said happily. "Do we wear graduation caps and gowns?"

"Yes, there will be an announcement tomorrow about renting them. They'll come to about five dollars."

Steve left, walking on air. He looked forward to the event, a reward for two years of hard work and sacrifice, and he guessed he'd have to dig into his savings for the cap and gown. It would be a once in a lifetime thing for him. He was a little troubled by her reference to his grades in Ohio, but he had been careful to transfer the names of the courses he had taken in Nebraska and the exact grades he had received. He regretted only that his mother could not be there to share the moment with him.

* * * * * * * *

He was sweeping the lower hall one afternoon when a student who worked in the school superintendent's office came to tell him that he was wanted there *right away.* The emphasis on the last two words told him that he would have to leave work, and he was a little puzzled by the summons. He climbed the steps to the third floor and walked slowly to the superintendent's office wondering what he could want. Perhaps it had something to do with the speech he was to give as valedictorian. He had spent a couple of hours working on it the evening before.

Miss Wickham, the school secretary, sat at her desk in the outer office. "Go right in, Steve, they're expecting you," she said.

He opened the door. There around the long, polished mahogany conference table sat the superintendent, the principal, Miss Edwards, a couple of teachers, and several members of the school board. Something was up, but what?

Superintendent Ford motioned to an empty chair at the end of the table. "Please have a seat, Mr. Whitfield."

Steve stiffened. It took only a second for the reality to sink in. It was not "Mr. Bowman." It was "Mr. Whitfield!" The game was up; there were no two ways about it—somehow, he had been found out.

"That's right isn't it, Steve?—Joseph Whitfield?"

He hung his head and stared at the burnished table, which reflected light from the big window behind Mr. Ford. How quickly his world had changed! "Yes sir," he admitted finally. "How did you find out?"

"When you were named valedictorian, some of us thought it would be nice if your *grandmother*," he put a slight touch of sarcasm on the word, "could come to the commencement exercises. You had said she wasn't much interested in you and couldn't get around very well, but we thought if we sent a car ... surely, since you were to be valedictorian ... Well, Miss Edwards and I went to see her this afternoon to invite her."

He paused a moment. Steve said nothing.

"You can imagine our surprise," he continued evenly, "when Mrs. Pike told us she was not your stepfather's mother and that you didn't even live with her! Moreover, she wasn't your legal guardian despite what the paper you gave us said. When we asked who had been signing your report cards, she said she had never seen any of them. I think we can assume that you have been forging her name on them. Is that correct, Joe?"

"Yes, sir," he said, looking down at the table.

"Naturally, we were curious about the transcript from the high school you attended in Ohio. What do you know about that?"

"I'm sorry, sir. I had to get into school somehow if I was ever to make something of myself, and I didn't know any other way. I made that up too—but those were the courses I took the first two years in Nebraska, and those were the real grades I got. I didn't know how else to do it. I had to go to school!"

"I thought so. Then we wondered if you hadn't been staying with Mrs. Pike, where you *had* been living. She mentioned an Aunt Mildred, and we suspected that you had made her up too. By coincidence, one of Mrs. Pike's neighbors, a Mrs. Meyer, and her little granddaughter were sitting in the swing with Mrs. Pike when we came by. As we speculated as to where you might be living, the strangest thing happened. A big orange striped cat came trotting up the front walk, jumped up on the porch, and rubbed against the little girl's leg for a few seconds. Then it went around the house toward the backyard, and the little girl jumped down and exclaimed, 'It's the magic cat! He's taking us to Prince Steven in the Magic Hideaway!'" He smiled. "She said something about our needing the cat to get there and that the cat trusted us. Then she ran into the backyard after the cat.

"We just stood there, wondering what to make of it, but her grandmother followed her on back, and when she returned with the little girl, she said, 'I think you'd better come see what I found back there.' She said she had seen a light in the shed out back once and had heard noises a couple of times and wondered why Steve came and went through the backyard so often. 'It all fits together now,' she said.

"So, we went back there to take a look around and went up to the room where you've been living. Needless to say, we were shocked by what we found."

Miss Edwards bowed her head and let out what sounded like a sob.

Mr. Ford continued. "Living back there in that old shed, nothing but a cot and a table. Cardboard walls! What did you do for heat in the winter?"

"I didn't have any heat, sir. I fixed it up with cardboard and covered myself with surplus blankets."

"It must have been freezing in there!" Miss Edwards said incredulously. "And in the summer … How could you stand it?"

"When you have no other choice, ma'am, you stand it," he said matter-of-factly. He seemed suddenly old beyond his years.

"And Mrs. Pike didn't give you any support at all?" asked the superintendent.

"No, sir. She's no kin to me. She had no idea I was living back there, and I never asked her for anything. We became good friends, but I took care of everything myself."

"What kind of work did you do? Miss Edwards tells me you held down three jobs."

"I worked at the printing office—that's how I was able to come up with the birth certificate and other documents. But those were my real grades on the transcript, honest," he insisted again. "I made up the high school in Ohio, but those were the right grades. And I worked at Banfield's and at the public library in the summer. I found whatever odd jobs I could—I worked raking leaves, spading gardens, and doing odd jobs around the neighborhood. Then you gave me a job sweeping up before and after school, and later I worked at the lunchroom. The ladies there sometimes gave me some leftover food."

"It must have been hard. I understand you sometimes went hungry."

The boy did not reply.

"Mr. Ford," interrupted Miss Edwards, "you remember the time he fainted in the hall."

"Yes, what happened, Steve?"

"Things were going along all right, but someone came into my room out behind Mrs. Pike's and stole all the money I had for food, all of the money I had saved during the summer for college. If you don't have any money, you just don't eat," he said. "Dr. Travis and the nurse were kind to me and gave me some food until I could get paid and get back on my feet. Then I made it on my own." A note of pride had crept into his voice.

"Well, I'm sorry you had such a tough time, and you certainly did well once you got yourself into this school. How could you study by that lantern?"

He did not expect an answer and continued, "And I guess this pretty much explains where you came from." He held up the newspaper clipping from the *St. Louis Post-Dispatch* reporting his disappearance two years earlier.

That explained how he knew his real name, Steve thought. They had apparently found it where he had tucked it into the Bible on the table.

"Why did you run away from home? You must have had a very good reason for you to go through all this!"

Steve looked down at the table for several moments. "I could never go back. I couldn't get along with my father, my real father—I tried—finally I couldn't take the abuse—beatings, taunts … humiliation. It just kept getting worse. I was afraid he was going to kill me, and one evening it got so bad, I just took off."

"How did you happen to land in Morefield? It's a long way from Nebraska."

"I hitched rides with truck drivers and salesmen hoping to get to Florida. I stopped in Morefield because I was tired and needed to find work to get some food. I met up with Mrs. Pike, moved into her shed, and never left. I had no place else to go. I looked for other places, but nothing worked out. I'm sorry for the lies, the lies about Mrs. Pike, the forgeries—I guess I defrauded the school when you get right down to it. But I didn't know what else to do … I had to get my diploma. Please. Please. Don't send me back to my father. *Please!*"

Miss Edwards appeared on the verge of tears, and a couple of the male members of the board shuffled the papers on the table before them.

The superintendent cleared his throat a couple of times and continued in a somewhat officious manner. "Well, Mr. Whitfield, the issue now is whether you can be allowed to graduate from this high school, and, if so, whether you should be valedictorian. Your whole existence here is based on an elaborate deception. We do not know that the transcript you concocted from a nonexistent school actually represents your true record."

"You can call my high school at Steadman Falls. Mr. George Richards is the superintendent, and he can verify my record for my freshman and sophomore years. It's all correct, the courses I took and the grades I received. I was careful about that. Please, sir, I've just got to graduate, and I need to go to college!"

"We'll see what we can find out from Nebraska, but I can't speak for the board. They will make the final decision. You'll have to admit that the whole situation is highly unusual. I cannot guarantee that the board will rule in your favor. As for your being sent back to your folks in Nebraska, you're still a minor—the county attorney down at the courthouse is checking into that right now. We'll have to see what the Nebraska law says."

Steve remembered with a start that the county attorney was Tom Marsh's father and exclaimed, "I can't go back! Don't let them send me back!"

"Well, we'll see. We'll put through a call to your high school in Nebraska right now so we can set things straight if we can before graduation. Meanwhile, you take a seat in the outer office, and we'll call you back as soon as we have reached a decision."

Steve got slowly to his feet, trying to hide the tears welling in his eyes. He turned and stumbled toward the door.

"I'm sorry. I tried … so hard … so hard," he said softly and went into the outer office.

Miss Wickham was busy at her desk sorting receipts and adding up a column of figures, and she took little notice of him. He sat down on a sofa near the outer door of the office, nervously flitting through a couple of *Time* magazines he found lying on an end table there. Nothing caught his interest as he pondered his fate now being weighed in the balance in the superintendent's office. His whole life seemed to him to be in jeopardy, everything he had worked for.

As the minutes began to tick by slowly, he could hear the muffled voices of the debaters in the office as they sat in judgment, sorting through the pieces of his life. He glanced up when the superintendent buzzed the secretary and asked her to put through a long-distance call. His anxiety seemed to have immobilized the hands of the Regulator clock on the wall.

After about half an hour, he looked up to see a city policeman enter the office and walk up to the secretary's desk. Although he did not appear to pay any attention to him, Steve's blood ran cold. While the officer was engaged in conversation with the secretary, Steve stood up slowly and, as nonchalantly as he could, stepped out the door and started down the long flight of steps toward the front entrance, picking up speed as he went. In the front hall, he passed his friend Rollie.

"See you after school, Steve."

"Yeah, see you," Steve replied, trying to act as if nothing unusual was in the wind. He cast a quick glance back up the stairs, relieved to see that the policeman had not followed him, and hurried on out the front door and down the walk. He was running now as fast as he could. He bolted across the street through traffic, and at the town square, he turned down the street that led to the black section of town. He slowed down to a normal walk to avoid attention and in fifteen minutes stepped up on the front porch of the Davis home. He was about to knock on the door when it opened suddenly and Tal stuck his head out.

"What's up, man?"

"Can I come in?" he asked, looking around nervously. Apparently, no one had followed him. Tal pushed the screen door open and he ducked inside.

"I've got to talk to you. They found out about me at school ..."

"That you're a runaway?"

"Yes, my real name and everything. I guess they're not going to let me graduate. The police came to pick me up."

"To send you back?"

"Yes, I've got to get out of town as quick as I can."

"Tonight?" asked Tal.

"Yeah, tonight. I don't know where I'm going to go. Probably up north somewhere . . . maybe Ohio. You want to go along? You said you'd go up north as soon as you got through school. Well, your school's out now, so how about it? Why don't you come along? I know it's short notice, but I'd sure be obliged if you would."

"We could help each other out," said Tal, clearly tempted.

"So, what do you say? I know your momma would approve. She told me there's nothing here for you last time I was here."

"Well, it's awful sudden. My folks are both still at the mill. I'm all for going, but I hate leaving without saying good-bye to them, 'specially Momma. She'll be home before long, but my dad won't be home till midnight."

"We can't get out on the road until it's dark anyway. Maybe we can just lie low here for a couple of hours, and then you can say good-bye to your mom."

"Okay. She'll get us some supper, and I'll pack up some things. You going by your place to get your stuff?"

"No, too risky. They'll be looking for me there." He thought regretfully about his clothes and the money he'd saved for college, now almost $145. And most of all he thought about Laura Lee and Mrs. Pike. What would they think? He couldn't even say good-bye to them.

* * * * * * * *

Meanwhile at the school, the call had been put through without delay to Steadman Falls, and Mr. Ford read the information from Steve's forged transcript to the superintendent there. He determined that the courses and marks received on the transcript covering Steve's first two years of high school were indeed correct, as Steve had insisted—down to the last letter.

There was general sympathy among those at the meeting for the boy, considering the trials he had had to endure and the mistreatment he had suffered at the hands of his father. However, a couple of the board members felt that the forging of documents for whatever reason was a serious offense and should not be rewarded. The faculty members who had worked with Steve for two years became advocates for his case, maintaining that the transcript had been correct as Steve had said, and his record at Morefield was one of the most outstanding in recent memory.

Superintendent Ford, normally thought to be a bit of a hard egg, took up for Steve as well. "The boy's deception, and I can't deny that his life in Morefield has been a tissue of lies, was undertaken solely for the purpose of getting an education, one which he has earned in an outstanding manner, and of staying out of the clutches of an abusive father. His performance under difficult circumstances has been outstanding, and I have no hesitancy in recommending that he be allowed to graduate. He's earned it."

Ultimately, the superintendent, supported staunchly by Miss Edwards, won the day, and when a vote was taken, a majority of the board voted to allow him to graduate. That decided, it seemed only logical that he also be allowed to be class valedictorian.

"Well, let's give the boy the good news," said Mr. Ford, a note of relief in his voice. "The long wait must have been agonizing for him." He buzzed his secretary on the intercom. "Miss Wickham, please send Steve Bowman in."

He turned to Miss Edwards. "You've been close to him, Myra. You can give him the good news. He'll be pleased, I know."

A moment later, the door opened, and the secretary stepped in. "Steve's not out here. He left over a half an hour ago. I was talking to Officer Fleming. He came in to pick up the month's lunchroom receipts to take to the bank like he always does, and I noticed Steve get up suddenly and leave. I thought he looked upset, but he didn't say a word. I didn't try to stop him—you didn't tell me he was supposed to wait. I hadn't paid much attention to him. I was working on the end-of-the-year report, and I thought he just stopped to read the magazines."

"Oh, dear!" exclaimed Miss Edwards. "He must have thought the police had come to get him. Oh, dear!"

"Quick!" Mr. Ford exclaimed. "See if you can find him! Everybody! Fan out and search the entire school! We've got to find him!"

"Suppose he's run away again? He said he'd never go back," said Miss Edwards, worry etched deeply in her face.

In a few minutes, the group had searched the building, asking teachers and students if they had seen the boy. Their frantic inquiries were in vain. Finally, Mr. Ford ran into Rollie, who was at his wall locker picking up his jacket to go home. "Have you seen Steve Bowman?"

"Yes, sir. I saw him about half an hour ago heading out the front door. He seemed to be in a real big hurry. What's wrong?"

A call was placed to the police station and the county sheriff, and a quickly organized search of the downtown area and Mrs. Pike's neighborhood failed to turn up the boy. It appeared that he had not returned to his room to pick up any of his belongings. He seemed to have vanished into thin air.

* * * * * * * *

When Tal's mother returned from the mill about eight, she reacted to her son's imminent departure with shock, tears, and finally resignation. Ultimately, she reasoned that it would be for the best, and she took some comfort from the thought that Steve would be with him and would look out for him. She quickly fixed some beef and barley soup for the boys and made some ham sandwiches for them to take along for the trip. Tal began to pack a large cardboard suitcase with a few clothes and other items he thought he might need. After supper, his mother came into his bedroom as he finished, dumped everything from the suitcase onto the bed, and repacked it, folding items of clothing carefully, putting some things aside, and pulling others from the bureau and closet and putting them into the suitcase, which soon seemed ready to burst like an overcooked sausage.

Tal pulled an item from the suitcase and held it up. "What's this?" he asked.

"Them's the red flammable pajamas I gave you las' Chrismus," she replied. "You'll need 'em. It gets cold up north nights."

"Yeah," Steve chimed in with a straight face. "They'll keep you good and warm."

"You listen to him, Tal," the mother replied. "He knows what it's like up there in Ohio."

Despite the desperate events of the day, Steve's spirits lifted somewhat as he listened to her motherly chatter, offering bits of advice as she bustled about the room looking for things her son might need. He wished he had more time to get to know her. She had a heart of gold, completely devoted to her youngest son. Now Steve was taking him away from her.

As she rushed about and fussed over little things, he realized that her behavior was in part a way of delaying dealing with the reality that her son would soon be gone, facing a new, uncertain life without her protection and guidance. When the suitcase had at last been packed to her satisfaction, she lowered the lid to close it, exciting a commotion within. Puzzled, she flipped the lid up and exclaimed, "Boomer! How'd you get in there! You sure ain't goin' to Ohio!" She gave him a whack. "You git on outta there!"

Boomer's front claw had gotten tangled in the pajamas, and the cat leaped halfway across the bedroom and hit the floor running, trailing the pajamas in a livid red streak behind him. In an instant, he banged the screen door open, bounded across the porch, and disappeared into the gathering darkness looking like a skyrocket gone sideways.

"Guess Granpa decided he didn't want to go with you after all," laughed Tal.

With a start, Steve thought of Man Friday for the first time that afternoon. He couldn't go back to the shed for him, and he couldn't take him along anyway. Who would feed him now? Who would take care of him? As the banter between mother and son continued, he fell silent, grieving for his old friend. It was a choice he had to make, but its justification did nothing to relieve his sadness and sense of guilt.

When at last it was time for them to leave, Mrs. Davis held her son close for a moment, then grabbed Steve and held him tight with her other arm. When Tal pulled away at last, she released them, and the boys stepped out onto the front porch and started up the darkened street.

"Bye, Steve."

"Bye, Mrs. Davis. I'll take good care of him, I promise."

"Write me, Tal, y'hear?" she called after him.

"I will, Momma, I will."

She stood in the door and watched them cross the pale orb cast by the farthest street light and step into the night beyond, then turned slowly, went inside, and sat down at the kitchen table, buried her head in her arms, and cried.

The boys slipped quickly up the alleyways toward downtown until they came to the street that forked off to the main highway. They stood in the shadows, surveying the street for police. A cement truck had stopped at the curb in front of the public library, and the driver was bending down to check a front wheel. Steve rushed over to him.

"Mister! You going on up toward Huntsville? My friend and I need a ride bad—my grandma is almost eighty and just had a bad fall, and I need to go look after her. My friend's got a job up that way. Could we hitch a ride with you, sir?"

The man gave them a quick once over. He eyed Tal suspiciously and said at length, "I guess so. Sure. I'll be done tightnin' this lug nut in a jiffy. Climb in."

The two jumped quickly up into the cab and hunched down to avoid being seen by passersby. After what seemed like an eternity to them, the driver got in, put the truck in gear, and they rumbled on up the darkened street toward the main highway. To Steve, the scenario was familiar, and it was as frightening as it had been the first time.

* * * * * * * *

As Steve left the life he had so painstakingly crafted in Morefield for two years, another brief chapter to his life there was added the following morning. A messenger from Western Union interrupted Mr. Ford as he chaired a faculty meeting. The telegram was from the University of Alabama in Tuscaloosa informing him that one of his students, Steven Bowman, had just won the Mitchell-Hawkins Scholarship. While he had not won the Drew Memorial, he had been a runner-up, and the committee had decided to award him another prestigious scholarship, which would cover many of his expenses at the university. His college education was virtually assured.

The following evening at the school's commencement exercises, a vacant chair in the graduate section symbolized his absence, and the program, printed three days earlier, listed the valedictory to be given by Steven Bowman among the evening's activities. The announcement of the awarding of the scholarship to him was met with thundering applause. It was a moment of triumph and of sadness. Although she knew her friend would not be present, Mrs. Pike had accepted the school's invitation to attend, and she sat proudly through tears during the announcement and the awarding of his diploma *in absentia.*

* * * * * * * *

The boy had simply vanished, and no clue as to where he might have gone was turned up for several days, not until the cement truck driver got back to town and heard the news of the boy's disappearance. The driver went to the police station to report having given him a ride, and although the police in Huntsville were quickly notified, no further trace of him could be found. Where he went and what new identity he might have assumed remained a mystery, and the irony of the fact that he never knew he had been permitted to graduate from high school and that he had won the scholarship was a frequent topic of conversation in Morefield and a source of deep regret for months afterward.

The request for the transcript made by telephone by Mr. Ford, had engendered a quick call to Steve's parents by Mr. Richards, the superintendent in Steadman Falls. His mother and brother were ecstatic, and even his father seemed to display a reluctant pleasure at the first indication they had had in two years that he was alive, and they began to talk about bringing him home.

Their excitement was quenched cruelly the next morning by the news that the boy had disappeared again. While his mother took comfort in knowing he was alive and was proud of her son's achievements at Morefield High, his father made no comment. It would be more than three years before they were to hear of him again.

CHAPTER 20

Darkness shines as light,
And faith's fair vision
changes into sight.

—Hugh Thompson Kerr

One summer evening, John and Edith Whitfield sat alone at the kitchen table eating supper. David had finally married his longtime fiancée and moved to Omaha to work in a packing plant. When his marriage didn't work out, he had enlisted in the army. Now that both of John's sons were gone, all of the chores and farm work had been left for him, and he had just finished separating the milk and feeding the calves himself.

It was at this time of day that the mother missed the younger boy most. She had often heard him singing as he returned from evening chores. When he was not upset and angry at his father, he often sat on the bench under the white elm in the backyard and sang until she called him for supper. The years had not dimmed the memory.

As they ate in silence, the front doorbell rang. She opened the door to find two men in military uniform, a captain and a staff sergeant, standing on the porch. They removed their caps and asked if they might come in.

The mother nodded and called out, "John!" In a moment, her husband appeared and looked at the unexpected visitors with a puzzled expression.

"Won't you sit down?" the mother asked uneasily.

"Thank you," the captain replied. The two sat down on the sofa, and he cleared his throat uncomfortably. "I'm Captain Grant and this is Sergeant Donaldson. We've come about your son."

"David?" asked the father.

"No, sir, about your son Joseph Whitfield."

"Joe?" said the mother. "About Joe?" She looked at her husband, not knowing whether to feel gladness or … What had the men in uniform to do with their son?

Mr. Whitfield broke the silence. "We ain't heard a word from him in, well, I guess goin' on six years now. What about him? Is he in the army too?"

"Yes, sir. I'm afraid it's bad news. He was wounded about two weeks ago in Korea."

"Korea?" said the mother, fear giving edge to her voice.

"Yes," replied the officer. "He was a company commander with the First Cavalry Division. He was wounded in action and evacuated to Fitzsimmons Army Hospital at Denver. They did all they could for him, but the wounds were just too severe. I'm sorry to have to tell you that he passed away early this morning."

"Passed away? … He's dead? Joe's dead?" She put her hands up to her face.

"I'm afraid so. They did all they could for him, but they couldn't save him. He was wounded rescuing one of his men who had been hit by enemy fire. You can be proud of him. He saved the man's life. He's almost certain to be awarded the Silver Star for his bravery and, of course, the Purple Heart. You can take some consolation in knowing that your son died a hero serving his country."

Edith sat in silence, not knowing what to make of the news, not wanting to come to terms with it. "W-where is he?" she asked at length, sobbing now. "He never came home. I never got to see him again."

"His body will arrive by plane in Lincoln tonight and will be taken by ambulance to the funeral home here tomorrow morning. The army is coordinating with them, and you can see him sometime in late afternoon. They will call you about funeral arrangements. There will be an honor guard if you want it."

The sergeant spoke for the first time. "You should know that the soldier that your son saved is accompanying the body, something he wanted very much to do. He can give you all of the details if you want. You'll meet him at the funeral home tomorrow."

The men got up, leaving a yellow telegram on the end table. "We're very sorry to have to give you such bad news," the captain said. "If there is anything . . ."

* * * * * * * *

The news spread quickly through the community, and the next afternoon when Steve's, or rather, Joe's parents, arrived at the funeral home, there were already more than fifty people looking solemn and grave lined up on the front sidewalk, some there in Sunday best suits and dresses, some in overalls and everyday dresses, some there in sympathy, some out of curiosity.

They waited silently along the sidewalk as Edith and John Whitfield with Uncle Robert and Aunt Mary walked between them and went inside. They were no strangers to the large room—the rows of gray metal folding chairs, the center aisle, the wicker stands with flowers at the front—but the sight of the closed, bronze casket covered by an American flag, its colors somehow too bright for the occasion, and a soldier in dress uniform standing at parade rest by the casket took them aback. The funeral director, Mr. Hensley, met them at the door, greeting them solemnly, talking in a low monotone as he escorted them up the aisle to the casket.

Joe's parents stood silently, his mother weeping and his father standing with his head bowed, eyes closed. "Can we see him?" asked Edith, her voice half swallowed in grief.

"Yes, of course." Mr. Hensley folded the flag back to the foot of the coffin and opened the lid, his body obscuring their view until he had reached in and adjusted something. Then he stepped back and they saw their son for the first time in more than five years. He was dressed in "pinks and greens," the dress uniform of a United States Army officer, the first lieutenant's bars on his shoulders gleaming under the spotlight that illuminated the casket. Two rows of bright ribbons decorated his left chest.

Although his mother still pictured him as the fifteen-year-old boy she knew, she looked now at a young man. He lay back in the silent, dignified repose that immediately separates those who have passed from life into death from the living. There was a solemnity in his face that seemed to say that his life was over, and he had gone on to other things. To be sure, it was her son. There was no doubt about that—the same broad brow, the same full lips, the same light brown hair. She reached to touch his face, running her fingers tenderly over the features she once knew, but he did not respond. She could not now share what he had been nor what he had become.

"He looks so peaceful," she said at last, withdrawing her hand but letting it rest on the edge of the casket. She noticed a jagged, red scar from a wound now healed running from the right side of his neck and underneath the collar of his khaki shirt. She turned to Mr. Hensley and pointed to the scar. "That isn't where he was hit, is it?"

"No, Mrs. Whitfield. That's an old wound. You see the purple ribbon with the metal clasp on it—he's been wounded twice before."

She and the father stood there for several minutes, she weeping, her husband stiff and uncomfortable, grim-faced and silent.

After a while, Mr. Hensley came over and took her by the elbow. "There's someone who wants to meet you," he said solemnly. He led them into an adjoining room where a young black sergeant in uniform sitting on a sofa got quickly to his feet and limped to meet them. His left arm was in a cast, and there was a bandage on the side of his neck. He appeared to be in his early twenties, tall and lean, with a look of confident amiability about him.

He smiled, looking solemn at the same time. "Mr. and Mrs. Whitfield, I'm Sergeant Taliaferro Davis. I was with Steve, er, Joe, when he was wounded and when he passed away at the hospital yesterday morning. I owe my life to him—he came and got me when I got hit, carried me back to the lines. That's how he got wounded. We've been friends since Alabama—I went north to Ohio with him."

"Ohio?" asked his father, trying to fit the pieces of his son's life together.

"Yes, sir. We left town sudden-like after they found out about him and hitched rides up north to Cincinnati to make a fresh start. We got jobs with the street department. He got his GED, and then he took classes at the university there. He wanted to be an engineer. We helped each other out, but it was hard just to make ends meet. He was having trouble coming up with the tuition and had to work an extra job, which cut into his study time. So, when the war in Korea broke out at the end of his freshman year, he decided the only way he'd ever manage to get through college was to join up so he could get the GI Bill when he got back out."

His mother began to weep again. "But he got to graduate from high school, and he had a scholarship! He didn't need to enlist!" she protested.

"He never knew anything about that. I guess my momma never knew that either—or she would have wrote, er *written* me. I wasn't doing much good either, so I went along with him. We looked out for each other, stayed together, went through basic at Fort Dix, and it wasn't long before we got sent to the same outfit in the First Cav in Korea.

"He was a smart and a brave man, Mr. and Mrs. Bow—Whitfield. Whatever he went after, he went after, if you know what I mean. We saw a lot of combat there, and he made sergeant in no time. You really get to know a man when you go through combat with him. When he got wounded in the neck a year and a half ago, he refused to even go back to the aid station until we'd taken the hill. And when the company commander was killed soon after that, he got a battlefield commission and took over the company. Got promoted! Wasn't a finer officer—or man, *Christian* man, in the United States Army. All of the men looked up to him. He was a square shooter, and he took care of his men. He saved my life!"

"He always was a good boy," his mother said.

His father nodded awkwardly and looked down at the floor.

"We were both evacuated to Fitzsimmons, and when he didn't make it, I asked if I could accompany him home—it's the least I could do for him. I wanted you to know what a fine man your son was and what he meant to me. We were friends, even in Alabama. Didn't make any difference to him that I was colored and he was white. He treated me like a human being, and that's something I'll remember all the rest of my life."

"Did he suffer?" asked Edith.

"He got shot up pretty bad, ma'am. He was hit in the right shoulder and lower left side. We were evacuated together two weeks ago—they thought he was going to be all right. I got over my wounds pretty much—still have this cast and a couple of bandages underneath and one on my leg.

"I was with him yesterday morning. He was sitting up in bed after breakfast. Said he felt fine, but he must have known that something wasn't right. He told me that when he got out of the hospital, he wanted to come back to Nebraska to see you. He talked about you and his brother a lot those last few days. He wanted very much to see you again and patch things up. If he didn't make it, he said he wanted to be buried here. He wanted me to come back and tell you that he loved you, and that he was sorry that he had caused you so much pain.

"I promised him I would, but I didn't take him serious much—I thought he'd be doing that hisself, er *himself*, when he got better. All of a sudden, he just raised up and looked at me for several moments and held out his hand for me to take. Then it was like he looked on past me, and his eyes brightened and he said, 'Tal—no shadows.' And he just slipped away. I yelled for the doctors and nurses, but they couldn't do anything to save him. They all felt bad. Wasn't nobody, *anybody*, didn't take a shine to *him*." The sergeant turned away. "I just can't believe he's gone."

* * * * * * * *

Joseph's disappearance had made him a local celebrity *in absentia* years before, and the story of his heroism in Korea brought out a large crowd for his funeral two days later, filling the sanctuary and basement of the Steadman Falls Methodist Church and spilling into the churchyard. At the cemetery, the American flag that had covered the casket was duly folded and presented to his mother. The firing squad gave full military honors, and the echoes of the volleys and the last, peaceful notes of "Taps" settled softly into silence, at one with the burnished fields and shaded valleys of his youth.

EPILOGUE

In the cold and snow of winter
there's a spring that waits to be,
unrevealed until its season,
something God alone can see.

—Natalie Sleeth

Awillah Pike had taken the news of the death of her young friend particularly hard, and there was a general feeling of profound regret and sorrow as word spread throughout Morefield. He had not been forgotten, and the account of his heroism in Korea served to add luster to the reputation he had earned there. However, for Mrs. Pike the loss was a personal one, and she reflected that if she wasn't his grandmother, she would like to have been.

One afternoon, as she sat in her customary place on the front porch, swinging gently back and forth and watching the late afternoon sun pour through the arching branches, leaving lacy shadows on the dust of the street, a figure stood for a moment at the gate, then pushed it open and started up the path. She squinted against the sun, and as it came near she saw that it was a young woman who was leading a little boy in short pants by the hand. He kicked at the roots in the walkway as he trudged along.

"Hello, Mrs. Pike. Do you remember me? I'm Laura Lee Chance. I used to be Laura Lee Andrews. I came to see you with Steven Bowman several years ago. This is my son Mark, Mark Chance. He's almost three."

"Oh, yes. Yes, I remember. How do you do, Mark?"

The little boy, freed by his mother, stomped loudly across the weather-beaten boards of the porch, shaking off some of the dust from his new shoes. The young woman sat down in the swing at Mrs. Pike's invitation, gracefully refusing the traditional offer of a cold drink.

"Of course I remember. It wasn't long before Steve disappeared."

"I guess you heard?"

The old woman nodded gravely. The question was a formality. She blinked her eyes a couple of times, trying to gain control of the tears that threatened to appear. "It's hard to believe someone so strong and full of life with so much ahead of him is gone. I can't seem to make the straight of it even yet, but he died for his country. I never heard from him after he left so sudden. Did you?"

"Yes, I got a letter from him a couple of months after he left. From Ohio. He apologized for not saying good-bye. He said things were hard there, and he loved me, but he couldn't offer me any kind of a future. He said I should get on with my life and forget him. There was no return address, and there was nothing until the story in the newspaper." She paused, then added wistfully, "Of course, I could never forget him."

"I felt so bad," the old woman said. "He was a good boy, almost like a son. If I'd only known, I'd have been proud to have him stay in the spare room here. He could have trusted me. Living like that back there by himself all that time, and I never knew! Never even suspected. It must have been so hard for him. And so lonely, no one to look after him and all. But he looked after *me.* He stayed by me day and night that time I had the flu so bad. He was a strong one, that boy, supporting himself like that and going through school at the top of the class. And the scholarship! My! I was so proud when I heard, but by then he was gone, and I never got to tell him that. But he made something of himself after all."

Laura Lee sensed that the old woman wanted to talk, sorting things out as she went, and she did not interrupt.

"He was like a son to me. Used to come by every day to bring in the mail going to and from his aunt's house—well, I guess that part wasn't so—but he'd sit on the porch a while and talk. He had a sense of humor. Liked to tease me. He accused me of being an unreconstructed rebel even though he knew full well my family didn't come south until after the war. But he'd tease me anyway, and I'd tell him he'd better watch out because 'the South will rise again.' He was just trying to get a rise out of *me!*" She smiled, and Laura smiled too, remembering their own give-and-take.

"We had our fun," the woman continued. "When he really wanted to get to me, he'd call me Willie. One day, when he was sitting right over there on the edge of the porch where he always sat, the milkman came by with the bill for the month's delivery. My feet were especially bad that day, so I asked Steve if he'd go into my bedroom and get my purse. I said I had a twenty-dollar bill in there. He came back with the purse and handed it to me, looking as innocent as a newborn babe. I opened it, and without paying any particular attention, fished the bill out and handed it to the milkman.

"He looked at it and said, 'Ma'am, I can't take this bill.'

"I said, 'What do you mean you can't take it?'

"He replied, 'This stuff ain't been worth anything for almost a hundred years,' and handed it back to me. It was a twenty-dollar bill all right—a twenty-dollar *Confederate* bill! Steve like to fell off the porch laughing. Somebody had given it to him, and he had switched the bills when he fetched my purse.

"He said to the milkman, 'Better keep it. The South's goin' t' rise agin—soon, and when it does you and Willie here will be in on the ground floor.'" The old woman laughed, then went on. "Before I could say a word to the rascal, he jumped down off the porch, vaulted over the fence, and disappeared on up the street. He was so full of life. But somehow, underneath the humor and the practical jokes, I always sensed there was a wistfulness, a kind of secret sadness about him. It was hard to put your finger on it, but it was there all right even when he was laughing. He never really confided in me, but I understand it now." Her laughter had quickly turned to sadness.

The little boy had been trying to catch a butterfly that flitted in and out of the honeysuckle vine on the porch trellis. When it flew off, his attention settled on a dandelion that had gone to seed, and he picked the white bloom carefully and came over to Mrs. Pike and held it out to her. She reached out to him, and his mother lifted him up, set him down on her lap, and smoothed back a shock of blond hair that had tumbled into his eyes. He closed his eyes tightly, puffed up his cheeks, and blew as hard as he could on the dandelion, sending little white parachutes floating gently into her tumbler of cranberry punch.

"Mark! Look what you've done!" his mother protested.

The old woman just chuckled. "Steve used to drink a lot of that on hot days. He loved it. Both of my boys did." She looked the little boy straight in the face for a moment, and he grinned up at her, his deep blue eyes flashing.

A shock of recognition crossed her face, and she gasped in surprise, "This is … *Steve's* child!"

"Yes," said Laura quietly. "We were very much in love. There was just the once. He never knew. I never got to tell him. I married Rollie Chance before Mark was born. He was Steve's friend, and he's adopted him as his own. He's good to us, a good father to Mark, so things have worked out. But I can't help wishing Steve could have known he had a son."

Mrs. Pike sat without speaking for a good while, holding the little boy and pushing the swing slowly back and forth with her foot, its rhythmic *squeee–squaaa*, *squeee–squaaa* marking the passage of time. A look of contentment, of calm resolution came at last to her face. Things had come round full circle as they were meant to. Shadows from the trees lengthened across the lawn as the summer sun went homeward for another night.

"Somehow," she said softly as if to herself, "it's almost like a benediction. To know that something so good, something so fine, lives on in this old world."

The End